A BRANCH TOO FAR

THE LEAFY HOLLOW MYSTERIES, BOOK 3

RICKIE BLAIR

BARKLEY
BOOKS

A BRANCH TOO FAR
Copyright © 2017 by Rickie Blair.
Published in Canada in 2017 by Barkley Books.

This book is a work of fiction. Names, characters, places and incidents are
products of the author's imagination or are used fictitiously. Any resemblance
to actual events or locales or persons, living or dead, is coincidental.

ISBN-13: 978-1-988881-01-0

To receive information about new releases and special offers, please sign up
for my mailing list at www.rickieblair.com.

Cover art by: www.coverkicks.com

CHAPTER ONE

THE WOMAN who emerged from the motor coach was a disappointment to the dozen protesters gathered at the Strathcona bus station. She was small and slight, her black hair showed gray roots, and wrinkles creased her lips.

Marjorie Rupert's dark, intense eyes surveyed the hand-lettered signs that greeted her.

Crawl Back to Your Web!

Killers Not Welcome Here!

How Many Others Will Die?

"A welcome party? How unexpected." She set a modest canvas suitcase on the pavement while slipping on sunglasses with her other hand.

A young woman with shiny fair hair jostled to the front, holding a wireless mic in her hand. A burly man in a red-checked shirt followed. He hoisted a video camera to his shoulder and tilted it to center his petite subject in the frame.

The young woman smoothed her hair before leveling her

mic. "Mrs. Rupert, why did you pick Strathcona as your new home?"

"Why shouldn't I?"

"You must know your parole is a contentious topic."

An undercurrent of muttering grew louder. The protesters pressed in, their eyes narrowed. Travelers rolling overnight cases past the line of parked buses stopped to see what was happening.

Rupert graced them all with a serene smile. "Only by those who reject the truth. Which is why I'm writing my memoirs—to tell the real story."

"We know that story," a voice called. The crowd parted to reveal a heavy woman with cropped brown hair, wearing khaki pants and a black cotton shirt. A pair of binoculars swung from her neck. She glared at Rupert. "We don't want you here."

Rupert appeared untroubled by this revelation. "You needn't worry. I'm simply passing through." She heaved an exaggerated sigh while casting her gaze over the crowd. "I know many of you are familiar with me only through the media's misleading accounts. It's true my life hasn't been a peaceful one—"

The woman with the binoculars gave a snort and pushed to the front, her cardboard sign parting the crowd like a knife.

Rupert held up a hand. "Please, hear me out."

More muttering. The spectators crept closer until they surrounded her.

A police officer leaning against the nearest bus with his arms crossed straightened up and approached the crowd, his mouth set in a grim line. "Stand back, please."

Rupert raised her hands before her audience, palms up, in a gesture of contrition. The loose cuffs of her shirt fell back, revealing frail wrists and papery skin.

With sheepish glances, the protesters fell back.

Rupert clasped a hand over her chest. "Losing my husband Ian was the most painful period of my life." A shadow darkened her eyes. "I feel the pain of our separation every day."

Some listeners looked puzzled, perhaps pondering how a husband found at the bottom of a well with enough barbiturates in his system to fell a grizzly could be considered lost.

The reporter thrust out her mic. "Some reports say Ian Rupert was the third husband you misplaced."

"Unconfirmed reports," Rupert said. She smiled sadly, then raised her voice to add, "Those of you fortunate enough to have loved ones waiting for you at home—cherish them. None of us knows what tomorrow will bring."

She took off her sunglasses to sweep the crowd with a sorrowful look. Several people in the front row stepped back to give her more room, looking embarrassed.

"You were convicted of second-degree murder," the reporter insisted, eliciting murmurs from a few people who now considered this query an indignity. "Surely—"

Rupert gripped the reporter's arm so hard the woman winced.

"That was a travesty. A mockery of justice. Even the name they gave me"—Rupert pursed her lips, looking disgusted—"*Black Widow Killer*." She scowled, flicking a hand at the protest signs with their hand-drawn webs and ineptly portrayed black widow spiders. "How perfectly absurd. A ridiculous name conjured up by the prosecution to hoodwink twelve simpleton jurors."

A gasp rolled through the crowd. Then a collective *"Boo"* rose from the emboldened protesters. They rattled their placards with gusto as the camera swept their ranks.

Rupert raised her voice. "Now that I'm free on parole, I intend to set the record straight."

The reporter peeled Rupert's fingers from her arm. "Yes, but—"

Rupert interrupted—her voice so suddenly booming, so incongruous with her petite size, that the crowd was shocked into silence. "I am returning to the place where I was happiest, in order to write the genuine tale of my dreadful experiences. The truth—and nothing but." She thrust out her chin. "I'm calling it *Justice Denied: A Widow's Ordeal.*"

It took a few seconds to sink in, but when it did, the protesters' mouths dropped open in unison. They pushed in, brandishing their signs until the bus bay was a forest of flapping cardboard.

The exasperated officer waded in to separate the group with his hands. "Move back, please."

"Mrs. Rupert," the reporter insisted, her voice rising about the tumult. "Your trial took three months to conclude, with dozens of witnesses. What can you tell us that we don't already know?"

Rupert leaned toward the camera with a conspiratorial air. "Secrets," she said, tapping a finger alongside her nose, "that were kept from the jury. It will all come out."

At the sound of a car engine, she jerked her head around.

An SUV pulled into an empty bay beside the bus. The

man at the wheel was wearing a fedora and huge sunglasses. He gave a toot of the horn.

Rupert opened the back door and tossed in her case. She slid in after it, reaching out to pull the door closed. The crowd surged forward, cell phone cameras flashing. The SUV backed out of the bay and sped off, rattling over speed bumps in the parking lot.

Inside, the driver twisted his head to address his passenger. "First stop?"

"Where else?" Rupert gave a gentle smile. "Leafy Hollow."

CHAPTER TWO

A QUICK SUGAR hit was the only thing on my mind when I pushed open the bright red door of the 5X Bakery that morning. If I had known what a chain of events was being set in motion, I would have abandoned my cherished maple-pecan butter tarts and marched right out again.

"Verity, thank goodness you're here. I'm desperate for lavender. It's an emergency."

With one hand holding the door open, I squinted at Emy Dionne, owner of the finest bakery in Leafy Hollow and my best friend.

"Lavender?" I asked. "Why do you need—"

"I've had a run on scones this morning. Could you pop over to Bertram's and grab me a bunch? And a six-pack of lemons? Please? I'm running low on everything today."

"Sure," I said, reminiscing fondly about Emy's lavender-lemon biscuits—a spin-off from her delectable poppyseed-lemon. "Anything for the scones." Letting the door close with a tinkle of its overhead bell, I turned in the direction of the grocer's.

Lorne Lewins usually ran Emy's "emergency" errands while waiting for me to show up each morning. Oddly, he hadn't arrived yet, even though I was fifteen minutes late. Slipping my cell phone out of my pocket, I checked my texts. Still nothing.

When not working as my paid landscaping assistant, Lorne took every opportunity to check in with his beloved. It was fine with me, because it meant I could start my workday with one of Emy's cheddar-parsley scones. Except on those days when I opted for caramel-walnut. I preferred not to be predictable.

Thankfully, my thin build, five-foot-ten height, and regular outdoor labor allowed for a little creativity when counting calories. Which was good, since Emy tested all her recipes on her friends. I feared we'd wake up one day to discover that time—and triple-chocolate brownies—had caught up with us, like that guy who kept his portrait in the attic. That didn't mean I'd turn down a lavender-lemon scone, though. I was only twenty-eight. Plenty of years ahead to worry about disturbing artwork.

Bertram's, the village's upscale grocer, was only two blocks away. I strolled along Main Street, nodding at passersby and enjoying Leafy Hollow's relaxed atmosphere— so different from the crowded streets of my former home.

Most of the village nestled at the foot of the Niagara Escarpment, a rugged rock face that runs for hundreds of miles through Ontario. The rest perched on the plateau above, where there was more room to spread out. That's where I lived, on

Lilac Lane. I'd moved into Rose Cottage, my aunt's abandoned home, after arriving in Leafy Hollow two months earlier. I glanced up, shading my eyes. With my finger in the air, I traced the two-lane road that zig-zagged up the escarpment, marveling at how much a person's life could change in eight weeks.

The highest local point, Pine Hill Peak, towered three hundred feet over Main Street. The peak's shale cliffs were cloaked with dense foliage and crowned with ancient pines standing like sentinels against the sky. Tiny figures perched on the main lookout, their T-shirts vivid pinpoints of color against the white rock.

It was unnerving how close to the edge visitors stood, especially since there was no fence on the lookout. Their casual waves made me uneasy, and I looked away with a shudder.

The grocer's was bustling with early morning visitors. Flats of field tomatoes, mushrooms, and imported figs flanked the front entrance. A crank-out black awning with *Bertram's —Est. 1922* in antique gold letters shaded the fruits and vegetables.

A curly-haired Labradoodle waited patiently outside, its leather leash wrapped around one of the village's replica lampposts. The dog's gaze was fixed on the organic butcher shop next door. Each time the door opened—emitting aromas irresistible to a canine nose—he whimpered and pawed the ground.

"Forget it, boy," I said on my way past. "I happen to know your owner's a vegan."

I pushed open Bertram's wooden screen door. The three

aisles that extended to the back of the shop were stacked with pasta, oils, and crackers. Odors of fresh basil, rosemary, and spinach filled my nostrils.

A half-dozen shoppers were lined up at the single till. The teenage clerk, her hair a vivid blue, looked up with a shy smile, nodding a greeting while she keyed in prices on the cash register. The five silver rings piercing her upper lip glinted under the overhead lights.

My quick scan of the flower containers at the checkout counter showed one bunch of purple lavender stalks among the herbs. I could grab it on my way out. With a brief wave at the clerk, I lifted a rattan basket from a stack by the door and headed down aisle number three in search of lemons.

White eggplants, purple heirloom carrots, and an artfully arranged pile of organic citrus fruit dominated the produce display. Sucking in my breath at the prices—Emy normally bought her ingredients at the big-box store on the highway—I placed six lemons in my shallow basket and headed for the lavender.

"Look out," a woman snapped.

I jerked back. The lemons rolled from one side of my basket to the other. "Sorry," I said. "Did I hit you?"

"No, but the way you were charging past me—well. Is there a fire?"

Her voice was so subdued I had to lean in to hear it, but there was a hint of steel under that tranquil tone. Taking a step forward, she blocked the aisle and fixed me with an unyielding stare from behind owl-rimmed glasses. I recognized the wispy brown hair and fragile bone structure of forty-something Lucy Carmichael, treasurer of The Leafy Hollow Original Book Club.

Lucy flicked her chin at my organic lemons. "You're not buying those, are you?"

Since I already had six in my basket, it seemed a pointless query. "Why not?"

Her blue-veined hand plucked a fruit from the display. "Look at the price. It's ridiculous." She tossed the lemon back with a grunt of distaste, then whispered, "I bet they're not even organic. They probably picked them up for a pittance at the Chinese grocer in Strathcona." Balancing her filled basket over one elbow, she rummaged in her shoulder bag for an antiseptic wipe, ripped it open, and carefully rubbed her palms. After a cursory glance around, Lucy dropped the used wipe on the wooden floor and kicked it under the edge of the fruit display.

I pursed my lips, but she ignored my sign of disapproval.

"I didn't know you shopped here, Verity."

I wanted to ask Lucy the same thing, since she regaled every book club meeting with details about her "amazing" deals. Bertram's was a delightful grocery with dedicated customers, but no one shopped there to save money. I curbed my curiosity. The day was getting away from me. If Lorne didn't show up soon, I'd have to start our lawn-cutting jobs without him, which meant they'd take twice as long.

With a smile, I tried to sidle past her. "I'm only here for the lavender."

Lucy whirled on her heel and walked briskly beside me to the checkout. Our rattan baskets clacked together in the narrow aisle, our steps accelerating as we neared our goal.

Lucy put on a last burst of speed—and a feint to the left that threw me off stride—to reach the checkout first.

I lined up behind her, eying her overflowing basket with an inward groan.

A woman with a gray pixie haircut and bright orange lipstick stepped into the queue behind me. "Beautiful day, isn't it?" she asked, beaming.

I reached for the last bunch of lavender, but Lucy plunked her now-empty basket on the counter in front of the vase, cutting off my access. I drew my hand back.

The teenage girl at the till read Lucy's total, holding out her hand for the cash.

"How much did you say?" Lucy asked with an incredulous air. "That's not right. The strawberries are on sale."

The clerk's forehead wrinkled. "No, I don't think so."

Lucy gave a snort of derision and reached for her cell phone. "I think they are, given that they're only $1.99 a quart at Wal-Mart. Look at this." She thrust the phone under the clerk's nose.

"We don't price-match, sorry."

"That's ridiculous. Take them off my bill, then." Lucy waved a hand.

Smiling weakly, the clerk put the berries to one side and announced the new total.

Lucy rummaged though her change purse, then her wallet, then the change purse again. "I think I'll use debit," she announced, putting the coin purse away a second time and pulling out her bank card.

The woman behind me loudly cleared her throat. Two

other shoppers had joined the line behind her. I heard muttering.

While the machine processed Lucy's debit charge, the clerk bagged her purchases. A box of granola, a sealed package of Canadian bacon, and a pint basket of gooseberries went into Lucy's environmentally friendly tote bag.

"Hold on," Lucy said, "what are you doing?"

The clerk froze, one hand holding the bag open and the other grasping a grapefruit.

"You can't put fresh fruit in the same bag with meat. You're asking for salmonella."

"But the bacon is wrapped," the clerk said, her eyes wide.

"I don't care. That's a health hazard. You'll have to remove all those contaminated items and start again with fresh ones."

The muttering grew louder. The woman behind me was no longer beaming. "Can't you hurry your friend up a bit?" she whispered loudly.

"She's not my—" The words caught in my throat as Lucy turned to give me a steely glance. "Salmonella is... bad," I said.

The three people in line behind me snorted in unison.

"I'm sorry," the clerk said nervously to Lucy. "I don't think—"

"You don't have to think. Why don't we let the manager decide. Is she around?" Lucy craned her neck to sweep the tiny store with an annoyed gaze.

"I can get her." The clerk's voice was wavering. She was close to a breaking point. If Lucy didn't let up, Emy would never get her lavender.

"This is ridiculous," a voice proclaimed from the queue. "Move it along, lady." It was the orange-lipsticked woman behind me. Her sunny day had clouded quickly.

Lucy planted her fists on either side of her waist and twisted to confront the grumbling lineup. "You should be thankful that I insist on proper food-handling hygiene. Obviously, this girl has not been properly trained."

The teenaged clerk blinked rapidly, and her silver rings quivered.

The shoppers fell silent, scanning shelves of gourmet vinegar with exaggerated interest.

I noted a suspicious twinkle in Lucy's eyes. She was enjoying herself.

As Lucy turned back to the counter, I dropped her empty basket onto the stack behind the till. Then I reached for the last of the lavender.

A delicate, white hand clamped onto my arm. "Hang on," Lucy said. "I was just about to add that to my order."

My mouth fell open as she plucked the lavender from the vase and flourished it in front of the clerk.

"I'll take this, too," she said.

With an indignant gasp, I snatched for the flowers. "No fair, Lucy—I told you I was buying those." I grabbed a corner of the lavender. "Let go."

The queue of shoppers stepped away with raised eyebrows as Lucy and I tugged at the bouquet. The rattan basket rocked on my elbow, and the six lemons leapt out one by one. I tap-danced around them, still clutching the lavender.

When Lucy released her grip without warning, I pitched

back, no longer able to avoid the rolling fruit. The first one squished under my running shoe with a splat. But the second and third were not giving up that easily. My feet planed across the lemons.

I landed heavily on my rear with a grunt of surprise, my empty basket hanging from one hand and a torn bouquet of lavender in the other.

Lucy bent over me and extended a hand. "Here, let me."

I raised my arm.

"Thank you," she said, plucking the lavender from my grasp. She straightened up, slapped it on the counter, and opened her change purse again.

"Hey," I squawked while struggling to my feet. "That's mine."

Lucy ignored me. "This is damaged," she said to the clerk. "I expect a discount."

By the time I'd paid for the battered lemons, Lucy was outside—with Emy's lavender.

I marched out the door, intending to give her a piece of my mind. At the very least, she should pay for the ruined fruit.

Lucy was standing beside her bundle buggy, eying the Labradoodle with disgust. The dog lowered its head and edged back as far as its leash would allow.

"Listen," I said, "about the lemons—"

"This is a disgrace." Lucy pointed to the dog. "That animal should not be in any store where food is sold. Someone should call the health department."

"It's not in the store."

She snorted. "It might as well be. Look—I think it drooled on those rutabagas."

I turned to look. The locally grown vegetables outside the entrance were at least a foot above the Labradoodle's head. Besides, he wasn't interested in rutabagas—unless they were wrapped in bacon. When I turned to explain this to Lucy, she was already marching up the sidewalk away from me. I jogged after her, hoping to open negotiations for the lavender.

"Lucy," I called.

I stopped in surprise as she halted beside a white Land Rover two car lengths from Bertram's front door. After placing her bag of groceries on the front seat, she folded up the bundle buggy and slid it into the back.

"Why do you need a bundle buggy if you're driving?" I asked.

She gave me a curious glance while latching the door. "Don't you care about the environment, Verity?"

Before I could answer, she opened the driver's door and got in. Lucy tucked a sprig of lavender behind her ear and tossed the rest of the bouquet onto her front dash. "See you at the book club meeting," she called through the open window as her white vehicle jerked into traffic and drove off.

A minivan shrieked to a halt to avoid hitting the Land Rover.

With a grimace of disgust, I pulled out my cell phone. Still no text from Lorne. I slipped the phone into my pocket and decided to fill in the time by harvesting the only lavender I could count on—the patch growing in my aunt's back garden.

I texted Emy, SLIGHT DELAY. BACK SOON. Then headed for my truck.

In Rose Cottage's kitchen, I laid my freshly cut lavender on the counter to even up the stalks and wrap them in paper. They weren't as pretty as the perfect flowers sold at Bertram's, but good enough to pinch hit.

"Verity."

I jerked my head up, listening. The voice had been so faint it could have been my imagination. I was alone in the kitchen. General Chang, my scruffy one-eyed tomcat, would usually be jonesing for a liver treat but today he was snoozing on the front porch. After glancing around the empty kitchen, I returned to my task.

"Verity. *Verity Hawkes.*"

There it was again. This time I identified the source—the basement. I tied a string around the flowers and placed them near the back entrance, where I could grab them in case of a hasty getaway.

"Verity!" The voice was louder now, with a definite petulant tone.

"Be right there," I called as I wrenched open the sticky basement door and started down the worn steps. At the bottom, I toggled the antique light switch and stepped into the dusty room, ducking under overhanging pipes.

The far wall normally displayed holographic shelves stocked with fake boxes of maple syrup and Molson Canadian. Today that wall was gone. In its place was a non-holographic swivel chair, a console with keyboard, and a double row of monitors. Identical gray heads—their sharp-edged faces reminiscent of Picasso's Cubist period, or perhaps ventriloquists' dummies—appeared on each screen.

Pairs of gray eyes watched me while I dropped into the chair. Other than my fingers tightening on the seat edges, I sat very still, painfully aware of a growing cramp in my chest. So far, I'd taken comfort in the no-news-is-good-news adage, but I'd been prodded awake more than once by an over-whelming fear that Aunt Adeline was gone for ever. Was this the day my nightmare came true? I decided to tackle my fears head-on.

"I've been waiting weeks for you to check in," I said, swallowing hard. "Do you have news?"

My aunt had been missing for over two months. After police pulled her ruined Ford Escort from the river, the authorities wrote her off as dead. I'd received enough cryptic notes to believe that wasn't true, but I had no idea when she would come home—or even if she could. Her next-door neighbor and long-time confidant, Gideon Picard, was out looking for her. So far, he'd shut me out of his search. The only thing I knew was that they had once both worked for a mysterious, black-ops marketing outfit called "Control."

And that this talking hologram in my basement was a direct link.

Perky black berets materialized on the puppets' heads. Their jaws moved in unison. "*Ma chérie*, we must talk. *Temps perdu*, and so on. Time waits for no—"

"Lose the accent, please," I said, through gritted teeth. "And the hat."

I didn't know what other talking holograms were like, but this one had always been pretty irritating.

"Just kidding, Verity." The berets disappeared with a *pouf*. "And we're sorry, but we have no news. Not yet."

The tightness in my chest eased. "Then what do you want?"

"We want to know why you're not in Niagara Falls. At HQ."

"I went there, as you instructed. No one contacted me. I couldn't even find HQ."

Emy, Lorne and I had walked aimlessly around Niagara Falls for hours. After contemplating the thundering water, we checked out everything from the dinosaur park to the power plant—even a forty-foot-wide chiming clock made out of flowers. Zinnas and creeping phlox, mostly. No one approached us.

"We told you to come alone."

"You did not," I sputtered.

The faces regarded each other quizzically. "No?"

"No. Also, you promised me information about my aunt. I'm still waiting."

"You don't understand the urgency of our demand."

"Why don't you explain it, then? And for starters, you can stop calling it a *demand*. You have no right to give me orders."

The faces swirled into multicolored ribbons before re-forming into identical contrite expressions. "Verity, we have embarked on the wrong foot. We apologize."

"Just tell me what you want me to do."

"Oh. We're not cleared for that."

I flicked my gaze upward with a sigh. "Then put me through to someone who is."

The heads twisted from side to side, exchanging glances, before facing me again. "They're not ready for you yet."

Through gritted teeth, I asked, "When will they be ready?"

Their faces brightened. "Ten days. Or maybe"—gray fingers tapped gray chins—"two weeks? Then again..."

"What about Gideon Picard?" I tapped the pocket of my yoga pants, where Gideon's latest message lay crumpled. I'd discovered it that morning while rummaging in the glove box of my aunt's truck for my Tim Hortons gift card.

The note simply said,

ADELINE FOUND

I recognized Gideon's handwriting, as well as his infuriating economy with words. Not to mention the fact that he could have knocked on the front door of Rose Cottage and told me this in person, instead of skulking around in ridiculous secret-agent mode. I pictured him plunging through the shrubbery, as usual.

I also cursed his brevity. *Adeline found?* Did that mean she was alive? Or—my chest contracted again—dead?

"Gideon can't be trusted," Control snapped. Then, with a sharp pivot of their heads accompanied by a beady stare, "Have you... heard from him?"

My fingers gripped my pocket as if it had suddenly become transparent. It occurred to me that *Adeline found* didn't necessarily mean Gideon had been the one to find her. I casually smoothed my hands down my thighs and adopted my best candid tone. "No. And unless you have actual news,

I have no time for this. Is there... anything you want to tell me?"

I waited.

Gray lips pursed, but said nothing.

"Fine." I jumped to my feet, scraping the chair across the floor, and turned to go. "We're done here. Call me." With an exhalation of disgust—to cover my disappointment—I headed for the stairs.

Behind me, metal panels clanged shut, locks snapped into place, and the basement wall shimmered back into cases of beer and syrup. I guess. To be honest, I didn't watch.

Or stop to wonder when I became so blasé about having a talking hologram in my basement.

On my way out the back door, my cell phone beeped with a text from Lorne.

DELAYED. SORRY.

HOW LONG? I texted back.

ONE HOUR.

Pausing on the threshold, I swept my gaze across my aunt's back garden. Tattered perennials, neglected vegetable plots, and magnificent herbaceous borders stretched four hundred feet before me, melding into the purple-hazed woodlands of Pine Hill Valley in the distance. I'd tried to restore the garden's faded glory, but there was so much to be done and never enough time to do it. Grinning, I set off to retrieve my gardening tools from the back of the truck. Emy wouldn't mind waiting another hour or so.

With the lavender on the front seat beside me, I drove my aunt's truck down the escarpment road and onto Main Street. A boy on a bicycle darted in front of me, and I slammed on the brakes. Then a man sprinted past, following the boy. I turned my head to see where they were going.

A crowd had gathered in a driveway directly under the Peak, where a garbage bin had disgorged its chicken bones, soggy kale leaves, and plastic milk bags across the road. The squashed receptacle looked as if it had been run over, but the flashing lights of a police cruiser suggested there was more at stake here than a vandalized garbage container. Or maybe not —this was Leafy Hollow, after all, where residents were infuriated by neighbors who mixed compost with non-recyclables.

I pulled the truck over to the shoulder to watch. Another police cruiser halted beside the first. With one hand on the gearshift, I debated driving off and staying out of their way.

Then Detective Constable Jeff Katsuro emerged from the second vehicle, settling his police cap over his jet-black hair.

I smiled. It couldn't hurt to say hello. And then—because Jeff was working—I'd get right back into my aunt's truck and drive away. I put it in park and got out.

There was no yellow tape up yet, so whatever this was must have occurred only minutes earlier. I sidled up to the group and craned my neck. One advantage to being five-ten— possibly the only advantage—is that I can see over most people's heads. The pavement was splattered with ripped cardboard, empty tin cans, takeout containers, and...

I sucked in my breath at the sight of a covered mound next to the garbage bin.

Exactly the size of a body.

"Fell off the Peak," a woman beside me whispered to her companion. "Just now." The woman with her nodded. They edged nearer, craning their necks.

"Did anyone see what happened?" the second woman asked.

"I don't think so. There was no one here when I arrived."

I tilted my head to look up at the cliff that soared above us. A fall from that height would be a long, terrifying drop. When I lowered my gaze, the first officer was placing numbered cones next to objects on the pavement. Number four sat next to... my breath quickened at the sight of a tattered stalk of lavender.

I squinted at the other objects, trying to make them out.

"Hey," the first woman asked, poking my arm. "I saw you at the grocer's, didn't I?"

I turned to face her gray pixie cut and orange lipstick.

"You were arguing with Lucy." She placed her hands on her hips. "It got pretty heated, as I recall."

"Lucy?" A cold hand gripped my heart as I inclined my head toward the body. "Is that... Lucy Carmichael?" I had trouble getting the words past my suddenly dry lips.

"Sure is. I found her body and called it in."

Her friend shook her head sadly. "What a tragedy. Poor Lucy."

Then both women looked suspiciously at me.

CHAPTER THREE

EMY WAS HUDDLED at the back table of the 5X Bakery with her mother, Thérèse. When the bell over the front door tinkled, they looked up at me with white faces.

I stood frozen in the doorway, recognizing their shocked expressions. It was an uncomfortable reminder that I had seen that look too many times.

"You already know?" I asked.

"About Lucy? Yes." Emy nodded miserably, exchanging a grim glance with her mother. Although Thérèse was older by twenty-five years, they could have been twins. The same petite five-foot-one frames, heart-shaped faces, and black hair. Only the wrinkles at the edges of Thérèse's brown eyes hinted at her age. That, and her elegant pencil skirt, silk blouse, and blunt-cut bob. Whereas Emy—cheeks flushed from the heat and humidity of her bakery kitchen—wore an enormous white apron over a T-shirt, yoga pants, and running shoes. It was all dusted with flour—including the tip of her upturned nose.

I walked past the glass-fronted counter that spanned a side wall of the narrow shop, drew up a third chair, and sank into it. I'd been conscripted into Thérèse's book club shortly after my arrival in the village, two months earlier, so I knew Lucy Carmichael well. Despite her annoying exterior, there was a lively intelligence in her eyes. Lucy had been a keen observer of life, if not an eager participant. As a world-class introvert myself, I recognized a fellow sufferer beneath that hard shell. And now...

"I simply can't take it in," I said, drumming my fingers on the table.

"You were there, weren't you?" Emy asked. "I'm sorry. It must have been awful."

"I didn't see anything. Not really."

"The police think she may have—"

Thérèse clamped a hand on Emy's arm. "It was an accident."

Something about her manner put me on my guard. From Emy's pursed lips, I could tell there was more, but I let it pass. No need to arouse the scrutiny of Leafy Hollow's chief librarian and unofficial Miss Manners, Thérèse Dionne.

"Why would Lucy be on the Peak?" I asked. "She was afraid of heights. It came up at our *Anna Karenina* meeting. When we were discussing the train scene."

Thérèse rose, brushing her skirt with one hand and reaching for her handbag with the other. "Don't forget, Verity —this month's meeting is on Sunday. Two days from now."

"Really? We're going ahead with it?"

Thérèse showed no sign that she'd heard. *"Alias Grace,* remember. Margaret Atwood." The heels of her pumps clicked on the floor as she strode to the door.

I watched her go, puzzled by her odd behavior. Why was Thérèse telling me something I already knew? And surely our meeting would be cancelled? Nevertheless, I made a mental note to set aside *Give Your Phobias the Chop: The Ninja Guide to Conquering Fear* and get cracking on the club's current selection.

Emy hustled after her. They exchanged a few words at the door, their voices too low for me to make out. While they talked, I got up and bent over the glass counter to check out Emy's latest creations. The tray of scones held only one offering, its pale glaze sprinkled with tiny purple blossoms.

I slapped a hand to my forehead. The lavender was still on the front seat of my aunt's truck.

Bells sounded, marking Thérèse's exit.

A second later, a finger poked my back. With a start, I whirled around to see Emy smiling at me.

"Get any closer and you'll leave nose prints on that glass." She walked behind the counter, put the scone on a plate, and handed it to me, followed by a cup and saucer. "Tea's coming up."

"Your lavender and lemons are in the truck. I'll go get them."

"Don't worry about it. Plenty of time." Emy gave an uneasy glance at the black-cat clock on the wall, watching its tail flick back and forth. "I wonder where Lorne is," she said before filling the kettle for tea.

I sat at the table, nibbling at my scone and watching Emy bustle behind the counter. "Your mother's taking this hard."

Emy blew out a breath while she measured loose tea into the pot. "Lucy was a founding member of the Originals, so they've been close friends for decades. But it's not just that. Mom's had something on her mind for weeks. Something to do with the club." She poured boiling water into the teapot, then added a comment that took my breath away. "Lucy didn't fall. It wasn't an accident."

She raised her head, and we locked glances.

"Are you saying it was suicide?"

"That's what the police think."

I sat back, dumbfounded. Lucy had been withdrawn and a little cranky, but I never got the impression that she was depressed.

Emy glanced at the pass-through door that connected her other shop—a vegan takeout—to the bakery. She snugged the teapot into a crocheted cozy and brought it to the table, sitting opposite me. "It wasn't suicide, either. Tea?"

"What, then?" I held out my cup, and she filled it.

Emy poured tea into her own cup before settling the pot onto a trivet and fixing me with a solemn expression.

I dropped the scone back onto my plate. "You're not suggesting that she was—"

"Pushed?" Emy asked, calmly lifting the teacup to her lips.

I slumped back, shocked. "Who would do that? Lucy was annoying, yes, but nobody gets murdered for jumping the queue at one-hour flash sales."

Emy put down her cup, looking grim. "So, what was she

doing up there? It's not safe to wander near that precipice. And you're right—Lucy was terrified of heights."

Nodding in agreement, I buttered the last morsel of scone and popped it into my mouth.

"She wouldn't even get on a Ferris wheel. Verity, we have to investigate."

"Wait... wha—?" I asked, my speech hampered by scone. "Is there buttermilk in this icing?" I asked in a muffled voice, pointing at my cheek.

"Don't change the subject. We have to find out the truth."

Swallowing, I shot her a warning glance. "Don't even think about it. You know what happened the last time." I tapped up the crumbs from my plate and licked them off my finger.

"You nailed a murderer. It was epic. People are still talking about it." Emy indicated my empty plate. "Butter tart?" she asked.

I gave her an indignant stare. "Stop plying me with baked goods. *Epic*? Have you forgotten I landed in the hospital?"

"Don't exaggerate. You were only there for observation."

That point was debatable. I was still prone to headaches from a minor concussion sustained in my face-off with a killer. It would be a waste of time to remind Emy of that, though. The Dionne clan was nothing if not persistent. I'd learned that the hard way, after being expected to speed-read all 864 pages of *Anna Karenina*.

Fortunately, Emy had come to my rescue with the DVD.

"Mom is devastated," she continued. "She thinks it's her fault—that she should have noticed Lucy was depressed.

With your talent for investigating, you could set her mind at ease."

"It's not a talent I want to pursue. You know that. I was in the right place at the wrong time, that's all. And I promised Jeff—I mean, local law enforcement—that I wouldn't meddle in any more murder cases."

Besides, this might not even be a murder. I considered Lucy Carmichael as unlikely to take her own life, but it wasn't possible to know someone else's mind. After the death of my husband Matthew in Vancouver, I suffered through black nights that could have... I pushed those memories away. "I agree it seems suspicious. But I fail to see what we're supposed to do about it. Did you share your doubts with Jeff? What did he say?"

Emy's face expressed disgust. "Suicide. Or an accident. He hasn't decided which."

"I'm sure he'll get to the bottom of it."

She pursed her lips, looking dubious.

I did not share those doubts. Jeff Katsuro was no slouch—either in the investigative department or the all-around manly division. I sighed, recalling how well he filled out a uniform. His dark, brooding good looks had attracted me from the day I arrived in the village. At one point, I even thought it was mutual. Until I spotted him escorting a blonde in four-inch heels out of the local steak joint.

"Speaking of Jeff..." Emy's eyebrows rose. "Any developments?"

I hoisted my teacup with a nonchalant air. "I don't know what you're talking about."

It was Emy's turn to lean back, looking incredulous. "You give up too easily."

"Hm-mmm. Could we talk about something else?"

She was right. But the thought of starting over—or worse, being rejected—coiled like a snake in my stomach, waiting to strike. The vein in my neck—the one that always warned of panic attacks—throbbed at the thought. I pawed at it with a surge of exasperation.

Emy relented. "Forget I mentioned it. Any news on your aunt?"

"Of a sort."

She leaned in, her attention riveted. "Did you hear from that... *thing* in the basement?"

"This morning. While I was trimming the lavender."

"Did you tell it we drove to Niagara Falls and found nothing?" Emy demanded.

I nodded.

"What did it want this time?"

"It told me to stand by. That something is coming up. In a week or two."

"Can't you just shut that thing off?"

"Not if I want to find my aunt."

Emy fingered the silver locket at her throat—a one-month anniversary gift from Lorne. She tucked the locket under her T-shirt. "You're more patient than me."

We looked up as the door bell tinkled.

Lorne walked in, brushing tangled brown locks from his forehead, his work boots clumping on the floor. Emy beamed and raised a hand as he bent his strapping, five-foot-ten frame to drop a kiss on her head.

He didn't even notice me.

I cleared my throat. "Hi, Lorne."

"Oh, Verity," he said brightly, twining his fingers through Emy's. "Sorry I'm late. I had a doctor's appointment. Routine," he said in response to Emy's look of alarm.

"Good, because we've got a full slate today," I said.

I'd been cutting lawns and trimming hedges since I arrived in Leafy Hollow. To date, only one client had ended up dead. So, customer service had definitely improved. But reviving my aunt's landscape business was more work than I'd expected.

Emy jumped up to fill a plate with goodies and pour a glass of milk.

Lorne accepted them with a grin. "Thanks." He tucked into a flaky sausage roll.

"Lorne," Emy said. "Verity needs you to fill in for her while she looks into a possible case."

My jaw dropped. "I'm doing what now?"

Lorne raised an eyebrow at me while he chewed. "No problem," he said, reaching for his milk. "What case?"

"Lucy Carmichael fell off Pine Hill Peak this morning," I said, eying Emy suspiciously.

He paused, the glass poised in his hand. "Is she..."

"Dead? I'm afraid so."

Lorne replaced the glass, and squeezed Emy's arm consolingly. "I'm sorry. That's a terrible accident."

"It wasn't an accident." Emy said. "She was murdered."

Uh-oh. I had been hoping to get out of there before anyone mentioned the "M" word.

"You don't know that for certain," I countered.

"It's not unusual for people to fall off the escarpment," Lorne said, running a hand up Emy's arm. "It happens every year."

"I know that." A smile tugged at her lips as she batted away his hand. "But they're generally drunk."

Lorne narrowed his eyes. "Could Lucy have been—"

"No!" Emy blurted. "What a notion."

"Although it's hard to imagine why anybody would walk that close to the edge," I said.

With a shrug, Lorne renewed his attack on the sausage roll. "Emy, remember the climbing team in high school?"

She darted him a wary glance. "What about it?"

He chewed and swallowed. "People are always climbing those cliffs."

"It's illegal, isn't it?"

"That's why they do it at night."

I leaned into their circle of two. "Are you talking about the type of climbing that involves ropes and hooks?"

Lorne nodded.

"People do that after dark? Really?"

"It's kind of a dare thing."

Emy pointed a finger at him. "You told me that climbing equipment in your parents' garage wasn't yours."

Lorne looked uneasy. "Did I?"

"Sometimes, I think you don't trust me."

Lorne grinned. "Well, if you weren't such a nag..."

"A nag?" She gave him a playful tap. "That's rich, coming from a..."

Their banter faded into the background as I focused on the mechanics. If Leafy Hollow residents routinely pitched over the escarpment—often enough that it didn't raise eyebrows—that made it an ideal murder method. There were no weapons to get rid of. No footprints, either, given that the trails were often slick with rain and furrowed by the hundreds of feet that tromped the path to the lookout every summer weekend. All a killer had to do was make sure no one was watching.

My troublesome curiosity was piqued. I closed my eyes, seeing pinpoints of color against the lookout's white rock. And watching them move ever closer to the edge.

"And besides..." Emy continued.

I snapped my eyes open. "Lucy's body was directly under the Peak."

Emy and Lorne turned puzzled expressions on me.

"So?" Emy asked.

"You can see the main lookout from Main Street. There's always someone up there hiking or sightseeing. Somebody should have seen her fall. Or heard her scream. But the woman who found Lucy's body said there was no one around."

"So?"

"So—what if Lucy fell from somewhere else? With all those tree branches and rocks on the way down, her body could have bounced around before it reached the ground." I winced at the image that produced. "She might have landed fifty feet from the point where she toppled over. Maybe more."

Emy narrowed her eyes to picture the scene. "When you're on the Peak, if you walk fifty feet to the right from the main lookout..." Her eyes widened, and she seized my arm excitedly. "That section is completely blocked by trees. If someone was standing there, you wouldn't see them from the ground."

"Exactly."

Lorne whistled. "Far out."

We gaped at him.

"What?" He shoved a second sausage roll into his mouth and looked at us, chewing.

With a brief shake of her head, Emy returned her attention to me. "That's brilliant. You have a sixth sense for this, Verity."

I nodded self-consciously, inwardly crediting my rapid scan in the checkout line of *Go Deeper: Psychic Breakthroughs That Stick.*

"Does this mean you'll investigate? Please?"

"I don't know, Emy. It's only a theory."

"Please? We have to help my mom."

I recalled Thérèse's distracted behavior. Emy's mother raised her alone after her father disappeared when she was an infant. I knew what that was like. Our deadbeat dads were something we had in common. A connection. My own mother was beyond my help. But I might be able to spare Thérèse further pain.

"Okay. The path to the Peak's not far from Rose Cottage. I'll take a quick look tomorrow morning." I raised a warning hand. "But that's all."

Emy clasped her hands in excitement. "Thank you. I know you'll figure it out."

Lorne, his mouth full of sausage roll, gave me a thumbs-up.

"There are a lot of trails there," I said. "How will I know which ones lead to the edge? Other than the main one, I mean?"

Emy looked thoughtful. "Some of those older trails are grown in, and a few are blocked off. I bet Sue Unger can tell you where they are."

"Sue...?"

"You know her. She's a book club member. Always wearing binoculars?"

"Right." I snapped my fingers. "The birder."

"That's the one. Or"—Emy paused dramatically before pointing a finger at me—"you could ask Jeff. Casual-like."

I gave her a stony look. "No."

She held up her hands in a gesture of resignation while I rose to my feet.

"We have work to do, Lorne."

He scrambled upright, dropped another kiss on Emy's head, and joined me at the entrance.

Outside, I gazed up at Pine Hill Peak. The first hundred feet down from the rim was a jagged wall of limestone. No one who plunged over that could survive.

It was odd nobody saw anything. And even odder that Lucy, with her fear of heights, had ventured that close to the edge. I narrowed my eyes, studying the cliffs.

Unless a close friend lured her there.

CHAPTER FOUR

STANDING OVER THE KITCHEN SINK, I gulped a quick coffee before heading out early the following morning. Dressed in jeans, rubber boots, and an old shirt of Matthew's, I trudged through the bush behind Sue Unger's home. Sue was in her mid-thirties, with no apparent source of income. Yet, she owned twenty acres of land bordering the Pine Hill Conservation Area. It was one mystery I didn't intend to probe. Our fellow book club member was notoriously irritable.

My attempts to reach Sue by phone had failed. After one ring, her line went to voice mail, filling my ears with trilled bird song. The notes barely faded before her curt, "That was a *Fringilla montifringilla*. If you've seen it, contact the Rare Bird Alert immediately. For everything else, leave a message."

I didn't bother. If Sue wasn't answering her phone, she was out birding. So, I had pulled on my Wellies, knowing I'd have to tramp around outside to find her.

A layer of spongy leaf mold muffled my footsteps as I plodded along, brushing aside branches soggy from an early morning rain and trying to avoid tripping on tree roots. The warm, moist air was rich with the pungent scent of rotting vegetation and the occasional sweet note of honeysuckle. Shafts of sunlight pierced the soaring canopy above my head.

Twice, I twisted around with a shiver of apprehension when twigs snapped behind me, but saw no one. If there was a killer on the loose, he wasn't following me.

Eventually, the forest gave way to a small clearing shaded by a wooden structure, about eight-by-twelve feet, perched twenty feet up in a massive pine.

I leaned my head back to study Sue's bird blind. Cut branches covered the blind's shingled roof and draped over its eaves. A shutter was propped up over a rectangular window that faced the conservation area. A ladder led from the ground to an opening in the floor.

"Sue? Are you up there?"

No answer.

I raised my voice. "Sue?"

A white face appeared in the opening. "Shh! What's the matter with you?" She looked puzzled when she realized who it was. "Verity? What do you want?"

"I need your help," I called.

"*Shh*. Not so loud. Come up, then." Her face disappeared.

The rickety ladder did not inspire confidence. Holding the rails with both hands, I trod cautiously on the first rung, bouncing a bit. It seemed sturdy enough, so I climbed—trying not to look down.

At the top, I stuck my head through the opening. A pair of large feet in sturdy hiking boots met me, and I craned my neck to see more. Sue was sitting in a chair that faced the open window. Her fleshy hands gripped a black scope, mounted on a tripod, that was aimed at the woods. A camouflage hat shaded her face.

"Emy said you could lead me to—"

"Do you have to make so much noise? Get up here and close the hatch."

Hoisting myself into the small room, I flipped shut the wooden door that lay against the wall. There was a small bench nearby, and I dragged it over to cover the opening. With a final thump of my foot on the hatch to make sure it was closed, I looked up.

Sue was shaking her head. She motioned to a fold-up camp chair beside her before turning her attention back to the scope. "Sit, and for Pete's sake, keep quiet. There's supposed to be a *Fringilla montifringilla* about, and I intend to see it." She flashed me a sideways glance. If you haven't already scared it away."

"A *fritter*... what?"

"A brambling." Seeing I was none the wiser, she added, "Brambling is its common name. It's a type of finch."

I nodded and peered out the window, trying to look knowledgable. Black ash and sugar maples, spruce and cedar, sassafras and tulip trees jostled for space. Despite squinting intensely at their foliage, I couldn't make out a single bird.

Instead, I turned my attention to a shelf on the back wall. Three pairs of binoculars were lined up under a topographical map of the conservation area marked with colored pins. On a shelf underneath, a huge leather book lay open, like the ones at hotel check-in desks.

I leaned in to read the headings along the top of the open page:

Species Name.

Weather.

Date.

Behavior.

I paused on that one, wondering what constituted wayward avian behavior. The entries included comments on tail bobs, head cocks, and wing stretches. It sounded like an aerobics class. Or a Justin Bieber video.

As I flipped through the pages, a loose paper caught my attention—a list of names with numbers beside them. I scanned the entries.

The Wicked Wallflower

The Officer Who Wasn't a Gentleman

The Rogue Not Taken

Puzzled, I looked up. "Are these bird sightings?"

Sue leaned an arm back over her chair to slam the book shut. I yanked my finger away just in time. "Don't mess with my journal," she said.

"Sorry. I've never heard of a Wallflower bird. Is that a local species?"

"Quiet, please," she said, without taking her eye from the scope.

"Sorry," I repeated, lowering myself into the camp chair, careful not to make a sound. Sue pointed to a spare camouflage hat, and I slipped it on. The floppy brim partially obscured my view, but at least I wouldn't spook any wildlife.

We sat in silence, Sue with her eye to the scope, and me watching for signs of... well, anything. A gust of wind rustled branches outside. One thumped against the roof.

"Sue, why do you like birds so much?"

She pursed her lips, not looking at me. Finally she said, "They don't judge you."

Before I could question her further, a trill of notes from outside the blind startled me. It sounded like the call on Sue's voice mail. "Was that the finch?" I asked brightly, angling my neck to peer out the window.

Sue gave me a weary glance. "Tree frog."

Another call, sounding like *chitter-chitter-dee-eeeeeee*. "Is that a—"

"Raccoon."

Chitter-cheep-cheep. Before I could open my mouth, Sue barked, "Red squirrel."

I crossed my arms over my chest. I was only trying to help.

"*Blast.* A red-tailed hawk." Sue flopped back in her chair, away from the scope. She flipped off her hat, revealing her cropped brown hair, and tossed it onto the table. "The brambling won't come here now. I'll have to wait for that raptor to leave." She burbled air through her lips with a disappointed look before sitting up straight and turning to me. "Not to be rude, but—why are you here?"

"I have something to ask you. But I'm interested in birds, too, especially bramblers. I've never seen one of those."

She gave me a pitying glance. "Bramb-*ling*. And of course you haven't. They're not native to North America. They're Eurasian."

I must have looked confused, because she added, "They get blown across the Bering Strait and end up in Alaska sometimes, but only a half-dozen have ever made it this far inland. That idiot who spotted it is probably wrong. Wouldn't be the first time. Last year, he claimed to have seen a Crested Caracara. Ridiculous."

She flipped open the lid of a small cooler at her feet. After plucking out a plastic bottle, she held it out to me. "Water?"

"Thanks." I snapped it open and took a swig, smiling at Sue. Then I put it on the floor—not the windowsill where it might topple out and scare off the brambling. The brim of my hat flopped down, and I pushed it out of my eyes.

Sue sipped her water, studying me. "I didn't know you were interested in birds. You've never mentioned it."

"My husband and I did a lot of hiking, so we saw plenty of birds."

Sue took another swig. "Such as?"

"Well, eagles and hawks and... others. Out West, mostly. Oh, and water birds. Lots of those." I smiled brightly.

Sue nodded. "Sure," she said with a noticeable lack of enthusiasm.

I glanced around. The blind was sturdily built. It even had a small wood stove connected to a chimney pipe that led through the wall. "Do you come here in winter?"

She nodded. "See lots of good birds in winter. At night, too."

"How can you tell what they are? Night goggles?"

"I identify them by their call."

"Don't birds sleep at night?" I paused. "Except for owls."

Sue sighed. "Plenty of birds are active at night. Common nighthawks, black-crowned night heron, woodcocks, screech owls, killdeers, Eastern whip-poor-wills. Most of the boreal forest birds migrate at night, and people who are really good can pick out their calls, no problem."

"Don't they all sound pretty much the same?"

Sue gave another sigh and sipped her water.

"Did you build this yourself?" I gestured around me.

"Good heavens, no. I'm not a carpenter. A guy in the village does this kind of work for me. You should come by the house. He built me a deck, over a hundred feet long, that overlooks the valley. I see a lot of good birds from there. Leafy Hollow is on a flyway."

I nodded, still trying to appear knowledgeable. But my confusion over what a flyway might be was superseded by curiosity about Sue's home. It sounded like a pricey place. Again, I wondered how she could afford it. I put that out of my mind. None of my business. More importantly, I'd promised Emy that I'd check out the Peak, and this chatter—however fascinating—wasn't helping.

"Sue, I was hoping you could show me the back trails at Pine Hill Peak. The ones that lead to other lookouts over the valley."

She shot me a quick glance. "How do you know about those?"

"Emy told me, but she's not certain how to reach them."

"They've been closed off for years. The conservation authority wanted that area to revert to the wild. Too many hikers. They were worried the edge might give way."

"Are the trails passable? You don't need a hatchet or anything, do you?"

Sue chuckled. "We're not in the tropics. You need boots and heavy pants, though." She pointed at my Wellies. "Those would do. And you have to watch for hornets."

"Yellow jackets?"

"No. They're usually harmless. I mean European hornets. Larger, blacker, and with a wicked temper. And they're active at night, so they're hard to kill."

"I'll keep an eye out. So where—"

"You haven't told me why you want to go there."

"Does it matter?"

"It does if you disturb the birds."

"I'm not doing anything like that. Lucy Carmichael fell from—"

"I heard. Shame."

"Yes, well, some of us think it may have been intentional."

Sue put down her water bottle. "Suicide?"

"No, we were thinking more like..." I raised both hands and winced.

"That's ridiculous." Sue gave a snort of derision, then got to her feet. "The trail begins a few hundred feet from Rose Cottage, actually. I'll show you where it branches off, but then you're on your own. I'm busy this afternoon."

"Birding?"

"No," she said bluntly. "The Society for the Protection of Leafy Hollow is meeting. There have been unsavory developments in the village lately."

"Oh." I'd never heard of this Society, but I quickly added, "You're very civic-minded."

Sue motioned for me to start down the ladder. Following, she muttered, "Somebody has to be."

Our path to the Peak wound upward under a treed canopy that dimmed the sunlight to flickering shadows. My rubber boots slipped on patches of mud from the night's rain as I followed Sue across a series of wooden footbridges.

A small, gray-and-white body trotted behind us. General Chang had left the cushioned comfort of his front-porch rocker to accompany me—despite my efforts to shoo him away.

Sue regarded him blackly. "You didn't say you were bringing a cat."

"Sorry."

"Does that thing kill birds?"

"Oh, I don't think so."

Sue looked unconvinced.

I picked up the General and deposited him on the trail to face in the opposite direction. "Go back to Rose Cottage," I said, then leaned down to whisper, "It's not safe up here."

He gave me a one-eyed look of disgust, then sat placidly, meticulously licking a paw while we walked off.

Eventually we reached a fork in the trail. On the left, our well-trodden path continued. On the right, a pile of fallen tree trunks and a nailed sign, "*Trail closed*," barred our way.

Sue pointed. "That's the beginning of the old network.

Watch your step, and stay well back from the edge." With a final wave, she turned to retrace our journey.

I scrambled over the tree trunks and onto a barely discernible path beyond. After ten minutes of tripping over roots and rocks, and battling branches that scratched my face, I reached a rotting bridge that extended across a twenty-foot-wide gully. I set my feet on the first planks, judging their strength. A little wobbly, but they would hold my weight. I took another step.

I'd been dimly aware of noises around me—the movements of small animals, the rustle of leaves, the sharp chatter of birds. Or maybe those were frogs. But a new sound caught me up short. It was a dull, throbbing undertone that had gradually grown in volume. I craned my neck to listen, trying to make it out. Was that—*buzzing*?

Grabbing the bridge's shaky railing, I bent to study the underside. A paper nest the size of a football clung to the far side. I raised my head to squint into the gloom ahead. Hornets were darting back and forth, their black bodies nearly invisible against the murky undergrowth.

My jeans and cotton shirt would protect my arms and legs. Unless the wasps swarmed my head, I'd get across the bridge without being stung. These were Leafy Hollow hornets though. If they were as bloodthirsty as some other residents of this supposedly tranquil village, I might be in for a rough passage. Not to mention the problem of my return trip. I envisaged a battalion of agitated wasps in military dress, deployed in rows to bar my retreat, wings buzzing as they readied their final charge.

Aunt Adeline would have known what to do. A childhood memory of her crisping grasshoppers in a frying pan before my saucer-sized eyes came to mind. "Insects are an excellent source of protein," she told me while dishing a few onto my plate and squeezing chocolate sauce over them. "If you're ever lost in the bush, a few juicy grubs could save your life."

I had not eaten grasshoppers since. They tasted like chicken, as I recalled, but with extremely tiny drumsticks.

My aunt had also insisted *they are more scared of you, Verity*. Too bad I couldn't recall her imparted knowledge about which insects to avoid. At least her Krav Maga lessons hadn't gone to waste, although my self-defense skills wouldn't be much use against these opponents.

In the end, I simply made a run for it. My work boots thundered on the planks as I sprinted across the bridge. But if these hornets feared me, they were skilled at conquering it. Maybe they'd read *The Ninja Guide To...*

"Ow!" I shrieked, slapping at my face. I squealed as another hornet jabbed my wrist while I raced up the path on the other side of the bridge, branches snapping me in the face.

After a hundred feet, I halted, panting. I bent over with my hands on my knees, spitting out leaf bits. The red welt on my wrist didn't look too bad—a glancing blow. My forehead, however, throbbed. Gingerly, I patted the lump rising over my eye.

The phone in my pocket rang. And rang. I puffed out a breath and considered not answering, but thought better of it. It might be a client. Still stooped over with one hand on my knee, I clicked the button with my other thumb and raised the cellphone to my ear without looking at it.

"Verity, I'm glad I caught you. The landlord still hasn't received your sublet agreement. Haven't you signed it yet? Maybe you forgot. I know how busy you are. You probably forgot. Do you want me to tell him—"

I pulled the phone away from my ear and squinted at the call display. Yep. Patty Ferris, my best friend in Vancouver, was checking in with her usual impeccable timing. I grinned, then winced at the pain it caused. Keeping my face as immobile as possible, I placed the phone against my ear.

"—and Clark said, stop calling her, she's probably busy and what did I know about running a business anyway? And of course he's right but still I knew you'd want to hear—"

"Patty," I broke in. "I'm on the road right now. Give me a minute to pull over."

Clutching the phone to my chest, I straightened up, stretched out my back with a groan, and trudged over to a fallen tree trunk. I sat, wiping the perspiration from my forehead with my sleeve—wincing when I hit the swollen bits—then raised the phone again.

"It's great to hear from you, Patty. What's up?"

"It's your sublet agreement—it's lost in the mail. Should I ask the landlord to send you another copy? It's no trouble, because—"

Patty kept talking, but I wasn't listening. My attention was focused on an image of the envelope that lay on my aunt's bureau in Rose Cottage. The sublet document had arrived weeks earlier. I only had to sign it and send it back to the landlord to relinquish my Vancouver apartment. And cut the last link to the West Coast city that had been my home for the past three years.

So why didn't I?

"Verity? Are you listening?"

Patty's voice jolted me back to the present.

"Yes, of course I am. I'm a bit busy at the moment though. You know. Work stuff." I glanced to my left. Daylight lit up the path ahead. Had I finally reached the edge of the escarpment? "Patty, hang on..."

I lowered the phone and walked toward the light.

Before me stretched the billowy green waves of Pine Hill Valley, intersected by the streets and lampposts of Leafy Hollow. On one side, the blue-gray expanse of Lake Ontario melted into the horizon. Sunlight broke through haze from the morning's downpour, glinting off a rainbow rising from the lake. Directly below, a train chugged along on a winding toy track. I drew in a lungful of rain-freshened air before looking at my feet.

Despite the difficult trail, the spot where I stood had been worn down by dozens of hikers. I imagined sightseers leaning over the edge of this unofficial lookout, daring fate.

The main lookout was on my right, fifty to one hundred feet away as the crow flies. I couldn't see it through the trees, although its broad, flat shelf of unfenced shale was easily visible from the ground below.

In my current spot, however, I was shielded by the dense foliage of surrounding trees and shrubs. To anyone looking up from the ground, I would be hidden from view. A knot formed in my belly. Someone could have pushed Lucy off here without being seen. I raised the phone to my ear.

Patty was still talking. "...and I said—"

"Patty, can I call you back? Tomorrow?"

"Oh. Sure." She sounded disappointed.

I slid the phone into my pocket and rubbed my goose-bumped arms. Had Lucy fallen from here? There were lots of rocks and shrubs, even the trunks of ancient white cedars, to hit on the way down.

I scanned the area, looking for clues. Several shrubs were flattened, as if they'd been trampled. Probably deer, settling in for the night. Although it seemed unlikely they would venture this close to the edge.

Another sight caught my eye, and I jerked back in surprise. Rustic fenceposts stuck up along the edge of the escarpment, in some places only a foot or two from the rim. They must have been installed years earlier, when this trail was open to hikers.

But that wasn't the surprising part.

Lorne and I didn't build fences. We turned those clients over to my competitor, the blond beefcake Ryker Fields, who built beautiful fences, gazebos and decks. He frequently helped me out and I was glad to repay the favor.

But I knew enough carpentry to see that this barrier was missing three crucial rails—the ones that should have spanned the gap of the makeshift lookout.

Wrapping my arms around a nearby tree trunk, I leaned over to peer at the posts that remained. I suspected mischief-makers, not murderers, had broken off the railings. Where was the fun in tempting fate if you couldn't actually fall?

Then I made the mistake of looking down.

My gut clenched and my breath caught in my throat. Yikes. It was so... far.

I jerked back, clutching the trunk to my chest and squeezing my eyes closed.

I'd never been afraid of heights. Crowds, enclosed spaces, and bad-tempered insects, sure. But never heights. So, after a little deep breathing, I approached the edge again. My throat tightened and my fingers twitched. The vein in my neck thrummed. I hadn't had an anxiety attack in weeks. Yet here I was, trembling at the prospect of standing on that precipice. Had I merely exchanged one irrational fear for another?

I released the tree and staggered over to an outcropping of shale a few yards away. After slumping onto it, I bent over and waited for my breathing to slow. *Three. Two. One.*

My "investigation" had been a bust. Far from gaining insight, I was more puzzled than ever. Lucy was afraid of heights. She never would have braved this trail. Not voluntarily.

With a shudder, I studied the scrap of blue sky that marked the edge of the escarpment. To the unwary, it might signal a peaceful clearing in the woods. A welcome break from the suffocating foliage. You could almost see Bambi frolicking nearby, a butterfly landing on her nose. A weary hiker might approach this spot eagerly, unaware that it actually marked the edge of the cliff and a long, horrifying drop.

But Lucy had lived in Leafy Hollow all her life. She would have known better. Besides, there had been no love lost between Lucy Carmichael and gentle woodland creatures.

There was no time to ponder further. Lorne was waiting

for me to tackle our jobs for the day. With a last glance over my shoulder, I stumbled back along the path.

Mud had slathered my boots, my T-shirt was in tatters, my bruises throbbed, and my forehead... I halted, realizing my eyelid had swollen so much that my eye was nearly closed. I tapped it gingerly with a muddy finger, wishing I had a mirror to check the damage.

At least I wasn't anxious anymore. Either my physical injuries had shouldered out the emotional ones, or my worry that I had developed a fear of heights was unfounded. Maybe I wouldn't have to reread *The Ninja Guide*. That would give me time to finish the Originals' pick for Sunday's meeting.

But thoughts of the book club only triggered more speculation about how Lucy met her death. There was another possibility—one that made my stomach churn.

What if she was dead before she fell?

CHAPTER FIVE

WHILE WALKING BACK along the trail, I decided to share my theory with Jeff. Perhaps it would convince him to take another look at Lucy's case.

Slogging along, I fine-tuned that plan. Explaining this to Jeff while looking like a battered prize fighter might detract from the point I was trying to make. He already thought I was a klutz, which was unfair. Yes, I'd once been attacked by a rooster I was trying to catch, and fallen into the river while eluding a coyote, and scraped the skin from my palms by sliding down a drainpipe. But mishaps like those could happen to anybody.

It was probably the bowling ball I dropped on his foot that sealed his opinion.

No matter. My theory was too important to withhold from local law enforcement. Still, it couldn't hurt to clean up a little before I passed it on.

Unfortunately, by the time I made it to the truck and

called Lorne to warn him I would be late, my eye was swollen shut. I peered at it in the mirror on the back of my visor before sliding my sunglasses on with a wince of pain.

Half an hour later, as my feet crunched over the gravel driveway of Rose Cottage, the village's most notorious handyman waved his pocket flask at me from the camp stool beside his pop-up tent-trailer. Carson Breuer had been living in my driveway since undertaking a leisurely restoration of Rose Cottage shortly after I arrived.

"Welcome back," he said. "Just takin' a break." The fingernails on his gnarled hand were split and blackened, and spidery veins crisscrossed his enormous nose.

I waved, shielding my swollen eye with my other hand as I headed for the porch.

Despite appearances, Carson's knowledge of historic structures far exceeded mine—or most people's. He had immediately identified my aunt's home as a mid-nineteenth century worker's cottage with post-and-beam construction, split fieldstone walls, and a gable roof. Usually, I nodded at his suggestions and tried to look knowledgeable. Today, though, for the umpteenth time I wondered where Carson... freshened up, since he never intruded on Rose Cottage with requests to use the indoor facilities.

I made a mental note to check the lawn for dead spots.

General Chang was stretched out on the faded cushion of a wicker rocker on the porch. His head and one paw dangled languidly over the front. The General swished his tail half-heartedly in my direction, obviously unconcerned about his owner's injuries.

Owner. I chuckled at that. The battered, one-eyed tom

who'd insinuated himself into Rose Cottage two days after I arrived was owned by nobody. I had convinced him to respond to his new name, however. He clearly considered being named after an infamous *Star Trek* villain to be an honor. Either that, or he recognized me as the procurer of his favorite liver treats.

I preferred to believe the former. I've always been a dreamer.

The General closed his eye and stretched farther until he was nearly half off the cushion.

My adopted rooster was avidly watching him from the porch railing. On my way up the steps, I ruffled Reuben's feathers, averting my eyes from the droppings in the flower bed below. At least he and General Chang got along now.

Although, since Chang seemed incapable of catching even the smallest mouse, he was far too lazy to take on a rooster. Especially one with a beak as sharp as Reuben's. I winced, remembering an earlier fowl encounter. My swollen eyelid throbbed in sympathetic protest.

Reuben stretched his throat and puffed out his chest.

I covered my ears, knowing what was coming.

Cock-a-doodle-doo.

Before Reuben could reload for another blast, I closed the door behind me and headed for the shower.

After I'd changed into fresh clothes, pressed a cold compress to my eye, and taken an antihistamine for the swelling, I was forty minutes late picking up Lorne. He'd happily spent the time with Emy at her bakery, but we had seven appointments to get through before dark. We couldn't afford any more delays.

So when I saw people bearing placards milling about in front of the bakery, and the flashing lights of a police car, I uttered a mild curse under my breath. I turned up the narrow lane in the center of the block, intending to park in the lot behind the bakery. But cars jammed that lot, unusual for a weekday morning. More lined the lane, despite the No Parking signs.

I found a spot three blocks away and jogged back to Main Street. As I approached, shouts grew louder. A ragged line of a dozen protesters were marching back and forth across the street, chanting:

"Killers. Not. Welcome. Here."

My mouth gaped. Sue Unger was leading the protest. She brought a referee whistle to her lips and blew. The marchers halted, shuffling their feet, as a car drove past. The vehicle's occupants appeared puzzled by the absence of a pickup hockey game that would have explained the unofficial street blocking.

The line reformed.

"Killers. Not. Welcome. Here."

I shook my head. Leafy Hollow had seen more than its share of killers, to be sure, but that hardly required a demonstration. It wasn't like the village was advertising on Craigslist for them.

"There she is," screamed the blue-haired, teenaged clerk

I'd seen at the grocer's. She pointed to a third-floor window above the hardware store.

The group surged into the street, causing an SUV and a delivery truck to screech to a halt. The SUV driver held up her hands over the steering wheel in exasperation, then slapped the horn, producing a loud *beep-beep*. None of the protesters moved.

I followed the girl's gesturing finger. On the third floor above, a middle-aged black-haired woman held back a lace curtain from an open window to peer at the street. Her lips were set in a straight line. She looked inoffensive for having sparked such a commotion.

That window and the two-room apartment behind it were well-known to me. I'd spent an anxious half-hour there once, before departing hastily through the skylight. I wondered if the new occupant knew her home was last inhabited by someone who'd been bludgeoned to death with a crowbar.

Across the street, a uniformed police officer stepped off the curb to hold up a cautionary hand to the SUV driver.

I assessed the cop. Tall and lean, with chiseled features and straight black hair—yep, it was Jeff. I sighed. Traffic control was not his responsibility, but he must have been passing through the village and noticed the commotion.

The front door of the hardware store swung open, and a skinny young man marched out. The logo of a national chain stretched across the dark gray apron that was tied tightly over his khakis and folded shirt sleeves. A frown further twisted the crooked chin of Derek Talbot, a clerk at the store and a member of the Originals book club.

He headed Jeff's way, ducking under the placards. "Can't you make this lot move along?"

"Good morning, Derek. I'll try to get them off the road."

Derek jingled the elaborate key chain that hung from his belt while he watched the protest with brows drawn. "Could you at least keep them from accosting the customers?"

Jeff rubbed the back of his neck with one hand. "No one's been accosted, Derek."

"Not yet."

Above us, the curtain twitched and dropped back over the window. The black-haired woman continued to watch through the lace. The demonstrators fell back, mumbling among themselves, to re-form their line.

It was a good time to make my move. I darted between two marchers, trying to avoid the placards blocking my path. At the last minute a sign swung out and whacked my hornet-stung forehead, causing a jolt of pain. Instinctively, I shoved it away—right into the face of its holder.

This elicited a loud, "Ow!"

"Sorry," I said. "But your sign—"

"She hit me." The blue-haired teen pointed an accusing finger. She looked close to tears. The silver rings along her upper lip quivered.

"I'm sorry. I didn't see you behind your sign. I didn't mean to—"

The others gathered around, muttering.

"That's Verity Hawkes," a protester said.

The others swung their heads in my direction before turning back to her with puzzled expressions.

"You know, the snooping gardener?"

"Oh, right," the others said in unison, turning chilly stares on me.

Sue thrust out her chin. "Tell me, Verity, are you in favor of murderers moving in? You like to study killers, don't you?"

"I don't know what you're talking about." I made another attempt. "Let me through, please."

The protesters joined ranks. As they surrounded me in a claustrophobic crush, my breathing quickened. If somebody didn't make a hole soon, I couldn't speak to the consequences. My fists tightened by my sides.

"Wait. Give Verity a flyer." Sue inclined her head at the man who stood beside her. He fumbled through his messenger bag and handed me a lurid sheet of red paper, printed in a dripping-dagger font:

Keep Black Widow Killer
out of Leafy Hollow

I took the page and squinted at the fuzzy photo in its center. I'd never heard of the "Black Widow Killer." Nor did I care.

"Nothing to do with me." I tried to hand Sue the flyer. "Can I go through now?"

Sue ignored my outstretched hand. "Three husbands, all dead." She flashed three fingers. "Three. Who's next? And now," she said, shoving her referee whistle in my face, "she's out on parole. After only eight years. It's a travesty."

I stuffed the flyer into my pocket as insight dawned. "Don't tell me—this is the Society for the Protection of Leafy Hollow, isn't it?"

"I'm the founder," Sue said. "You should come to our meetings."

"No thanks." I clasped a hand to my chest, trying to breathe, and searched again for an exit. "If this woman is on parole, there must be a good reason," I said. "The courts—"

"The courts are wrong."

I recognized that tone, because I'd heard it about myself. Not all Leafy Hollow residents were welcoming when I first arrived. Given that I was a murder suspect at the time, that wasn't surprising. Still, I knew from personal experience that rushing to judgment could be wrong. I took a deep breath, determined not to respond.

One of the protesters stepped closer and poked a finger into my shoulder.

I flinched and pulled back. "Get out of my way," I muttered.

My eye throbbed and itched, my stomach rumbled— reminding me I'd had nothing but coffee for breakfast—and at that moment, my phone thrummed with a text. Probably Lorne, wondering where I was. I was cranky, okay?

Still, I wasn't proud of what I did next.

I shoved her.

It's not a Krav Maga move, The Shove. But I didn't want to risk anything more effective. A hearty push is usually enough. Unless you miscalculate and your opponent trips. And then pitches against the next person in the line, who also goes over, landing against the next person who... Think of ten-pin bowling with pins that fight back.

Also screaming. Lots of screaming.

Jeff frowned under his peaked cap and started in our direction.

Before he could reach us, someone gripped my arm above the elbow. A woman's voice trilled in my ear.

"Time to go, Verity. Quick march."

What the... I glanced over to see the flawless makeup and blunt-cut bob of Thérèse Dionne.

"Thérèse? What are you—"

She didn't listen. Nor did she release her death grip on my elbow. Instead, she beamed at the protesters and waved expansively with her other hand. "Let us through, please," she said. "Please? My goodness, what a crowd."

The group parted, looking ashamed of themselves. Thérèse had that effect on people. Or perhaps they were cowed by her classically understated French manicure. Someone had just been to the nail salon. Unfortunately, several of those freshly lacquered nails were poking into my arm.

Thérèse was generally soft-spoken, even when negotiating overdue book fines that stretched back to the last century. Yet today, my arm stung under her forceful grasp. It was totally out of character.

I was so shocked, in fact, I hardly noticed the protestors fall away as Thérèse marched me into Emy's bakery.

CHAPTER SIX

THÉRÈSE STEERED me into the 5X Bakery. The chanting receded as the door closed behind us.

Emy stood behind the counter, glaring. "What the heck were you doing out there?"

"Me?" I answered, checking my arm for puncture wounds. "What was *I* doing? Is that what you're asking?" An incredulous look crossed my face.

Emy placed her arms on her hips. "Isn't it bad enough those people are scaring off customers without you aggravating them?"

I opened my mouth to protest. Lorne was leaning against the far wall, shaking his head at me with one of his *don't-go-there* smirks. I closed my mouth.

"Now ladies," Thérèse said with a tone of forced jollity. "Let's not argue."

Emy and I stared at her. In the silence that followed, chants of *"Killers. Not. Welcome. Here,"* competed with the tick-tock of the black cat on the wall. Its tail swung back and forth. *Tick-tock. Tick-tock.* After every fifth *tock*, its round eyes slowly blinked.

I waited for an apology. If not from Emy, then maybe Thérèse. Anybody would do.

Emy found her voice first. "I'm sorry, Verity. That chanting is making me crazy. I shouldn't have taken it out on you." She leaned over the counter, sighing heavily. Her expression changed to one of horror when she saw my eye. "*Crackers*—what happened to your face?"

Tentatively, I touched my eyebrow and winced. "It's nothing. A hornet stung me at the Peak."

Emy darted out from behind the counter. "Sit down," she said, ushering me to the table in the back and pulling out a chair. "I'll get a cold compress for that, and you'll need a cup of tea. Mom, can I get you a cup?" she asked over her shoulder.

"No thanks, Emy. I'm needed at the library. Another time."

Thérèse walked out, pausing with her hand on the door handle long enough to deliver a weak smile. The chanting rose again when she opened the door, then dissipated when it closed.

Her hasty departure filled me with a vague sense of uneasiness. *That was a weird encounter.*

Emy put a dish towel to soak under the cold water tap and turned on the kettle.

Lorne winked at me. *Nice work*, he mouthed while gesturing at his eye. I made a face at him.

Emy hurried back with a plate of bacon-cheddar scones

and set them in front of me. "Tea's on its way. Now tell me how you did that." She peered anxiously at my swollen brow.

"It's nothing," I said.

"Don't be silly. You need to take care of that." Emy hustled back behind the counter to wring out the compress and returned with it. "Hold this against your eye."

I did as she instructed. "I can't stay, Emy. We have work to do."

"Nonsense. Lorne can do it without you."

Lorne pushed off from the wall. "I'll get the equipment off the truck."

"No," I protested, trying not to drip water on the table. "That's not necessary."

"It's no problem, Verity," he said. "Look after that eye." As he pulled open the door, the chanting grew louder.

I raised my voice. "No, really—"

Lorne waved through the window as he walked away.

Emy placed a filled teapot by my elbow. "I'm so sorry. I shouldn't have asked you to go up there."

I flipped the compress and pressed the other, cooler, side to my brow. It was ridiculously soothing. The perfect antidote to my crazy morning.

"So?" Emy asked, sitting down. She poured me a cup of tea from the pot and added milk. "How did it happen?"

She listened carefully while I described my encounter with the hornets and my reconnaissance at the Peak.

Then she sat back, tapping her fingers on the table. "I'm more convinced than ever that something's not right. It couldn't have been suicide."

We sipped our tea, mulling this over.

Emy replaced her cup on its saucer with a slight frown. "I wonder what the autopsy will find."

"Have they done an autopsy?"

"Not yet, but they will. Suspicious death and all that. I don't think they can avoid it when someone dies like that, can they?"

I shrugged. "Dunno." No need to speculate whether Lucy was injured before her fall. From my repeated viewings of *Mystery Theater*, I knew an autopsy would take care of that.

Emy scrunched her eyes at me. "Jeff would know." She took the now-warm compress from me and rose to re-soak it in the sink behind the counter. "He's right outside. You could ask—"

I pointed at the window, anxious to change the topic. "Why are those people here, anyway?"

Emy turned to follow my gesture. Derek had emerged from the hardware store again to scowl at the protestors. We watched as Jeff guided the marchers down the street to the jewelry store, one building down. They shuffled along the sidewalk to their new positions and resumed their chanting.

The jeweler—a thin-lipped woman with amazing earrings—glared at them through her plate-glass window.

"Who is the Black Widow Killer?" I asked.

"It was years ago. I don't remember much about it. Mom knows the details."

I nodded in agreement. Thérèse was not only Leafy Hollow's chief librarian, but also its primary repository of village lore. She would definitely have the facts.

"Any clippings in that scrapbook of hers?"

"I'm sure there are, but it's not here anymore. Mom took it home. Something about us being too nosy." Emy grinned. "But she did tell me that both of Mrs. Rupert's husbands— that's her real name, Marjorie Rupert—died under mysterious circumstances, and Marjorie went to prison."

"So why do those protest signs have spider webs on them?"

"You know—black widow spiders?"

"What about them?" I asked, remembering an incident from my childhood when Aunt Adeline had nonchalantly dispatched one with a paring knife. *Thwack.* I was so impressed.

"They kill their mates. That's why women who murder their spouses are called Black Widow Killers. Especially if they've done it more than once."

"Sue mentioned three husbands." I held up my fingers in a parody of her emphatic gesture.

"I don't know—maybe that's true."

"Why does she care?"

"I don't know that, either, but she's been going door to door, trying to get people to sign a petition to have the Black Widow run out of town."

"Can they do that?"

Emy snorted in amusement. "No. But Sue claims to have inside information. A few people have taken her seriously, but not many. Most prefer to let it alone."

"Why would she care about an old murder case?" I asked.

Emy shrugged. "Why would anyone? This Black Widow isn't a danger to anybody except a new husband, and who'd be dumb enough to marry her?"

"Why is she here?"

"According to Mom, she owns the building where the new restaurant is opening. That's why it's been empty for so long. She refused to rent it out while she was in prison."

I picked up my cup to walk over to the front window. Sipping my tea, I studied the protestors.

"Derek doesn't look happy," I said.

"Who?"

"Derek Talbot—from the book club?"

She walked over to stand by my side. "Oh, right. I didn't see him there. He's probably been told by his boss to shut down the protest. Derek does what he's told."

I nodded. At book club meetings, Derek always agreed with Thérèse's interpretation of the book's theme. But then, I did too. It was easier and, besides—Thérèse was always right.

I pulled the crumpled flyer from my pocket and smoothed it out on the window. The newspaper photo printed on the flyer showed a black-haired woman getting into an SUV at the bus station. The caption read, "Marjorie Rupert arrives in Strathcona."

But it was the driver who caught my attention. A mustache darkened his upper lip, but sunglasses, a fedora, and the turned-up collar of a windbreaker obscured the rest of his face.

I pointed to the photo. "Maybe there *are* men willing to get involved. One, anyway."

Emy gave my arm a playful tap. "That's probably a relative."

"Have you ever seen him before?"

Emy studied the clipping. "I don't think so. It could be a hired driver."

Outside, Sue sounded a blast on her whistle. I looked up. The entire group was heading our way.

"C'mon," Emy said, pulling me to the door. "This is a perfect opportunity. Go talk to Jeff."

She dragged me across the floor and shoved me out the door so hard that I tripped over my feet and nearly ran into a lamppost. Cursing my awkwardness under my breath, I looked up.

Jeff smiled down at me. "You don't strike me as the protesting type," he said, extending a steadying hand.

"I'm not protesting anything," I objected. "I'm only—"

He caught sight of my forehead and narrowed his eyes. "Did they hit you with that sign?"

"It's a hornet sting." At his puzzled glance, I launched into an explanation.

"Never mind," he said with a grin. "It would be more surprising if you *didn't* have signs of battle."

"That's not fair," I sputtered.

He bent toward me, inspecting my injury with his lips slightly parted. For a moment I couldn't breathe—or take my eyes off his mouth.

"Just kidding," he said. "Get that looked at, though. By a professional."

Jeff didn't specify what type of professional, and since he was looking at it, that was enough for me. I felt better already, so I gave him what was probably a goofy grin.

He started to speak. "Verity—"

My stomach churned. What if his comment had nothing

to do with hornet stings or protesters? What if it was more personal? Did I want to hear it?

"I got this at the Peak," I broke in, tapping my swollen eyebrow, "while I was investigating the spot where Lucy Carmichael fell."

Jeff gave me a startled glance. He took a step back, and his expression changed. "Investigating? Why?"

I tugged at my T-shirt. "Did I say investigating? I meant sightseeing. I was sightseeing—"

"On a weekday morning?"

"The sunrise is beautiful from there."

"The sun rose four hours ago."

Before he could say anything else, I rushed through my assessment of the scene, tumbling my words together.

Jeff uttered a long sigh. "Verity, you haven't been in Leafy Hollow long—"

When I opened my mouth to jump in, he held up a hand.

"—enough to know it's not unusual for someone to fall off the escarpment. We do our best to warn people, but the ridge goes on for miles. There's no way to prevent every accident. That's what Lucy's death was—a tragic accident." He paused again. "Or suicide. We scoured the scene, believe me, and there was nothing to indicate foul play. Nothing." He emphasized the last word.

"But the fence—"

"There's no fence, partial or otherwise, on the lookout where she toppled off. And no fence pieces at the bottom where we found her body. I'm sorry."

A protest rose in my throat, but Jeff's expression reminded me that he was no stranger to sorrow. He would never take someone's death lightly. I bit my lip and looked away.

"We haven't closed the case yet. And we won't until we've talked to all of her friends and family. But so far, there's no evidence anyone else was involved." He bent his head to catch my gaze. "Okay?"

"Are they doing an autopsy?"

"Yes. It's standard procedure."

While we were talking, the demonstrators had reconsidered their new position and crossed the street again.

The jeweler barreled out of her door, scowling. "Get out of here," she said, shoving the nearest placard carrier.

It happened to be blue-haired girl, who had regained her composure since her encounter with me. "Fascist," she yelled, whacking the jeweler over the head with her sign.

Jeff rubbed a hand over his face, shaking his head. "I have to go, Verity. Look after that eye." With a brief smile, he crossed the street and approached the combatants.

I watched him go, assessing the cut of his... uniform.

With a spring in my step, I whirled around—and walked straight into the village's resident blond Adonis.

CHAPTER SEVEN

I RETREATED WITH A HASTY "SORRY!" until my back was up against the lamp post. When I saw who I'd run into, I fisted my hands on my hips. "Are you following me again?"

Ryker Fields regarded me with his lips pressed into a thin line.

I immediately felt bad. Yes, he once followed me—and if he hadn't, I might be dead now. Leafy Hollow's heartthrob would never stalk women. If anything, it was the other way around.

"Sorry. I don't know why I said that."

"Perfectly understandable." Ryker leaned in, flashing his trademark sexy grin and flaunting his impressive pecs. "Which reminds me—what about that dinner date you promised me?"

"I never promised any such thing." I smiled despite myself.

"You've probably forgotten. You were unconscious at the time."

"If you're referring to that day by the river, then yes, I was unconscious. That's how I know I never..."

His eyebrows lifted. "A guy could get a complex when you go out with him only to make someone else jealous."

"I never did that," I blustered. "I..."

Biting my lip, I remembered our shared dinner. It was at Kirby's, a popular steak house on the highway outside the village. Ryker and I had been drinking at the bar, but I agreed to escalate our encounter to dinner after spotting Jeff flirting with that blonde. When Jeff had leaned in to share a spoonful of whipped cream with her, I hid my reaction—I thought.

"You saw that?" I asked sheepishly.

Ryker's eyebrows rose even higher. "If you mean the look on your face when you spotted our resident crime-buster and his date—then yes, I did."

Briefly closing my eyes, I hoped the flush I felt didn't mean my face was beet red. "It wasn't like that," I said, opening my eyes.

"Of course not." Ryker smiled. "Now, dinner. How about right here? Tonight?" He gestured at the window behind us.

I pivoted to take a look. We were standing in front of Anonymous, Leafy Hollow's trendy new gourmet restaurant. A banner over the window read, "*Grand opening tonight.*"

The three-story brick building had housed a restaurant on its ground floor for many years. But when I arrived in Leafy Hollow, the leatherette booths and laminated counter were gathering dust. That was before Fritz Cameron blew into town. The redheaded hipster somehow lured a noted chef from Strathcona to re-open the old place. After a renovation that included everything from mahogany tables-for-two to Irish linen napkins, Fritz renamed the restaurant and announced the opening. All the area's notables were attending. Most of them, I suspected, had been promised free meals by the media-savvy restaurateur.

My invitation, sadly, was lost in the mail. But I knew every detail about the new eatery because Fritz had hired Emy to craft the desserts. They'd been conferring over them nonstop. Emy couldn't stop talking about it since Anonymous —and its online marketing campaign—might attract restaurant critics from as far as Toronto.

"How did you get an invitation?" I asked Ryker.

He slapped a hand over his heart and raised his eyes to the heavens. "Another low blow," he said, before lowering his head with a grin. "Also not relevant. Nice hair."

At least he'd elected not to mention my swollen eye. Nervously, I patted my wavy brunette locks. I had taken a little more trouble with my appearance of late, but only because Lorne was such a tremendous help at Coming Up Roses Landscaping that I had the time. It didn't mean I was looking for romance. At least Ryker didn't set my heartbeat racing, so I wasn't likely to make a fool of myself. Which was a point in his favor. Or was it? I made a face, trying to sort out my tangled feelings.

"Are you in or not?" he asked.

I mulled it over. On the one hand, I was curious to see the village's latest eatery in action—as well as provide Emy with moral support. But the restaurant would be packed. Threading my way through a crowd always made me queasy.

"Well..." A movement inside the restaurant caught my eye. Fritz was in the rear, near the kitchen, talking to a man in a white jacket and chef's hat whose back was to me.

Fritz caught sight of me looking in the window. *Verity!* he mouthed and pointed to the front door.

I froze, wondering whether that meant I should go in, or he was coming out. When I glanced at Ryker, he shrugged.

Fritz pushed open the door and stepped onto the sidewalk, wearing a big smile. His brown eyes twinkled behind his rimless glasses and his red hair, graying at the temples, was shorn into a poufy haircut that faded into a close crop underneath. Obviously, Fritz spent more time at the hairdresser than I did.

"Hey, you two," he said, patting his upper lip.

With a start, I noticed his trim red mustache. *That's new.*

Ryker took a step back. "See you tonight, Verity."

"Uh," I mumbled with my usual poise, turning my back on Fritz while mouthing to Ryker, *Don't leave!*

"Ciao," Ryker said with a smirk, then strode off.

Great. Now I'd have to listen to a hipster blowhard tell me about his fabulous new restaurant. I hoped Fritz didn't want to debate thread counts again.

"He seems like a nice guy," Fritz said as Ryker walked away.

"Yes." I glanced around, hoping for an excuse to get the heck out of there. "You know, I have to..."

"Verity, I'm glad I ran into you. I'd like your thoughts on a few marketing ideas of mine. If you have time."

I cast a longing glance up the street. No sign of Lorne,

who must be off cutting lawns by now. "I know nothing about marketing."

"That can't be true," Fritz responded with an easy laugh. "Everyone says you resurrected your aunt's landscaping business single-handed. That must have taken marketing skills."

Everyone? I stared at him. "Who..."

He flicked a hand, cutting me off. "Emy Dionne. She has a very high opinion of you."

"We're friends, but—" I tried to remember any marketing efforts I might have made. As far as I knew, they consisted entirely of having the faded and peeling *Coming Up Roses* logo re-stenciled on the doors of my aunt's aging pickup.

Across the street, the chanting rose in volume.

"Killers. Not. Welcome. Here."

"Let's walk," Fritz said. He grasped my hand at the elbow and guided me down the street, away from the marchers.

I tried to disengage my arm while suppressing an urge to whack it across his smirking face. This was a perfect example of why I had so much trouble warming up to Fritz Cameron. He would zero in—so close I could count the freckles on his corded neck—and then, before the encounter got really awkward, back off with an affable grin.

It was also surprising that a successful restaurateur had picked such a sleepy village to host his new venture. Emy had dismissed my concerns, claiming I was too suspicious. I countered that by insisting she was too trusting. We agreed to disagree.

Fritz pointed down the street. "Let's go this way. I've wanted to take a closer look at the statue in the square since I arrived. Founder's Day is coming up, isn't it?"

"On Saturday—a week from today. But there's not much to the statue," I replied, thinking of the bronze Loyalist in his buttoned-up waistcoat, tight pants, and riding boots. Either the original had been height-challenged—like his contemporary, Napoleon—or the village fathers had a tight budget when they commissioned his bronze likeness in the mid-nineteenth century. Perhaps they didn't have enough funds for a life-sized figure. Better short than armless, I guessed.

Fritz towered over the statue by at least a foot. He sank onto the nearby bench and patted the seat beside him. "Sit," he said.

I did, but sidled over to the far side on the pretext of wanting to lean on the wooden arm. Sparrows flocked at our feet to peck at the pavement, no doubt hoping for bits of stale hot dog buns. Or, now that Fritz had arrived, perhaps artichokes and goat cheese?

"So... marketing?" I asked.

Fritz stretched his arm along the back of the bench in my direction and crossed his leg so that one Italian leather loafer pointed toward me. "Tell me about yourself." He lifted his right hand and frowned at an unruly cuticle.

I forced a laugh. "Haven't you heard it all from Emy?"

"I like to get alternative viewpoints."

Alternative viewpoints? I suspected the reason for this interrogation was that Fritz had the hots for Emy—which wouldn't be unusual. Not only was she adorable, with a smile that melted most men's hearts, but she made a killer lemon meringue. Whereas, my idea of gourmet cooking was adding frozen peas to Kraft Dinner. Also, it had been three years since my last professional manicure, and my notion of girly attire was digging out a clean T-shirt.

I did have a dress—I just couldn't remember where I'd put it.

So, I was positive the hip and well-groomed Fritz Cameron wasn't interested in me. It was possible he thought befriending Emy's best friend would bring Emy herself closer. He'd have no luck there. Lorne would cut him off at the knees, graying temples and all. My landscaping assistant presented a shy exterior to the world, but if anyone made a move on Emy—especially an unwelcome one—he'd chase them off with hedge trimmers. Maybe even a lawnmower.

Whatever. I simply didn't feel comfortable around Fritz. Waving my hand airily, I forced a smile. "I think your story is much more interesting."

He looked at me, his expression blank. "My story?"

"Why are you in Leafy Hollow, re-opening a restaurant that failed years ago? There must be better prospects."

"Oh. No, you're wrong. The original restaurant didn't fail. The owner simply left the area and refused to lease it." He leaned in and double-tapped his forehead. "A bit eccentric, apparently. But that's why it's been empty for so long. It's an excellent location. I was lucky to get it."

Eccentric seemed a rather charitable assessment of a convicted murderer. But before I could ask Fritz about it, he jumped in with another question.

"What about you? Why did you come to Leafy Hollow two months ago?"

"How do you know I did?"

He shrugged. "Emy mentioned it."

I walked my fingers along the bench's sun-warmed arm. "My aunt disappeared, and I came here to look after her estate."

He nodded solemnly. "I'm sorry for your loss. Your aunt sounded like a wonderful woman."

Fritz had never met Aunt Adeline. His concern seemed genuine, but it irked me. "She's not dead," I blurted.

Darn it. I hadn't meant to say that. I bit my lip and looked away.

"Oh? Have you heard from her?"

While I pondered how to answer that without lying, a sparrow hopped onto the bench between us. Fritz flicked it off without taking his eyes from mine.

"Nooo," I said, finally. "I haven't."

"Ah," he said, settling against the bench with a loud exhale. "Wishful thinking, then."

I bristled and opened my mouth for a snarky retort.

Before I could deliver it, he added, "I've lost a loved one. It's tough."

The look on his face deflated my anger. "I'm sorry," I said. "Accident?"

A flash of anger crossed his face, but it lasted barely a second. "Never mind. Mustn't dwell on the past. We have to move forward." Clapping his hands on his knees, he stretched out his legs and then bounced to his feet. "See you later, Verity."

"What?"

"Aren't you coming to my opening? I thought Ryker—"

"Oh. I guess I am."

Darn it. I had been so overwhelmed by the day's events

that I'd agreed to a second date with perennial ladies' man and determined heartbreaker Ryker Fields.

As Fritz walked off, I wondered if my expression gave me away when I claimed not to have heard from my aunt. I had faith in Gideon, but I wished I knew exactly where he was.

But first, I had a more immediate goal: Find something to wear to the village's most hotly anticipated event of the summer.

CHAPTER EIGHT

THAT EVENING AT ROSE COTTAGE, I stood in my underwear, facing the tiny closet in my aunt's bedroom and contemplating the outfit I'd purchased that afternoon. It was sleek, black, and probably sexy. Although my recollection of what constituted sexy was a little dim.

I pulled the slinky dress from its hanger and tossed it onto Aunt Adeline's four-poster bed while recalling my conversation with Fritz. It seemed strange he should be so interested in me. It almost felt a little creepy. I bit my lip, making a mental note not to share that observation with Emy. She would be horrified. Fritz wasn't exactly her friend, but she admired him.

I was searching my aunt's closet for a shawl when my cell phone rang. The screen read, Patty Ferris.

Darn. I had completely forgotten to call her back. I grabbed the phone. "Hi. I was just about to call you."

Patty had been my lifeline while I was holed up in my

high-rise apartment in Vancouver. In the beginning, she saw me as one of her charity projects. I didn't mind. It always brightened my day when she waltzed through my door, blonde ponytail swinging, holding aloft a plate of her baked goods. They were usually inedible, but I never told her that.

"Verity, it's me."

"I know—call display, remember?"

"Yeah," she said dejectedly.

I'd meant it as a joke, but Patty was surprisingly subdued. The sounds of a soccer game—or "football" as her husband Clark called it—came from their big-screen TV. Clark never missed a match of his beloved Leeds United.

"Are you baking, Patty?"

"Not at the moment."

Patty was rarely this reluctant to talk—even while working out a new recipe, she kept the phone on speaker and maintained a nonstop commentary. She loved to share her creations with me. The last email she sent me included instructions for her Pickled Beets 'n Raisins Layer Cake. I had deleted it with a shudder.

To be honest, I wasn't sure why she bothered. If it didn't come in a box with "Betty Crocker" on the front, I wouldn't be making it.

Still, I comforted myself with the knowledge that the world was full of bakers. And they needed non-bakers, like myself, to appreciate their work. So, my lack of skill in the kitchen was really a public service.

I took a deep breath and plunged in. "I'm so sorry I didn't call you back before this. How's the sale going?"

"Great," she said, her voice immediately more perky. I

could almost see her ponytail bounce as she talked. "You'll be thrilled with the total. The last buyer is picking up your bedroom set tomorrow."

That sparked a twinge. Matthew and I bought that set at IKEA—after searching for the exit so long we laughed and said they'd find our bodies propped up against the Billy bookcases.

It was a joke. I never thought I'd actually be a widow three years later.

Coming so soon after my mother's death—my father, living in Australia with wife number three, was no help—Matthew's illness was too much. For two years after his death, I retreated to our apartment, living among a growing army of dust bunnies and stacks of self-help books. I might still be there, except for a fateful phone call about my missing aunt that brought me to Leafy Hollow and a new life.

I missed Patty though.

Maybe that was why I hadn't signed my sublet agreement. I glanced at the bedroom bureau, where the torn edge of an envelope revealed the document inside.

"...and the kitchen cupboards are empty now. That just leaves..."

I put the phone on speaker and resumed the scrutiny of my aunt's closet. "Patty, you've saved me a huge headache. The landscaping business is good right now. I don't need the money from the furniture. Why don't you and Clark use it for a weekend away? Banff, maybe?"

"Are you sure?"

"Absolutely."

"Well," she said. "We have been thinking about a vacation."

"There you go then. It's perfect."

A roar in the background signaled a goal. "Was that Leeds?" I asked.

"Sadly, no," she answered. Clark groaned. The noise died down, so I figured Patty had taken her phone into the bedroom.

"It doesn't look like they'll make the playoffs," she said.

"Clark won't be happy."

"No, but it means we can go away without me having to sabotage the hotel's cable."

We both giggled. "Good one," I said.

"You get the Sports Network at Rose Cottage, right?"

"I'm afraid not."

"Any plans to add it?"

Suspecting one of Patty's veiled ploys to discover if I was dating again, I fended off a potential *"time to move on"* pep talk. "No one here watches sports much," I said.

That was an understatement—the General and I lived alone in Rose Cottage. Although I watched the occasional hockey or basketball game, he had eyes only for Animal Planet. "If I want to see a game, I can go next door. I have a key to Gideon's place, and he has a huge wall-screen TV that gets everything. Even NASA, I think." I recalled the satellite surveillance footage I'd noticed once when I dropped by to check the fridge for mold. It might have been the science fiction channel.

"Gotta go," Patty said. "Talk to you tomorrow."

She hung up without waiting for my reply. I looked at the

phone with misgivings. Surely Patty wasn't... With a sigh, I tossed it onto the ottoman and rummaged in the closet for an evening bag. Within minutes, I found a feathered cross-body, a kiss-lock beaded tube purse, and an embroidered *baguette* clutch. My aunt's social life was clearly more interesting than mine.

I had insisted on meeting Ryker at the restaurant, hoping that would make it seem less like a date. Anonymous was hopping by the time I made my entrance.

Each linen-covered table was occupied, and a hopeful lineup of uninvited guests had formed outside. Indoors, a sheet of water trailed over the restaurant's back wall and gurgled into a channel at the base. Small overhead spotlights glinted off the mahogany chairs and silver fixtures.

Emy hustled over when she saw me at the door. "You look fabulous." She paused for a complete assessment of my outfit, forcing me to twirl uneasily. "Where did you get that dress?"

"Is it okay?" I whispered, acutely aware the black spandex was both short and rather tight. I brandished the pink shawl I'd thrown over it. "I found this in my aunt's cupboard. It's vintage, I think."

"It's gorgeous," squealed Emy, fingering the embroidered silk. She leaned in to whisper, "Ryker's already here."

We swiveled our heads to a table near the back where Ryker's blond head towered over the diners seated nearby. He wore a navy jacket over a shirt open at the neck. A gold watch gleamed on his wrist as he extended his arm over the back of the empty chair beside him and flashed his eyebrows at me.

"Lorne and I are over here," Emy said, inclining her head at a table nearer the front, where Lorne was talking to a waiter. She placed her hand on my arm with a worried look. "Let me know what you think about the desserts."

"They're terrific. You have nothing to worry about."

Lorne and I had been willing guinea pigs for Emy's creations. Her rum baba with cardamom-scented Chantilly cream and violet-petal garnish was exquisite.

She leaned in. "You always say that. Just try to hear what people say about them."

I patted her arm reassuringly. "I will."

Emy returned to her seat.

I walked to Ryker's table, aware I hadn't worn heels this high in a long time. Any second now, my ankle might... *Oops.* I stumbled, thrusting out a hand for balance.

My palm flattened across the stomach of a well-upholstered man at a table to my left. He gave a brief "Oof" and drew back, looking alarmed.

"Sorry," I said with a wince.

Ryker was grinning when I reached our table. "Long trip?" He stood and pulled out a chair for me. "I would have asked for a table nearer the door if I'd known it was a problem."

I whacked his arm with my aunt's *baguette* clutch before sitting down. "Very funny."

He sat and reached across the table for my hand with an appreciative glance at my dress. "You should wear shorts on the job. With those legs, you'd attract a lot more clients."

I pulled my hand away and tugged at the hem of my dress. "Stop flirting. This is *not* a date."

He pulled his hand back with a smirk and flipped open the leather-bound wine list. "Right. I forgot. You're... how did you put it? *Investigating.*" He flexed his eyebrows again before calling over the nearest server and pointing to an entry. "We'll have this one, please, Theresa. But only if you recommend it."

I craned my neck to check the price. "Too expensive. Get the house wine."

Ryker ignored me, focusing on the waitress.

Theresa didn't even notice me. I could have tripped flat on my face and taken out her entire section and she wouldn't have seen a thing.

"Excellent choice. One of my favorites." Giggling, she took the wine list from Ryker.

"Great." He tossed her a seductive grin. "One bottle, to start."

"I'll be back with your menu," she said breathily, clutching the wine list to her bosom. Ryker watched her walk away with rapt attention before returning his gaze to me. I rolled my eyes at him.

I didn't care about the wine, but I was curious about the food. Fritz had hired a celebrated chef, so the dishes at Anonymous should be excellent. Most chefs rose at dawn to visit farmers' markets and fishmongers, organize menus, and prep dishes. And their day wasn't over until the last diner left and the kitchen was spotless again. But running a restaurant entailed long hours for the owner, too. One of Patty's friends in Vancouver was married to a restaurateur. I'd often heard her moaning about his work day while we shared a pot of tea over Patty's coffee table. I wondered how Fritz was coping.

Waiters bustled in and out with laden trays. Theresa returned to place a single parchment page in front of each of us.

TASTING MENU

ANONYMOUS

GRAND OPENING

The seven courses included potato and sea urchin, foie gras with sunchokes, and... I couldn't read the rest, because my eyes were mesmerized by the price. "We're splitting this," I whispered, tilting my head and pointing at the menu.

Ryker smiled. "No, we're not."

"This is *not* a date," I insisted, leaning in.

Just then, the kitchen door swung open to admit a waiter with another laden tray. Behind him, two figures sat at a table even tinier than the ones in the dining room. Leafy Hollow councilor and lawyer Wilf Mullins had snagged a seat at the chef's table—naturally. Trust Wilf to wangle the most coveted spot. I wondered if he'd brought his upholstered booster seat. At four feet tall, he needed a little help.

Opposite him, the impeccably groomed and blond-haired Nellie Quintero, the village's favorite realtor and Wilf's BFF, lifted a bite of course number four—steelhead trout with crème fraîche and sorrel—to her lips. The door swung shut, and I lost sight of them. But not before seeing Fritz lean over their table to whisper in Nellie's ear—and her friendly smile in response.

I swept my gaze around the main dining room. Sue Unger sat at a table for two against the far wall. Her lipstick was a near-psychedelic red. It was her only concession to fashion, since the rest of her outfit consisted of khaki pants, heavy sandals, and a black cotton shirt open at the neck. As she studied the tasting menu, I studied her. Fritz wasn't the kind of businessman who left anything to chance. He must have offered Sue a free meal so she wouldn't cause trouble at his opening. My hunch was confirmed when Fritz swept past to deposit a glass of bubbly by her elbow.

"With my compliments," he said. "Enjoy your dinner."

Sue looked up and smiled. I wondered what she thought of the Irish linen.

Fritz knew how to work a crowd. At this rate, Anonymous would be an enormous success. Smirking, I returned my attention to the tasting menu.

"Have you heard what Sue's been up to?" I asked.

Ryker pushed his menu to one side and leaned over the table. "Who?"

"Sue Unger. The woman with the whistle?"

He glanced at Sue with a flicker of interest, then looked away. "I ignore people like that. Rupert did her time. Everybody else should move on." He ran a finger down the menu. "Looks good," he said with a smile, changing the subject.

I knew about Ryker's brushes with the law when he was a teenager. That could be why he objected to the persecution of former cons. But he'd also warned me some Leafy Hollow residents were more dangerous than they seemed. Could he have been talking about Marjorie Rupert?

"That's quite a shiner. How did you get it?" Ryker indicated my eye, which was now partially open, giving me the rakish appearance of a perpetual half-wink. "Not that it looks bad or anything," he hastily added.

"That's okay, I know what it looks like." A rueful grin puckered my lips while I gingerly tapped my swollen brow. I had considered covering it with makeup, but it only would have made things worse. Besides the fact that I didn't have any makeup that would do the job.

"It happened up on the Peak, when I was checking the spot where the police think Lucy Carmichael fell."

"Think? Do they have doubts?"

"No, but I do."

"I don't blame you," he said. "Tumbling off the Pine Hill Peak lookout in broad daylight? It's a bit unusual."

Theresa returned with our first course—hearts of palm with pineapple pear. Before we could lift our forks, Fritz swept up with two glasses of champagne.

"On the house," he said, placing them on our table with an unctuous smile. Although he spoke to both of us, he looked only at me. "I hope you'll grace Anonymous with your presence many times in the future."

Fritz disappeared into the kitchen. As the door closed behind him, I smiled at Wilf's cackle. Our ebullient councilor never missed the opportunity for a good belly laugh.

We were only two courses in when Sue made her presence felt.

"Hey." She waved at the server. "More champagne here,

please." Sue looked as if she'd had plenty already, but the server hurried over.

The waitress bent over her table and spoke in a murmur.

Sue responded with a scowl. "I don't have to pay for it. I'm an invited guest. The champagne is on the house."

Shamelessly, I leaned in to listen.

"That's only the first glass," the server said. "And you've already had three. I have to charge you for the next one."

"Absolutely not," Sue insisted, her voice rising. "Does Fritz know about this?" She twisted in her chair to face the kitchen, sweeping her arm around. Her hand caught the lip of her water glass. It crashed to the floor, soaking the table-cloth and the server.

"Fritz!" Sue called, unconcerned about the now-dripping Irish linen.

I snickered at Ryker, who snickered back.

"Ms. Unger," a calm—and familiar—voice broke in. "Is there a problem?"

I jerked my head around. Jeff was standing by Sue's table. I gave Ryker a questioning glance. He tilted his head toward a table on the other side of the room where a woman sat oppo-site an empty chair. Her gray-streaked black hair was swept back into an elegant chignon and her black eyes watched Jeff with unmistakable pride. I did a double take. Jeff Katsuro had brought his mother to Anonymous's grand opening.

Within minutes, Jeff calmed Sue, the server mopped up the spilled water and broken glass, and the hum of conversa-tion resumed.

Jeff returned to his seat without ever looking at me. At least, I assumed so. When he walked by, I had my head down, studiously examining my ballotine of quail with bacon-infused polenta.

"He's not really into that hot nurse, you know," Ryker said, flipping his spoon between his fingers with a smile.

"It's no concern of mine," I muttered, crushing the quail under my fork until the bones splintered. "I'm not interested."

I looked up to see Ryker grinning. "Noo," he said, nodding at the carnage on my plate. "Of course you're not."

CHAPTER NINE

FROM HER THIRD-FLOOR window across the street, Marjorie Rupert watched the last of the evening's diners stumble out of Anonymous, laughing under the street lamps, to mingle on the sidewalk.

A tall, muscular man with blond hair caught her eye. He resembled Ian—her late husband, the love of her life, gone forever. With a sigh, Marjorie brushed the lace curtain aside for a closer look. Her eyes narrowed when a slim woman in a black dress—far too short for any decent woman to wear— walked out behind him.

Ian turned and threw an arm around the young woman's shoulder.

No, not Ian. Marjorie shook her head. This was someone else. Ian was gone.

As they walked away, along the sidewalk, the woman reached up to brush his arm away. He took a step back, held up both hands, and grinned in mock apology. She playfully tapped his arm with her purse, and they resumed their stroll.

Marjorie recognized the young woman. She had been at the protest that morning. On this very street, arguing with the marchers. They called her *Verity*. And then something else: *You like to study killers, don't you?*

Feeling a chill, Marjorie pulled the window sash shut and let the curtain fall. She stood there, watching through the lace.

Waiters dressed in white and black tromped wearily out the door, bowties trailing limply from the men's necks. The kitchen staff followed. One man stopped on the threshold, cupping his hand to light a cigarette, before moving off.

Finally, the red-haired restaurateur stepped out and locked the door.

He raised his head to scan the windows across the street. Marjorie wondered if he could see her through the curtain. Then he climbed into a copper-colored convertible, revved the engine a few times, and sped off. At the corner, his car turned and disappeared behind a building. She wondered idly if he was circling the block.

She pulled the lace curtain back to study the street again. It was quiet, the empty parking meters flashing red. Two raccoons scampered across the pavement, their chattering audible even through the closed window. They disappeared up an alley, followed a few moments later by the clatter of an overturned bin.

Marjorie twitched the lace back over the window. Footsteps were climbing the fire escape from the parking lot behind her building. A knock sounded on her door, a soft *rat-*

a-tat-tat meant only for her. Her visitor obviously didn't want to alert the neighbors.

There was one other flat in the building, on the second floor underneath hers. A retired couple. Most of the time, the husband was drunk. Marjorie barely spoke to them, other than unavoidable chatter on the fire escape while the husband sucked in his gut so she could sidle past. She had immediately pegged the wife as a busybody. More than once, she'd caught the woman studying her face, as if she expected to find something concealed behind Marjorie's eyes. At those times, Marjorie merely smiled and nodded.

The *rat-a-tat-tat* sounded again.

Marjorie thought about ignoring it, but that wasn't an option. She would have to deal with this. Make a statement if necessary. Put an end to it.

She crossed the room and pulled open the door to admit her visitor, then softly closed it, hearing it latch. She turned around, glaring.

"I told you to stay away."

"That's not fair. I helped you against my better judgment. You wouldn't be here without me. And now you have to—"

She cut off the tirade, catching a whiff of alcohol-laden breath as she leaned in. "You made a few calls. Everything else I did myself." Marjorie gestured impatiently with a gnarled finger. "You don't understand what I've been through. Don't tell me what to do."

"Is that it? Your memoir?"

She swiveled her head to follow her visitor's fascinated gaze. Tiny scribbled script covered a stack of papers under the window. An expanding folder lay open in the middle, more papers spilling out of it. She walked over to slam the folder shut, and placed it on top of the stack, anchoring it.

"None of your business," she said.

"I know it's been hard—"

"Hard?" She whirled around, eyes flashing. "Hard? Solitary confinement? A concrete room and a light on twenty-four hours a day?" She snorted. "You don't know hard."

"I did what you asked. At great personal cost. You have no right to tell me—"

A vicious slap echoed throughout the room. Marjorie pulled her hand away, her palm tingling.

Her visitor gasped, eyes watering, and took a step back. "What was that for?"

"You've been drinking."

"What if I have?"

"You're disgusting. Get out."

"No."

Marjorie's nostrils flared as she took in her visitor's belligerence—the crossed arms, the sneer. For a moment, she felt a thrill of fear. *Ridiculous.* She pushed away the unease as her visitor spoke.

"You can't toss me aside after what it cost me. You think you're safe here? I'll cause so much trouble, you'll never be safe again."

"You forget what I've done for you."

Her visitor paused. "What you've done for me? You're confused. Like before."

There it was again, a whiff of alcohol. Then, suddenly, a

warm breath against her ear. She held up a hand to shield her face, turning away. Fingers dug into her arm.

"You can't remember, can you?"

"I can." She looked at the scribbled pages on the bureau.

Her visitor turned sharply to follow her gaze.

"I wrote it down," she whispered. "I wrote it all down." She yanked her arm away, thrust out her chin, and raised her voice. "I remember everything."

"The ravings of an old woman? Who would believe you?"

The visitor strode to the bureau, shoved the bound volume aside, and scanned a handful of loose pages.

Marjorie followed, plucking at the papers. "Give me those."

"This is gibberish." The papers fluttered to the floor. "You've lost touch with reality. Keep this up, and you'll be back inside. Soon. And this time, I won't help you."

Marjorie gave a snort of fury and turned to face the window, her hands trembling.

She jumped as the door slammed. Footsteps pounded down the fire escape. Marjorie twisted her head to look at the closed door, her lips pursed. Obviously, she would have to make an example of someone.

You like to study killers, don't you?

And she knew just where to start.

CHAPTER TEN

IT WAS an extraordinary book club meeting in Thérèse's living room that Sunday evening—one that would go down in Originals history.

As the dozen members gathered, choosing places to sit, I glanced at Thérèse. She stood at the entrance to her kitchen, staring into the distance while adjusting the flawless collar of her silk blouse—an uncharacteristic display of nerves. Touching clothing can signify inner turmoil, as I knew from *Reading People for Fun and Profit*.

But a sign of what? Grief? Or guilt?

Emy didn't attend. Although an honorary member, she had special dispensation from her mother to skip the meetings because she rose at four a.m. to start her day at the bakery. For the rest of the Originals, attendance was mandatory.

Not that Thérèse ever said so. As the village's overworked chief librarian, volunteer literacy coach, and book club founder, her style and work ethic inspired us all. Nobody wanted to let her down. And now—well, we knew how hard Lucy's death had been for her.

Or perhaps I should say that *most* of us did.

I watched Thérèse from my perch on the dining room chair nearest the door. Emy often chided me for sitting near the exit. She thought I should be more sociable. That was fine for her. Emy was an extrovert, well-liked in the village that had been her home since birth. Whereas I was... happy to sit by the door.

Thérèse forced a smile and walked into the room. Her stiff posture and anxious expression softened as she mingled with her guests. She filled a wine glass here, chuckled at a joke there, and read out loud an excerpt from a held-open book. Warm smiles and nods greeted her passage.

With my attention focused on Thérèse, my guard was down. So I was startled when Sue Unger dropped her hefty frame into the armchair beside me with an impact that shook the floor. She slipped off her hiking boots before stretching out her stocking feet and flopping her arms over the sides of the chair. One bare toe poked out of a striped sock.

Sue raised her eyebrows at me. "Awful news, eh?" she asked in a conspiratorial whisper.

I couldn't shake the notion that Sue's mid-thirties frame was inhabited by a much older, and ill-spirited, busybody. I leaned in, keeping my voice low. "I didn't know her well, but I liked Lucy. It was a terrible shock."

Sue drew back. "Lucy?" She narrowed her eyes. "Yeah, that was a shock all right, but I meant"—she indicated our hostess with a flick of her eyes—"the rumor about Thérèse."

I must have looked confused, because Sue leaned in even closer and added, "About the bequest?" She swiveled her head to study Thérèse, but continued talking out of the side of her mouth. "Nobody believes it, of course. It's all nonsense. Darned interesting though, don't you think?"

She turned her gaze on me, obviously expecting a response.

"Perhaps," I stammered. "I'm afraid I don't know what—"

My reply was cut short by a crash in the hallway. Thérèse whipped her head around and then hurried through the doorway. Raised voices followed.

"Sorry, Thérèse. That was clumsy of me," a man said.

"It's all right, don't..." Thérèse said. "No, please, don't—"

Sue chuckled. "That must be Derek. Probably knocked something over again."

"Ouch! Darn it! I'm so sorry."

"Please, Derek, leave it. You're bleeding—"

A muffled curse came from the hall. A few of the women in the living room snickered.

Closing my eyes, I pictured Derek Talbot knocking over a vase or dropping a plate of cookies or putting his elbow through a picture. Despite his slight build, he seemed to take up a lot of room. No one knew why he joined a book club full of women although most suspected he was there for the fabulous baked goods. Since Emy didn't have to attend the meetings, she was happy to provide the snacks.

For my part, I suspected Derek was one of Thérèse's former literacy students. Lorne had made such progress under her tutelage that he'd enrolled in community college courses for the fall. Thérèse and I were proud of him, but he was too embarrassed to tell Emy. I thought he should, but I kept out of it—an unusual display of discretion on my part. Jeff would have been proud.

Derek appeared in the doorway with a dinner napkin wrapped around his hand. Thérèse swept past, holding a broom in one hand and a dustpan piled with broken china in the other.

She indicated the bathroom down the hall with a nod of her head. "Hydrogen peroxide and Band-Aids. Now." Pointing the broom handle at Sue, she said, "Can you help Derek, please?"

Sue rose and headed for the hall, but not before bestowing a smirk on the rest of us. She would be cracking jokes all week about Derek's latest misadventure.

I jumped to my feet and put a hand on her arm to hold her back. "I'll do it. I have first aid training."

That was a bit of a stretch. My aunt taught me the basics on our field trips when I was a child. But the only remedy that I could remember—how to fix a dislocated shoulder while ignoring the victim's screams—would be overkill in this case. Too bad, really. I'd always wanted to try it.

Sue dropped into her chair with a shrug. "Be my guest."

I followed Derek into the bathroom. He sat on the edge of the tub while I opened the medicine cabinet over the sink and pulled out a spray bottle of hydrogen peroxide and a box of bandages.

"It's only a scratch," he objected.

"Can I see it?"

He shrugged, unwound the napkin from his hand, and

held it out palm up. "Kind of the blind leading the lame, isn't it?" he asked, giving my swollen eye a pointed glance.

"Very funny. You're lucky there's no iodine in that cabinet."

Derek smiled. His chin was crooked, his eyes a watery gray, and his face pockmarked from teenage battles with acne. I'd always liked him. He made thoughtful comments on our books, even though many in the group failed to listen. Speaking up was difficult for someone so subdued, I guessed. Or maybe he felt the same way I did, and being the center of attention made him uncomfortable. That line of thinking gave me pause. Did I agree with Thérèse because she was right, or because it saved me from speaking up?

I paused a moment, the bottle in my hand.

Nah. Thérèse *was* always right.

I sprayed Derek's scratches with hydrogen peroxide and dabbed at them with a cotton pad. "What did you break, anyway?"

"That blue-and-white vase in the hall."

"Oh. Thérèse likes that one. It belonged to her..." I glanced up, meeting his gaze. "I don't know why I said that. It's a vase. She can get another."

He looked away as I covered the gashes on his palm with crisscrossed bandages. "Some of these are days old," I said, remembering Derek was a clerk at the hardware store. "Did you cut yourself at work?"

He pulled his hand away with a grimace. "I'm always doing something stupid. Or hadn't you heard?" Flexing his fingers, he stood up. "I dropped a paper bag of nails on the floor, and it burst. Then I tried to scoop them up with my hands. Dumb, like I said. Thank you for this."

"No problem." The local hardware store was one of the few places that still sold nails by the pound, instead of in those hyper-irritating bubble-wrapped packages. Carson, the handyman who was repairing Rose Cottage, bought all his nails there. I smiled at Derek. "Next time, use a dustpan."

He nodded grimly and turned into the hall, his key chain jangling at his waist. I wondered why he wore it when he wasn't at work. The disjointed head of a bobble doll dangled from the ring—a pink face with a receding hairline, thin lips, and goggle-rimmed glasses. Its truncated collar bore the initials TPB. With a chuckle, I recognized "Bubbles," one of television's Trailer Park Boys.

I threw the soiled cotton into the trash and returned the hydrogen peroxide to the cabinet before following Derek.

Thérèse had started the main event, a synopsis of our current book, *Alias Grace* by Margaret Atwood. She smiled at Derek as he took a seat at the edge of the group. He gave her an embarrassed nod in return.

A spirited discussion followed, which grew more heated as the meeting wore on—and more wine bottles were opened. At the end of our debate, Thérèse rose to her feet and smiled weakly. There was no mistaking her subdued air.

"A good discussion tonight, Originals. But before we break for refreshments, we have a piece of business to address." Her lip trembled, and she took a shaky breath before continuing. "A sad business, I'm afraid. Someone must continue Lucy's work as treasurer. Any volunteers?"

She looked around expectantly.

The room fell silent. Out in the kitchen, Thérèse's ancient Frigidaire roared into life.

Sue's hand shot up. "I'll do it."

Thérèse gave her a curious glance. "Really?"

"Sure. I've got some ideas about how we organize our business affairs. I'd like the chance to implement them. Lucy did a good job, as far as it went. But new blood is always welcome."

On my chair beside Sue, I kept my gaze rooted to the floor, painfully conscious of the raised eyebrows around us. Lucy had been dead only two days. Sue was not known for diplomacy, but this was a new low.

"Thank you," Thérèse said stiffly. "I'll download the records at... her house. I'll see that you get them."

There was an awkward pause while Sue considered this statement with her brows drawn. "You don't have a copy?"

"I'm afraid not. Lucy kept it on her computer at home."

Murmurs rolled around the room.

Sue cleared her throat, readying a fresh objection.

"Hey," said Hannah, Thérèse's co-worker and assistant librarian at the Leafy Hollow Library. "I see some terrific goodies over there." She pointed to the table in the dining area, laden with shortbreads, scones, and pastel-colored French macarons. "Race ya'."

Thérèse gave her a weak smile. *"Thanks,"* she silently mouthed.

With an audible sigh of relief, the group rose and followed Hannah to the table.

I stayed back, hoping to question Sue about the myste-rious "bequest" she'd mentioned. After that, I intended to grill the group about Lucy's fear of heights. The Originals loved to gossip over their desserts, so this was an ideal time to probe.

I tapped Sue's hand as she passed me, and she gave me an inquiring glance.

After checking to make sure Thérèse couldn't hear us— she was at the table in the next room, pouring tea and coffee —I leaned in, my voice low. "What were you talking about earlier? That bequest you mentioned?"

"You haven't heard? Lucy left her estate to Thérèse."

"That huge house of hers?" I sat up straight, shocked. Lucy had inherited her childhood home when her parents died in a car crash. She reveled in the heritage status of the Victorian-era mansion. I'd been in it only once, to borrow a book, but recalled rooms jammed with antiques. Lucy had an office on the second floor, but I didn't see it. That was where she did the part-time accounting work that brought in enough money to pay for her continuous restorations and upgrades. Business must have been good, because cash never seemed to be a problem. Not only did Lucy drive an expensive Land Rover, she took a vacation every year to visit her cousin in Moose Jaw.

My musings evaporated at Sue's next comment.

"The police asked Thérèse to come in for a chat." Her eyebrows rose.

"I don't believe you," I sputtered, trying to quell the sinking feeling in my gut. "That's malicious gossip."

Sue's lips curled in a smile. "Is it? Thérèse has no alibi for the morning Lucy was pushed off the Peak."

"That's not true. I saw her myself at Emy's bakery."

"That was later."

"And what do you mean, pushed? The police think it was suicide."

"That's not what you told Jeff Katsuro."

I narrowed my eyes, assessing Sue's smirk. "How do you know about—"

A voice behind me called, "Verity!"

I held up a finger to Sue—"Hold that thought"—and whirled around.

Hannah, the assistant librarian, was gesturing wildly with one hand, her other gripping a plate piled high with cookies. "Get over here," Hannah said, her plate tilting precariously. "We have questions."

Thérèse was no longer pouring tea, so I assumed she was in the kitchen getting refills. With a sigh, I walked over to the table and picked up a plate. Our gathering had taken a grim turn, but that was no reason to reject Emy's lavender-lemon scones. Especially after what I went through to get the lavender. I picked up a scone and slathered on a spoonful of clotted cream. "What do you want to know?"

"We heard you went up to the Peak in search of evidence," Hannah said eagerly. "Sorry about your eye, by the way. It looks painful," she added with a wince. "Anyhow... did you find anything?"

The other women around the table—and Derek, the sole male—stopped in mid-munch to stare at me.

I took a bite of my crumbly scone and chewed it thoroughly. No one looked away. "Not much," I said, raising the scone for another bite.

Hannah placed an impatient hand on my arm. "We know that's not true."

I put the scone on my plate. "Okay, here's what I think. Lucy was scared of heights. She didn't go up there willingly."

"I knew it," Hannah crowed. "What else?"

Curious faces leaned toward me, and I tried to curb the feeling of being hemmed in. Maybe I shouldn't share my findings, given that one of these people could be a killer. Then I gave my head a shake. That was ridiculous. The Originals were nondescript bookworms who harbored a quiet affection for each other. Even Lucy's prickly behavior had never sparked a serious argument.

But if one of the Originals was hiding something that might shed light on Lucy's death—maybe something they didn't realize they knew—a blunt attack was the best way to flush it out.

"I found a section of broken fence at the rim of the escarpment. On one of the closed trails. It was at least fifty feet from the spot where the police believe Lucy fell. I think they could be wrong about her... trajectory."

Eleven people inhaled all at once. I could almost feel the oxygen level drop in the room.

"Oh, my gosh," said a tremulous voice. "Does that mean there's a killer on the loose?"

The women shared shocked glances around the table. Then the muttering started, gradually growing in volume.

Sue's loud comment brought it to a halt. "Oh, come on," she said with a scowl. "If anything was suspicious, it was Lucy's hobby." She spit out the word with obvious contempt.

This was news to me. "What hobby?"

Before she could reply, Hannah leaned in. "None of us know. But she spent a lot of time in her office working on her computer."

"She did bookkeeping," I said. "To pay the bills."

Sue snorted. "I don't know anyone in town who used Lucy as a bookkeeper." She scanned the solemn faces around the table. "Does anybody?"

All heads shook emphatically.

"If someone wanted her dead..." Sue raised her eyebrows. A few women directed furtive glances at the kitchen where Thérèse was bustling about.

I didn't like the direction this was taking.

"Nobody knows for sure what happened," I stammered, wishing I'd stayed in my comfortable chair beside the exit. I crammed the rest of the scone into my mouth and regarded them solemnly, chewing.

Sue leaned over to whisper something to the woman standing beside her. My mind filled with a sudden flashback of a previous meeting, when Sue and Lucy had ducked out into the hall together. They conferred in low tones for nearly ten minutes, until Sue gave Lucy a vicious poke with her finger. "That's not what you promised me," she hissed. I heard her clearly from my perch near the door. But Lucy only whirled around and walked back into the living room. For the rest of the evening, they had not spoken to each other. I assumed it was a minor disagreement.

Today, as Sue chuckled and reached for a pistachio macaron, I wondered if I had been wrong.

Sue plunked the cookie onto her plate. "I'd like to see the will, that's for sure."

"What will?" said a voice from the doorway.

At the sound of Thérèse's voice, I nearly choked on my scone. She had returned from the kitchen while we were talking, a teapot in one hand and a coffee carafe in the other.

We whirled to face her.

"What will?" Thérèse repeated, her hand trembling under the weight of the carafe.

Derek stepped forward, fingering his injured palm. "Lucy committed suicide," he said loudly. "Everybody knows that. Those railings have been broken for years." His glance darted around the room, lighting on each of us in turn. It was an unusual show of defiance for the soft-spoken hardware clerk.

For a moment, I wondered how Derek knew about the fence. But maybe everybody in Leafy Hollow did. It was a popular hiking spot and not everyone respected the new boundaries.

"Well, Derek, you should know—with all the skulking about that you do," Sue said. "Follow one of your girlfriends up there, did you?" She smirked at the group, inviting us to share in the joke. A few titters broke out, but withered away under Thérèse's warning glance.

Derek whirled on Sue. "You bitch," he snapped. "I never went near that place."

Sue regarded him with an air of surprise.

Derek pivoted on his heel and stalked out of the room. A few seconds later, the front door slammed with such force that glass tinkled in the kitchen.

"I hope he didn't break anything else," Sue said with a smirk.

Thérèse thumped the carafe down on the table, followed by the teapot. Tea spurted from the spout and onto the table-cloth. "Can I refill that for you?" she asked evenly, reaching for the nearest cup.

The group broke up after that, leaving half-empty cups and dessert plates scattered around the room. I stayed to gather up the remaining pastries and seal them into a Tupperware container from the kitchen.

Thérèse flicked a hand. "Never mind that, Verity." She paused, biting her lip. "But I do need your help for something else."

My stomach dropped. *Now what?* I'd fulfilled my promise to look into Lucy's death and only made everything worse. Hopefully Thérèse wasn't about to blame me for that.

"You're an accountant, right?"

"Sort of," I countered. "I never sat the exams. More of a casual bookkeeper, really."

"Good enough. I want you to look over the club's accounts." She walked to a desk at the side of the living room, pulled open the main drawer, and drew out a USB flash drive. After she closed the drawer and returned to my side, she held it out.

Confused, I took it from her. "I thought all the records were at Lucy's."

"No need for Sue to know." Thérèse sighed. "She has such a suspicious mind."

"Why do you want me to look at this?"

"I think there are... discrepancies." She inclined her head at the stick of metal in my hand. "I need someone to confirm it. Then I can decide what to do next."

"Can I take it home?"

She nodded, and I dropped the flash drive into my purse.

Thérèse walked me to the front door. At the entrance, I turned to face her.

"I don't understand why this is important. The book club doesn't have much money, does it?"

Thérèse studied the hall carpet for a moment before replying. "Normally, no. But we did a fundraiser last year, before you arrived in Leafy Hollow, for a literacy training program at the high school. All the village businesses contributed. We raised a lot of money—over fifty thousand dollars. Lucy put it into a separate account, so it wouldn't get mixed in with our book club money. There are two accounts on that flash drive, our regular account and a second one for the charity drive.

"Two weeks ago, I wrote a check on the charity account for eighty-five dollars to pay for the first study guides. It was a small order because we wanted to check them over before launching the full program. And..."

Thérèse flinched, squeezing her eyes shut for a second.

"Yes?" I leaned in.

Heaving a sigh, she sank onto the hallway's carpeted stairs and reached up an arm to steady herself on the railing before replying.

"The check bounced. I think the money is gone."

CHAPTER ELEVEN

EMY and I had not expected to attend the reading of Lucy Carmichael's will. Yet, there we were—sitting in leather armchairs arrayed in front of the massive mahogany desk of Wilf Mullins, Leafy Hollow councilor and village lawyer.

Wilf beamed at us from behind the executive workstation in his inner sanctum. "Everybody comfy?" he asked, rubbing his hands together.

We nodded.

Twenty minutes earlier, I had been having an early-morning tea break at the 5X Bakery when Thérèse walked in.

"Girls," she said. "I need your help."

She asked if we'd accompany her to Wilf's office. Thérèse explained that she was a beneficiary of Lucy's will. She expected that her friend had bequeathed her one or two coveted first editions from the antique glass bookcase in the mansion's front hall. Nothing more.

Although her request surprised me, I was delighted to comply—if only so that later, I could refute Sue Unger's ridiculous allegations.

"Thank you, girls," Thérèse said with a small smile. "I appreciate it."

During our short walk to Wilf's office, a few doors away on Main Street, Emy had leaned in to whisper, "Mom's pretty cut up about Lucy's death. She wants us for moral support. I think she's afraid she might break down and cry in Wilf's office."

The thought made me wince. A public display of emotion like that would mortify Thérèse. The only time I'd seen her even remotely affected in public was during her talk on *Anna Karenina*—the suicide scene, as it happened. If my presence helped her maintain her composure, I was happy to help. And yes, it also meant I could satisfy my curiosity about Lucy's will. But that was an unexpected bonus.

Wilf's assistant, the elegant gray-haired Harriet, had ushered us in. "Mr. Mullins will be here shortly," she said, placing a leather portfolio on the mahogany surface. She aligned it with the edges of the desk before walking out, leaving the door ajar.

I craned my head, trying to peek at the folder's contents, and then reached for it with one hand. Emy slapped my fingers, and I withdrew.

"Wilf's going to read it to us anyway," I whispered. "It can't hurt to take a little peek."

She glared at me and glanced over at her mother. Thérèse was staring at the pull-down map on the far wall that outlined Wilf's latest business venture—The Cameron Wurst Waterpark. She seemed mesmerized by the dancing sausages that decorated the edges.

The door opened and four-foot-tall Wilf strode in, followed by realtor Nellie Quintero. Harriet slipped in behind them with a steno notebook in her hand. She closed the door before sitting on a straight-backed chair along the far wall.

"Good morning, ladies," Wilf said, grinning broadly as he shook each of our hands before walking behind his desk and hopping onto his leather chair. With the whirr of an electric motor, the chair rose until Wilf's face—still smiling—was level with ours.

Nellie slid into a seat directly behind mine where I couldn't see her without contorting my neck. I was baffled by her presence, but I suspected it might have something to do with her status as Wilf's BFF. The listing for Lucy's house would be lucrative, and Wilf might be giving her an advance peek. Either that, or Nellie simply wheedled him into it. Given his finely honed sense of political survival, Wilf hated to say no to a constituent. Any constituent.

Wilf adopted his most solemn lawyerly expression before flipping open the folder with a dramatic air. He paused to scan it. More theatrics. He'd prepared Lucy's will, so he must know what it contained.

Stifling a sigh, I gave my watch a sideways glance. Lorne and I had a lot of bookings today, and I hoped Wilf would move this along.

I also hoped the reading would end the public insinuations about Lucy's death. That evening I intended to go through the book club account. Hopefully then I could close this volume forever.

Although, if money really was missing, Thérèse would have to report it. What if she didn't? Would that make me an accomplice? That made me think of Jeff. I shifted uneasily on my seat. Why couldn't I put him out of my mind?

"Let's begin," Wilf said.

We settled in our chairs, giving Wilf our full attention.

A tap sounded on the office door, and it creaked open.

"Hallo in there," called a woman's gruff voice.

Wilf looked up, startled. The door opened completely, revealing Sue Unger's considerable bulk. "Am I too late for the reading of Lucy's will?"

Harriet got to her feet, dropping her steno pad on the chair behind her and reaching for the door handle. "I'm afraid this is private, Sue. You'll have to come back."

"I need to be here," Sue said as she pushed through the door, pulled over the nearest chair, and sat. She steepled her fingers on her lap. "I'm the new treasurer for the Leafy Hollow Original Book Club, and Lucy's computer is part of the estate. The book club's accounts are on that computer. I'm hoping her last will and testament will reveal all."

Wilf looked confused. "What accounts?"

"For the book club. And the charity drive. There seem to be no other copies." Sue nodded sagely.

I exchanged glances with Thérèse. There were definitely copies. The flash drive that contained them was sitting on the dining table at Rose Cottage where I'd placed it after the book club meeting. I waited for Thérèse to explain this.

She merely brushed both hands down the length of her immaculate skirt, no doubt contemplating the fabric's mysterious lack of wrinkles.

Wilf pursed his lips, but I knew he wouldn't ask Sue to leave. Our diminutive councilor never caused a scene, unless he was at the center of it. Although... the last time Wilf was annoyed in public, scores of chocolate cupcakes were destroyed in a fusillade of baked goods.

He raised the document and tapped it on his desk to align the pages. "Let's get started then..."

Before he could read a word, the door creaked open again.

"Are we too late?" asked an elderly woman. Her bare arms resembled the desiccated skeleton of a bird I'd found as a child. She fluttered her hands anxiously. Behind her stood a man with a thatch of white hair, who also looked anxious but had more bulk to back it up.

Ignoring Wilf's consternation, the woman strode into the room and held out her hand. "I'm Anne Sage, and this is my husband Owen." She indicated the man behind her, who gave us a worried nod.

Wilf limply shook her hand, his mouth falling open.

"Are these seats free?" Anne asked, pointing to two straight-backed chairs against the wall.

Harriet looked askance—one of her specialties—and rose to her feet. "I don't think..."

"We're Lucy's neighbors," Anne said, urging her husband toward the empty chairs. He dragged them over to the back row, next to Nellie.

"We used to be neighbors, that is," Anne said with a

heavy sigh, hands on her hips. "What an awful thing." She glanced at each of us in turn. "Such a loss."

She settled into the new seating. Owen sat beside her, staring at the floor.

"Uh-huh," Wilf said, no doubt evaluating their two council votes against the need to eject onlookers from a private meeting. "And you're here because..."

His words hung in the air.

"Because of the house, of course," Anne said, shrugging and glancing about for affirmation. "We live next door. We need to know what's going to happen to it. Who our new neighbors will be, and so forth."

She poked Owen with her elbow. With a start, he sat up straight. "That's right. Neighbors."

"Oh." Wilf studied the newcomers. "It's really not a public process, I'm afraid."

"You don't understand." Anne's formerly friendly tone turned harsh. "That Carmichael woman owes us. Tell him, Owen." She elbowed her husband. Before he could open his mouth, Anne added, "She made him do things."

Every eyebrow in the room shot up.

"Things?" Wilf asked with a tentative air.

"Tell him, Owen," Anne said, then carried on without him. "She claimed to have vertigo." Anne sniffed. "As if. Nothing wrong with her. But Owen did all sorts of chores for her, getting up on ladders and fences and rooftops. Look at him. Is this a man who should be climbing ladders?"

Owen hung his head sadly.

"Ah..." Wilf said. "I don't—"

"And did she ever pay us for it? Not. One. Penny. And what about the notes?" Anne snapped open the clasp on her purse and stuck in a hand. She pulled out a handful of business cards, rose to drop a few on Wilf's desk and then passed the rest around. "Look at those."

We regarded the white cards. They were blank except for ??? in the middle. In red ink.

"I don't get it," Wilf said, peering at the cards.

"Lucy left one of those every time we did something she didn't like. Our neighbors got them as well." Anne glanced around the room. "I'm surprised none of them have shown up yet."

Harriet shot a worried glance at the door.

"What did Lucy object to?" Wilf ventured, although I suspected he would rather not know.

"Once." Anne leaned forward, and we held our breath. "It was because we didn't deadhead our zinnias. She said it made the street look *trashy*." Anne settled back in her chair. "We're considering a lawsuit, to be honest. No matter how high the fees."

Wilf perked up at the word *lawsuit*. Or maybe it was *fees* that did it.

"I guess you can stay." He looked around. "Unless anyone objects."

There was a general murmur of approval.

"All right, then. Harriet, would you please close the—"

Another knock.

Wilf's sigh was heartrending. "Now what?"

Jeff stuck his head into the room. He regarded the crowd

with surprise. Then he nodded at me with the hint of a smile before turning to our host.

"A word, Wilf?"

I'd known Wilf long enough—he was my aunt's lawyer and so mine by default—to know his smile was not genuine. He flicked on the chair's motor.

No one spoke as he descended silently, lips pressed together.

Wilf shut the door when he left. There was a muffled conversation in the anteroom. The men returned, leaving the door open.

Harriet rose, her leather flats silent on the plush carpet, to close the door. This time, the lock snicked softly before she regained her seat and picked up her steno pad and pencil.

Jeff removed his peaked cap and leaned against the far wall. Wilf flicked on the chair motor and waited silently while it rose. He flipped over the first of the papers.

There was no preamble this time.

"I, Lucy Grenadine Carmichael, declare this to be my last will and testament. I hereby revoke, annul, and cancel all wills and codicils previously made by me..."

Wilf's voice droned on. I checked my watch again. Eventually, he got to the good stuff.

"...other than the codicils noted below, I leave the entirety of my estate to Thérèse Dionne."

Several people gasped, myself included.

Wilf pretended not to notice. He continued by reading out minor bequests—many of them to other book club members. A first edition here, a china set there. Nothing of immense value.

Sue leaned in with a puzzled expression. "Are you saying that Lucy left everything to... Thérèse?"

Wilf nodded. "That's correct, except for the bequests I just read."

"Which are worthless."

Wilf flinched. "I'm sure those items carry a special significance to the deceased's friends. They will serve as a fond remembrance..."

"Yeah, worthless." Sue slumped back with a snort. "This will be a shock to a few people."

"Whatever do you mean?" Wilf demanded. "Are you implying—"

She held up her hand. "Nothing at all. But that old house is worth a lot of money, isn't it?"

On the other side of the room, Harriet cleared her throat. We turned to face her. "It's an extraordinary example of a Victorian home and is in wonderful condition. It is historically significant as well."

Lucy had recounted her home's long history to me during a book club meeting. I zoned out during most of her exposition, but I remembered something about Loyalists and the American Revolution. The house had been in her family for generations, she said. An official plaque attached to the exterior wall near her front door attested to its significance.

"Never mind the history lesson," Sue said with a snort of disgust. "What's it worth?" She swiveled in her chair to look at Nellie. "Well?"

The realtor tossed her hair and gave Wilf a questioning glance.

He shrugged in one of his *why-not* looks. "Go ahead," he said.

"The last time I did an appraisal for Lucy," Nellie said, "we estimated the house at half a million or more. But that was several years ago."

More gasps. *Half a million?* I mouthed to Emy, whose eyes were wide.

"And then there's the contents," Nellie continued. "Lucy's family had a number of exceptional antiques, both furniture and artworks."

Sue narrowed her eyes. "Lucy had a lot of restoration work done in the past few years. Must have cost plenty."

"I can't comment on that, but the house is in incredible condition," Nellie said. "Everything in it exceeds the building code, yet Lucy took care to maintain the original structure. She even had the Leafy Hollow Historical Society advise on the restoration. So, really, the entire estate is worth substantially more than half a million."

Wilf cleared his throat. "There's also her investment portfolio."

You could have cut the astonishment in that room with a Loyalist butter knife. Lucy Carmichael, who had no visible sign of employment other than phantom bookkeeping gigs, possessed an investment portfolio?

"How much is that worth?" Sue asked.

"I believe that's a matter for her inheritor," Wilf said firmly. "I can't comment. It has nothing to do with her neighbors or the book club."

Everyone in the room gawked at Thérèse, whose gaze was fixed firmly on the carpet. She raised her head, smiled feebly, and said, "I'm not trying to hide anything, Wilf. You might as well tell them."

My eyes swiveled sideways, taking in Emy's pained expression, but I forced my attention back to the front.

"Well, if you insist," Wilf said, "we have a printout here, and the total comes to..." He took a deep breath, scanning the sheet. "Another half-million, give or take a few thousand." He scanned the paper in his hand, his lips moving silently as if he were checking it one more time, then placed it on the other papers in the portfolio and shut the cover.

Conscious that my mouth was hanging open, I closed it.

Thérèse lowered her head into her hands with a soft sob. Emy slid close and flung an arm around her shoulders. I rummaged in my purse for a tissue and handed it over. Emy took it gratefully and gave it to Thérèse, who slipped it under her hand and dabbed at her eyes.

Sue raised her eyebrows. "Nice haul, eh?"

I glared at her. "Wow. That's... insensitive."

"Well, I'm sorry," she huffed. "But that's a heck of a lot of money." She looked at Anne and Owen Sage, Lucy's neighbors, who seemed unable to move. "Wouldn't you say? I mean, where did it come from? Lucy's father was a school teacher, and her mother was a housewife. She didn't get it from them."

I sat ramrod straight, staring at Wilf's desk, trying—and failing—not to picture that flash drive in Rose Cottage.

Sue flopped back in her chair with a chuckle. "Wow, Thérèse," she said. "Do you realize this makes you a prime suspect in Lucy's death?"

Emy stiffened, but Thérèse didn't appear to have heard.

I turned to face Sue. "That's ridiculous."

"Relax..." She held up a roughened hand. "I'm just kidding."

As I flounced around to face the front, I caught a glimpse of Jeff. His dark eyes were intent on Thérèse and Emy. He seemed to be gauging their reaction to Sue's outrageous comment. Jeff would have heard the village gossip after Lucy's death. Up to now, there'd been no reason to think any of it deserved a second hearing.

That had just changed. Big time.

"Wait," I said, anxious to deflect attention from Thérèse. "Lucy had a cousin in Moose Jaw, didn't she? What about her?"

"I don't know anything about a cousin," Wilf said. "Lucy Carmichael had no relatives that I'm aware of." He gestured at the will. "She certainly never mentioned any to me when I prepared this will last year."

Jeff pushed off from the wall and straightened up. "Speculation is not helpful. So let's end it now. Thérèse, where were you on Friday morning between the hours of nine and eleven?"

I recognized that was roughly the elapsed time between my encounter with Lucy at Bertram's and the discovery of her body below the Peak.

Everyone faced Thérèse, who continued to stare at the floor, seemingly unaware of the question. Emy shook her arm.

Thérèse slowly raised her head. "Excuse me?" she asked.

Jeff repeated his query.

We waited.

Thérèse straightened up. "I'm afraid I can't tell you that."

"Mom," Emy urged, her eyes wide.

"I can't. I'm sorry." Thérèse weakly waved a hand. "Obviously, I had nothing to do with Lucy's death. But I can't tell you where I was."

CHAPTER TWELVE

EMY HUSTLED her dazed mother out of Wilf's office and down the street to the bakery. I followed, conscious of Jeff's intense gaze on our departing backs. I hoped he wouldn't press Thérèse for an alibi. Not yet, anyway. Not until she had her story straight.

Yet, the very thought that Thérèse Dionne needed an alibi was crazy.

The minute we walked through the entrance, Emy flipped her OPEN sign to CLOSED, locked the door, and pointed to the table in the back. Thérèse and I meekly sat while Emy put her hands on her hips and gawked at her mother.

"What on earth was that about?" she demanded. "You can't tell us where you were? This isn't dinner theater, Mom. Tell Jeff what he wants to know, so he can eliminate you as a suspect and find the real killer." She narrowed her eyes. "And frankly, I'm a little curious myself."

"I can't tell you."

"Mom, stop." Emy dropped into the chair beside her. "You're scaring me."

"I'm sorry, sweetie, but I can't tell you," Thérèse said. "And it doesn't matter, anyway. I didn't... I couldn't..." She tapped the silver brooch at her throat and looked away.

Emy took her mother's hand. "Just tell me. Then we can explain it to Jeff and put an end to this."

Thérèse shook her head and pulled her hand away. "I can't."

Emy slumped back and gave her mother an astonished look. "Are you seriously refusing to—"

I cleared my throat, and both women turned their attention to me.

"You're getting ahead of yourself, Emy. It doesn't matter where Thérèse was. Lucy may have taken her own life. Which would mean there is no killer. We won't know for certain until—" I clapped my mouth shut at her warning glance.

Thérèse looked stricken. "Lucy wouldn't do that, would she?" She rocked forward with her head in her hands. "It's my fault. I should have done something."

"Mom, don't say that." Emy gave a frantic glance to the locked front door. "Especially not when Jeff gets here. Whatever happened—it wasn't your fault." She pried her mother's fingers away from her face. "Are you listening? It wasn't your fault."

"Wasn't it?" Smiling grimly, Thérèse straightened up, wiped a tear from her cheek, and leaned back. "Remember the house tour, Emy?"

"Last Christmas—to raise money for the library? Sure."

"I tried for years to convince Lucy to take part, and last year she agreed. But she let only two people at a time indoors, and followed them around. 'Don't touch anything' she said, over and over." Thérèse shook her head. "That was embarrassing enough. But when somebody picked up an antique paperweight to take a closer look..." Her voice trailed off.

She didn't have to continue, because we knew the story. Everybody did. Screaming at the top of her lungs, Lucy had shoved everyone out the door—including Thérèse. Then she slammed and locked it, leaving them outdoors in the cold.

Villagers swear they heard her ranting inside.

A few minutes later, Lucy flung open the door, marched down the walk, and tugged the "Holiday House Tour" sign from her lawn. "Tour's over," she screamed at the crowd milling about on the sidewalk. She flapped the cardboard at them. *"Go home."*

Then she rushed the stragglers, holding her sign like a matador's sword.

Even today, you could elicit chuckles from Leafy Hollow villagers simply by uttering the words, "Lucy Carmichael's house tour."

"I don't see the relevance," Emy said.

"Well, it wasn't normal, was it?" Thérèse entreated. "The way she was acting. I should have known something was wrong. I should have tried to help her."

Thérèse's gloomy expression made me cast about for other explanations. Some of the ideas I came up with were pretty far-fetched. For instance, what if Lucy had changed her will before killing herself, knowing Thérèse would be blamed? Perhaps Lucy had a terminal illness, and decided to punish Thérèse for some imagined slight before she died.

Perhaps I read too much Agatha Christie.

Emy's words jerked me out of my trance.

"C'mon, Mom. You can't possibly believe that it's your fault."

If anybody could pry an alibi out of Thérèse, it would be Emy. I was only getting in the way. Plus, I'd promised to delve into the book club accounts.

I pushed my chair back. "I should go."

Neither of them looked up. After unlocking the front door, I slipped out onto the sidewalk. A glance back through the window showed two black heads touching over the table. Emy was holding her mother's hand.

Originally, I agreed to a brief probe of Lucy's death only to reassure Emy and satisfy my own curiosity. I hadn't intended to do more than poke around Pine Hill Peak and report back.

The reading of Lucy's will had changed everything.

I thought back to the trampled shrubs at the second lookout, the broken fence railings, and Lucy's professed fear of heights. Something didn't add up. But until the police faced up to that fact, the only way I could help Thérése was to conduct an enquiry of my own.

And the most promising lead was sitting on my aunt's desk at Rose Cottage.

I inserted the flash drive into my aunt's laptop, opened her bookkeeping program, and started in on the files Thérèse had given me.

An hour later, I gave up in confusion. After examining every entry for the past six months, I couldn't find a single discrepancy. The charity account showed all the money collected in the fundraiser was still in the bank. Yet a check with the bank showed that account was empty.

If only Thérèse had confronted Lucy with the bounced check when it was still possible to prove Thérèse wasn't involved. It was too late now, I realized with a sinking feeling as I closed the laptop and slid a finger along its cover. Where did the money go? I longed to find an explanation other than the one that stared me in the face.

Worse, what if Thérèse did confront Lucy about the loss, and they argued? Could that have led to violence?

The scrape of my pushed-back chair startled the General awake from his snooze. He gave me an exasperated, one-eyed glare before flopping back down on the sofa. I wanted to join him in a catnap, but my head was pounding and the walls were closing in. Should I sit still and do breathing exercises, or pace the floor? The distraction of pacing won out. At least it would work off a few scone-induced calories.

But thoughts of scones led to thoughts of Emy, and that led back to her mother and the missing funds. So much for distraction. I headed for the kitchen instead, where I peered into my near-empty fridge with dismay before selecting the only viable option.

Sucking on my beer while leaning against the counter, I reviewed the facts.

Someone—probably Lucy—withdrew fifty thousand dollars from the book club's charity account.

Thérèse discovered the fraud.

Lucy died in suspicious circumstances.

Thérèse benefited from Lucy's death.

The setup didn't look good. No one who knew Thérèse Dionne could suspect her of fraud, never mind murder. But the police weren't always concerned with a suspect's reputation, as I knew from experience.

Lucy's betrayal might have infuriated Thérèse. How could she explain to the other Originals that she'd given her trust—and their money—to a thief? At minimum, Thérèse would suffer a terminal blow to her reputation. Worse, she might face conspiracy charges.

Not to mention the serious setback to her favorite charity.

I made another circuit of the cottage, beer in hand. This time, the General merely opened his good eye to watch my progress, not willing to leave his comfy perch for anything less than a handful of liver treats.

A new idea brought me up short.

How well did I know Thérèse? She was Emy's mother, and Emy was my best friend, but the only personal contact I'd had with Thérèse was asking her to help Lorne. I couldn't vouch for her ethics, not really. But I could attest to her temper. Thérèse had once chewed me out for a good ten minutes after an unavoidable incident that may, or may not, have involved surveillance of an illicit tryst that turned out to be, well... something else entirely. Not my fault, really. I would have realized our error and ordered a hasty retreat if it hadn't been for the wet leaves hanging over my face from my

camouflage hat. Which had proved to be a completely inade-
quate defense against local wildlife, by the way. Long story.

In any event, I winced at my recollection of the language
Thérèse had used.

With a loud sigh, I dropped onto the sofa, shaking the
cushions.

The General uttered an annoyed *"Mrack"* and jumped
onto the floor. He stalked into the kitchen, tail waving, probably checking to see if kibble had appeared while I was
pacing. Perhaps he expected Rose Cottage's imagined tenant,
the rumored Loyalist ghost, to top up his bowl.

"Regardless of what you've heard, there's only one of
me," I called after him. "No twin."

With a solid slap to my forehead, I sat up straight as real-
ization hit. *For heaven's sake.* What a dunce I was.

Then I bent over with a groan. Was it so hard to
remember a swollen eye?

Gingerly patting my forehead, I assessed my break-
through. It was obvious, really. Lucy set up two accounts for
the book club's charity—a classic smokescreen, as I knew
from my bookkeeping days. She prepared a fake account for
Thérèse—with fake transactions—while using the real
account to track her own withdrawals. All I had to do was
find Lucy's record of the real account. Then we'd know
where the money went. I crossed my fingers. Hopefully it
would be on her home computer and not hidden somewhere
else. That's what I would do, if I was embezzling thousands
of dollars—hide it elsewhere.

Wow. It was entirely possible my new life was teaching
me things I really shouldn't know.

Meanwhile, uncovering the real account would clear Thérèse of fraud allegations because it would prove she didn't know about Lucy's deception.

It wouldn't clear her of the suspicion that she pushed her friend off Pine Hill Peak, but accomplishing that would have to wait. First, I had to learn more about the mysterious hobby Sue mentioned at the book club meeting. It couldn't be fraud, since Sue seemed genuinely surprised by the generous amount of Lucy's legacy. But if not fraud, then what else was Lucy involved in?

I was back. And this time, carrying bribes.

"Sue," I called from the gloom underneath her tree blind. "Are you there?"

No reply.

"I have sandwiches," I called, brandishing a Tim's paper bag in one hand. A breeze lifted a tendril of hair from my face while a bird twittered overhead. Or maybe that was a squirrel. "And cappuccinos," I added, holding up a cardboard tray in my other hand.

The hatch swung open, and Sue's face appeared.

"Donuts?"

"Of course. Maple-glazed."

"Come on up."

We shared our food and coffee in companionable silence, sitting in the chairs facing the open window. Branches shivered in the breeze, and there was a hint of rain in the air.

I waited until Sue selected a donut before broaching the reason for my visit.

"When I was here last time, we talked about Lucy."

She chewed and swallowed. "So?"

"Well, I have a question. At the book club meeting, you mentioned she had a hobby. What was it?"

Sue took a sip of her cappuccino and wiped maple icing from her mouth with a napkin before replying. "Shouldn't have said that."

"You did, though, and I'm curious. Was she a pole dancer or something? Is that why you don't want to tell me?"

An unfortunate visual sprang to mind of Lucy in a bikini, plucking bills from her G-string and swabbing them with antiseptic wipes. I chuckled, then stilled my expression. After all, I was talking about a dead woman.

"It was nothing like that." Sue leaned in with a scowl. "Lucy wasn't the paragon you obviously thought. You and Thérèse both." She gave a snort of derision. "For a smart woman, Thérèse Dionne was easy to fool."

The coffee threatened to curdle in my stomach. "What do you mean? Fooled how?"

"Lucy had enemies."

My muscles tightened. "Were you one of them?"

"Me?" She chortled. "Don't be ridiculous."

"Then who—"

Sue slumped back in her chair and tilted her exasperated gaze at the ceiling. "All right." She straightened up. "I don't know what she was doing. But I was in her office several times to discuss... club business, and there was a lot of instant messaging going on. Her computer was beeping non-stop."

"Did she ignore it while you were talking?"

"No, that's the thing. At every single beep, Lucy would say something dumb like, *let's put a pin in that*, and whirl around to type a reply. And it wasn't just the computer. Her darn cell phone was going off all the time, too."

"Who was she messaging?"

"No idea. But I caught sight of a few, and they weren't about bookkeeping." Sue dropped her donut and leaned toward the window with an indrawn breath, her gaze fixed on the forest. "Oh... that's interesting," she whispered. She dragged her chair back up to the telescope and fitted her eye to the scope. "Check Lucy's computer. It's probably all there."

"But how would I—"

"Shhhh." Sue flapped a hand at me. She adjusted the focusing knob, then turned to face me. "You can let yourself out, right?"

"Sure," I muttered. "No problem. I climb ladders all day. All day."

Back on the ground, I slogged along the trail until I reached the lawn behind Sue's house. My boots sank into the uncut grass, reminding me I still had a full day's work ahead. I walked to the road while sliding out my phone to text Emy.

Do U have Lucy's house key?

I waited a few seconds for the beep of a reply. In the distance, a bird sang. I cocked my head, trying to zero in. Was that a *Fringilla montifringilla*? Or maybe a— My phone beeped and I looked down.

Mom does. At home.

Can U get it?

THIS AFTERNOON.

DO IT. TALK TO U LATER.

I shut off my phone and tromped down the hill.

CHAPTER THIRTEEN

LORNE and I raced through our jobs the next morning so our afternoon would be clear. By the time I dropped him off outside the 5X Bakery, my muscles were aching and my stomach rumbling. Emy's vegan takeout shared a shopfront with her bakery, and I could have picked up a sandwich. But I needed something more substantial than braised vegetables to prepare me for the task ahead.

As I cruised along Main Street, my gaze rested on the grinning, three-foot-high purple bird that marked the Tipsy Jay. Sue often complained that the sign did not resemble any known avian species, but she missed the point. It exactly captured the personality of the Jay's owner and main chef, Katia Oldani, who was famous for her comfort food. Her macaroni and cheese, beefy shepherd's pie, and scalloped potatoes were legendary. As for dessert—a helping of sticky toffee pudding might ease my pain.

Grinning, I pulled up to a parking meter.

Inside, I ignored the half-dozen tables in favor of a seat at the bar, where the service would be faster. I had no time to waste.

"Hi, Verity," said the plump, middle-aged woman wiping glasses behind the bar.

"Katia," I said. "Any mac 'n cheese left?"

"For you, always. Need a menu?"

"Not necessary." I paused, mentally totaled up the calories I'd eaten in the past few days, and changed my mind. "Better make that a house salad," I said with a grimace.

Katia nodded. "And to follow...?"

I paused again, considering. I'd already sacrificed my favorite mac 'n cheese. "One of your wonderful hot fudge sundaes," I said decisively. "And don't hold the fudge."

Katia grinned. "Tough day?"

I rested my elbows on the bar to prop up my chin. "You have no idea."

The big-screen television over the bar was tuned to one of Katia's soaps—*The Young and the Clueless*, I thought. Once the late-afternoon crowd arrived, the channel would change to a sports network. Meanwhile, I found myself getting caught up in the plot. One of the characters was having a clandestine afternoon with two other characters. Negligees were involved. Then came a knock on their motel unit's door. The actors froze, eyes locked. And then—

"There you go, love. House salad," Katia said as she slid a generous helping under my nose. I inhaled the aroma of balsamic dressing with a sigh.

"I added bacon," Katia said. "You looked like you needed it." She gave me a wink.

I picked up my fork, the shenanigans on *The Young and the Clueless* forgotten. "Thanks."

"Let me know when you're ready for that fudge sundae. I'm trying out a new version with raspberry sorbet and white chocolate."

"Ooh," I said with my fork paused halfway to my mouth, momentarily distracted. "That sounds fabulous."

The door opened, and a couple walked in to sit at a table. Katia stepped out from behind the bar to deliver their menus.

While she talked to the newcomers, I dug into my salad. Even though it was delicious, I couldn't shake my uneasiness over the week's events. I toyed with my greens, pushing radicchio leaves from side to side.

In the two months I'd been in Leafy Hollow, my life had changed completely. I'd gone from being a shut-in unable to leave her apartment to a small business owner and member of a community. I'd made new friends. My anxiety attacks had receded. I still got anxious, and I would never be entirely comfortable in a crowd, but now it was manageable.

Yet, something was missing.

Back in Vancouver, while struggling to come to grips with Matthew's death, I read travel books and planned adventures. I could drift up the Amazon on a raft. Act in a Bollywood movie. Scale tall buildings with grappling hooks. I could do anything, I told myself. Go anywhere. But in truth, I couldn't even buy groceries. A heavy chain tethered my heart to that apartment.

Maybe I'd still be there if Leafy Hollow hadn't intervened. One phone call had been enough to send me on a crazy cross-country mission to save my missing aunt. And here I was, two months later, with nothing to show for it other than a few cryptic messages, an annoying hologram, and overwhelming guilt.

Worse, I was still alone. With Matthew's photo and an old shirt to remind me what I had lost.

In Vancouver, Patty advised me to move on. Here in Leafy Hollow, Emy said the same. And they were right. But how could I? Whenever I tried to take the first step, even just flirt a little, my heart pounded and my stomach churned.

I thought I'd made progress—with Jeff. Then I saw him escorting that blonde out of Kirby's and my anxiety came roaring back. Ryker insisted Leafy Hollow's crime fighter wasn't involved with anyone, which seemed to be confirmed when Jeff showed up at Anonymous's opening with his mother.

And how sweet was that? A hard-nosed cop out on a date with his mom? The memory brought a smile to my face. But it was too late to rekindle our first flashes of attraction. Pushing my now-empty plate aside, with a twinge of regret I remembered pushing Jeff away in much the same way.

I slumped on the bar with my chin resting on my hands.

"No good?" Katia asked, whisking away my plate.

"Terrific, as always," I said without moving. "Thanks."

"You wait there," she said. "Chocolate always cheers me up."

I lowered my hands and smiled at her. "Me, too."

Twiddling nervously with my dessert fork, I looked up as the front door opened and stayed open. Sunlight streaming through the doorway framed Jeff's straight black hair, razor-sharp cheekbones, and dark eyes.

My breath caught in my throat as he looked at me.

He smiled, closed the door, and came over to the bar.

"Hello," he said. "Haven't seen you for a while." He sat on the stool beside me and slid a menu out from behind the condiments holder.

Despite three empty stools at the bar, he had picked the one right next to me. Possibly he wanted to leave two seats at the end, in case a couple came in and wanted to sit together. Or perhaps—more likely—he hadn't given his seat location a thought. On the other hand—

I mentally slapped myself. *Verity, get a grip.*

Jeff flipped the menu closed and slid it back behind the ketchup bottle with a wry grin. "Don't know why I bother—I always order the same thing." He looked up as our hostess walked over. "The usual, thanks, Katia."

"Just once you could try something new," she said, smiling.

"Creature of habit," he replied with a shake of his head. Katia retreated to the kitchen.

"It hasn't been that long," I said.

Jeff gave me a puzzled look.

"Since you've seen me, I mean. I was at the reading of Lucy's will."

"Which reminds me..." His brow furrowed. "Why were you there?"

"Oh." I flicked my hand with a hoped-for air of nonchalance. "Friend of the family."

His brow remained wrinkled. "Which family? Lucy's?"

"No," I said hastily. "Emy's family. Her mother, to be exact. Thérèse." Since he still looked unconvinced, I rattled on, unable to stop myself. "That room was definitely crowded, when you come to think of it. Most of those people had nothing to do with the will, did they? I wasn't the only onlooker. Any more and they would have had to send out for folding chairs. And Harriet's head might have imploded."

One half of Jeff's mouth bent upward in the kind of smile one bestowed on a puppy. Or a precocious toddler.

I took that as my cue to stop talking. *Nice work, Verity. Now he thinks you're a puppy.* Not the effect one hoped to have on an available hunk who was so close you could smell his Old Spice. I leaned in for a covert whiff, and sighed. Nice.

Then I frowned. Was Jeff available? Or was that wishful thinking?

"The look on Wilf's face was priceless, though," I babbled. "I thought maybe he summoned you to clear the room."

Holy cow. I had to leave before I made a complete fool of myself. "Katia," I called, intending to cancel my hot fudge sundae.

Too late.

"Yes?" she asked, returning from the kitchen with a tray. Katia placed a toasted chicken and tomato sandwich in front of Jeff, and for me...

"Wow." I contemplated a mound of raspberry sorbet crowned with a dome of white chocolate. "That looks incredible."

She smiled. "Wait." And then she poured a pitcher of hot chocolate sauce over the whole thing. I gasped in delight, before spooning up a helping of white chocolate, hot fudge, and cool sorbet as they melted together. As the flavors blended on my tongue, I closed my eyes. I might have moaned a little.

"Amazing," I said, flicking my eyelids open.

A smile spread across Jeff's face. "You seem to be enjoying that." He picked up the first half of his sandwich.

"You can say that again." I spooned up more chocolate.

Katia smiled at us. "My work here is done." The couple across the room waved to get her attention. "Be right there, hon," she called.

Jeff and I concentrated on our food, not looking at each other.

Eventually, he pushed his plate away. "I'm glad you attended that reading only as a friend, Verity. Because after your last investigation, I hoped you wouldn't do that again."

"Do what?" I asked, a tad defensively.

He gave a little cluck-cluck of his lips, but he was smiling. Somehow, I found it hard to look away from his mouth. To cement my resolve, I called up a mental image of the time I'd dropped that bowling ball. *Ouch.*

"I think you know," he said.

"That is so unfair," I sputtered. "I've been in the wrong place at the wrong time once or twice"—I ignored his raised eyebrow—"but it wasn't my fault."

His lips twitched. "No," he said, nodding solemnly.

Jeff fiddled with the menu holder again. If I didn't know better, I would have suspected the village's unflappable detective was... nervous? I watched his hands. Tidy cuticles and nails. Not quite a manicure—but the mark of a man who looked after himself.

He released the menu and sat up straight, facing the

menu holder. "I don't mean to lecture you. It's just that when I saw you in that hospital bed..." He swallowed hard before turning his soulful gaze directly on me.

I nearly slid off my stool and into his lap—as I had contemplating doing once in the kitchen of Rose Cottage. Those flashes of attraction were roaring back. I must have blanked out for a bit, because my alluring reply was reduced to a feeble, "I'm fine now."

Then my foot tapped the bar, making *whack-whack-whack* sounds. Like a small child at the movies. *First a puppy, and now an irritating theater goer. Great.* I halted my foot in mid-whack.

"Sorry," he said. "I know you're fine. At the hospital, you resented me barging in and, um..." His fingers tapped the table.

Tap-tap-tap.

Holy cow. Now he was doing it, too.

Unable to take the tension, I started babbling again. "How's your nurse?" I asked brightly. I scrunched my eyes shut in horror. *Did I really just say that?* My foot hit the bar with a thump that brought me back to my senses. I opened my eyes.

Jeff tilted his head to one side. "What nurse?" He looked puzzled. If he was faking it, he was doing an admirable job. Of course, he was a cop. This might be one of those fabled interrogation techniques they use to beat down a suspect's resistance.

I scooped up a last spoonful of fudge sauce and sorbet. Maybe if I ignored him, he'd attribute my comment to the television characters screaming at each other over our heads.

"Oh," he said finally. "You meant..." He shook his head. "We're not involved."

Interesting. I licked the sauce off my spoon and set it aside, watching him.

"How did you know about—"

"I saw you at Kirby's. You looked friendly."

I could see his wheels turning. "Kirby's? That was a while ago."

"It's none of my business."

Jeff leaned in. "It could be your business." He shrugged and straightened up, seeming almost embarrassed. "I mean, if you wanted."

For such a good-looking guy, his patter was pathetic. Almost as bad as mine. I looked into those dark eyes and made a mental note to ask Katia to turn up the air conditioning.

Running a finger along the counter, I asked, "Are you talking about more bowling?"

A smile broke through his embarrassment. "We both know that's a lost cause."

"Hey."

"No offense. I meant we could... go out sometime. If you want."

I narrowed my eyes, brushing back the butterflies in my stomach. "Like on a date?"

There. I'd said it.

"Yeah." His smile broadened. "Like a date."

My cell phone buzzed in my pocket, and I slid it out.

DEPLOYED. WAITING ON U.

With a sidelong glance at Jeff, I slid the phone back into

my pocket. "I have to go. Trouble on the job front." Inwardly, I winced. We hadn't had our first date yet, but I'd already lied to him. Then I brightened. If the team's assault succeeded, I'd be able to tell him all about it.

Jeff placed his diet Coke back on its coaster. "Before you go... Dinner? Friday night?"

There were few moments in life that one could look back on and say, *That was it. That was when everything changed.* Still, I almost blew mine.

"Ah..." My heart thrashed about like an overactive toddler and I found it difficult to breathe. "Ah..."

Jeff turned away. "Sorry. I don't know what I—"

"Yes," I blurted. "That would be... yes."

He smiled. "Great. I'll pick you up at seven."

I steadied myself with my hands on the counter. "Where are we going?"

"It's a surprise."

"Not... Anonymous? I don't think I can face sea urchin again."

He snorted in laughter. "No."

"Dress code?"

"Well... I kinda liked that outfit you had on, the black one. I mean..." he added hastily. "You should wear whatever you want."

I hadn't thought he'd noticed my dress. Smiling, I said, "I'll see what I can do." Actually, I was relieved since it meant I wouldn't have to go shopping again. Also, the bookkeeper in me approved of the fifty-percent reduction in the per-wear cost.

I left a bill on the counter to cover my lunch and pranced

out the door. Outside, I slipped on my sunglasses and beamed at the storefronts, grinning at total strangers while I strolled to my aunt's truck. It might be a mistake to start up another relationship, but I was willing to take that chance.

Then everything else would fall into place.

After all, if I could crack the romance code, how hard could a murder probe be?

CHAPTER FOURTEEN

LUCY'S HOUSE was in an area of the village where Victorian-era mansions lined the streets and sunlight filtered through the branches of hundred-year-old trees. Grass flowed from house to house, curving around flower beds filled with late-summer daisies and day lilies.

After parking my aunt's truck, I scrambled into Emy's waiting neon-yellow Fiat 500. An aging pickup with Coming Up Roses stenciled on the side was too conspicuous for undercover work. Lorne was twisted like a pretzel in the back of the Fiat. Emy pulled away from the curb for our three-block drive to Elm Street.

Good sense told me not to ask, but curiosity always trumps good sense. Or is that just me? Anyway, I plunged ahead. "Did your mom say anything about her—"

"No." Emy's lips made a tight line. "She won't give me any idea where she was on Friday morning."

Lorne leaned over the front seat. It was hard not to, since

he was already hunched over in the tiny vehicle. "It won't matter, Emy. No one could possibly believe your mom had anything to do with that."

Emy slammed on the brakes, and we shot forward against our seat belts. "What is *that*, Lorne?" she asked, glaring at him in the rearview mirror and biting her lip. She looked close to tears.

Lorne and I exchanged glances.

"Nothing at all," he said, scanning the scenery with great interest.

We passed the rest of our brief trip in silence. Emy was still biting her lip, looking more worried than I'd ever seen her.

We cruised by the gingerbread trim and mullioned windows of Lucy's three-story red brick house. A wrought-iron fence surrounded the front yard, curving into an elaborate pergola over the front gate. The hollyhocks, asters, and chrysanthemums that lined both sides of the walk would have been familiar to any Victorian gardener. They swept up to a wraparound porch that lacked only women in floor-length skirts, gathered in the wicker chairs to sip lemonade, to make the picture complete.

The only person on the porch today, however, was a twenty-first-century police constable, standing in front of the puce-painted door with his arms crossed.

"Should I pull over?" Emy asked.

I ducked my head. "Keep going. We don't want that cop to see us, and..." *Report back to Jeff*, I thought, but didn't say. "Lucy's property runs through to the other side of the block. Drive around the corner and park at the back."

Once we'd pulled up outside Lucy's back garden, Emy slid the gear into park and turned to face me. "Now what?"

"Did you bring the key?"

"Yes. I got it at Mom's this morning. She doesn't know I took it." Emy made a face. "Not yet, anyway."

"We can go in the back door."

"Won't that police officer hear us?"

Lorne leaned over the front seat. "What if I tell him I saw a break-in in progress down the street? He'd have to investigate, wouldn't he?"

Emy turned to him, looking contrite. "Lorne, I'm so sorry—"

He squeezed her hand. "Never mind," he said softly.

While they cooed at each other, I mulled over Lorne's suggestion. "It's not a bad plan," I said, "but he'll be able to identify you if this goes wrong."

"We're not doing anything illegal," Emy pointed out. "We have a key."

"Yes, but if we walked up to the front door with it, that cop would stop us. He must be there for a reason."

Unfortunately, that reason was probably that Jeff knew me too well.

Or not well enough, depending on how you looked at it. I had once vowed not to get involved with him, and here I was, anticipating our first date. *What if it didn't work out?* Should I really be getting my hopes up? What if—

Emy poked my arm, and I jumped.

"Earth to Verity. Any ideas?"

I studied the back of the house. "Let's get out for a closer look."

We ducked through the bushes that lined the fence, taking care to stay out of sight. At the back of the house, I stuck my head out to peer around the side. Then I pulled out my phone and disabled Call Display before tapping in the number. A fake emergency call was probably illegal in Leafy Hollow. Or frowned upon, anyway.

After four rings, a woman's voice answered.

"Leafy Hollow Village Hall."

"Hello, dear," I croaked, doing my best to sound elderly. "Someone's forcing a door near Elm Street. I think they're breaking in."

"Best you call the police, then."

"Could you do that for me?" I wheedled, my voice breaking. "I'm in a phone booth. There's no telephone directory here."

"I'm sorry but—"

"Why are there no telephone directories any more, dear? Does someone steal them?"

"I don't know. But you can call nine-one-one—"

"To report the missing phone directory?"

"No, no. To tell them about the break-in."

"Oh, I can't do that, dear. I don't have my glasses on."

The woman sighed. "Where is this break-in?"

I gave her the address of a house three blocks up and one block over, and hung up.

It took less than a minute before the constable's radio crackled. He trotted to his cruiser and, with a brief wail of the siren, drove away. Once he'd turned the corner, I motioned to the others. Keeping low, we darted up to the back door.

Emy inserted the key while Lorne acted as lookout.

Within seconds, we were in the darkened kitchen at the back of the house.

"Lucy's office is upstairs," I whispered.

My phone beeped with an incoming text, a reminder that my phone's GPS was tracking me—and our clandestine operation. Ignoring the text, I turned the phone off before tucking it into my pocket. "Let's go."

Emy started up the wooden steps at the back of the house. In the nineteenth century, these uneven and painted planks would have been the servants' stairs. The spacious staircase at the front of the house, lined with Oriental carpet, would have been reserved for the family.

Emy halted, and I ran into her with a jolt that made my swollen eye sting. Lorne ran into me, causing another jolt.

"Oh, man," I said, rubbing my eye.

We paused to untangle our limbs.

"Emy, what were you doing?" I asked. "Why did you stop?"

"The stairs," she hissed back. "They're creaking."

I leaned my head back with an exasperated sigh. "Who cares? No one's here but us. *Move.*" I gave her a little push.

Emy resumed her climb. The stairs did squeak. Practically every step, in fact. Must have been Lucy's insistence on authenticity. The Victorians wouldn't have cared if the servants' stairs creaked. In fact, it might have helped them ensure the hired help was actually working.

At the top, we fanned out to check the rooms.

I was pleased with the team's precision movements. We'd come a long way since our first covert ops. Some people wouldn't consider that a desirable accomplishment. Still, if it

helped Thérèse... I shut my mind to the possible consequences.

Lucy's office was at the back of the house, overlooking the
lavish shrub borders of the back garden. That was a plus for
us, since no one on Elm Street could see us rifling through a
dead woman's home. I gestured to a table where newspaper
clippings and scrapbooks had fanned out from overturned
library boxes. "Lorne, can you look through those? And check
the cupboard?"

We set to work.

Emy slid into a chair at Lucy's desk and clicked the
mouse while I leaned over her shoulder. The machine woke
with a musical chime.

"What am I looking for?"

"Anything unusual. Start with her chat history."

Emy scrolled through the files while I watched.

"What is... that?" Lorne blurted from the other side of
the room.

Emy and I jerked our heads up. Lorne had opened the
cupboard door. And halted.

A life-sized cardboard cutout of a woman in a bikini and
black-ribboned sailor's cap winked at us. A royal blue banner
rested diagonally across her chest with S.S. *Sea U Later*
printed on it. But that wasn't the interesting part.

The woman winking at us was Lucy Carmichael.

We stared at this nautical apparition. Then we took a
step nearer and stared some more.

"Well," Emy said finally. "I think we can assume Lucy
did not spend her vacations with a cousin in Moose Jaw." She
opened the photo library on Lucy's computer. It didn't take

long to find mementos of her vacations. Lucy had taken luxury cruises to every continent. One photo in particular made my jaw drop—a much younger Lucy, parasailing above the Gulf of Mexico.

"So she wasn't afraid of heights?" Emy asked.

"I guess not. Unless... something changed." I pointed to a long list of bookmarks. "Try those."

Emy clicked on the first. A buxom woman appeared, holding a stick of dynamite in one hand and a burning match in the other.

"Is that an online dating site?"

"It is, and so are these." Emy opened several at random. "Lucy was surprisingly popular. She has multiple accounts on a dozen sites."

Beep.

A message winked on at the top of the screen.

U THERE BABY?

"Type something," I urged Emy.

With a giggle, she complied. OOOH BABY AM I...

Beep.

YEESS SOOOO HOT...

"Ick." Emy hastily closed the link.

Other messages popped up.

Beep.

S HOME EARLY. CAN'T TALK

Beep.

TARENTINO RETRO 2NITE U WATCHING?

Beep.

WHICH I U LIKE?

This query was accompanied by a selfie of a young

woman displaying two skintight tube shifts in a retail dressing room.

"Don't answer that," I cautioned.

"Really?" Emy smirked. "Shouldn't we tell her the green one clashes with her hair?"

I gave her arm a tap. "Never mind that. Check the history on that chat."

Emy scrolled through a mind-numbing list of OOH BABIES and WHATCHA DOIN'S, until one message stood out.

U OWE $600.

Similar messages turned up on the other chats. The amounts "owing" ranged from three hundred dollars to three thousand. I jotted them down on a scrap of paper to see if there was a pattern.

Emy's brow burrowed. "I don't get it. Owing for what?"

My mind churned through half a dozen potential frauds until I hit on the obvious. "I think I know what Lucy was doing."

Beep. Beep. Beep.

Half a dozen messages blinked simultaneously.

Emy ignored them. "Which was?"

"Online flirting for other people."

"Why? They could do that themselves."

"Not everybody is comfortable talking to strangers, Emy."

"But still..."

"Faint text never won fair lady. Think Cyrano de Bergerac, but digital."

"It's a bit creepy, isn't it? Pretending to be someone else?"

"No use asking me. I find all online dating weird."

Emy narrowed her eyes. "You know, you could—"

"Don't even think about it."

Beep.

Emy's mouse hovered over the exit key.

I put a hand on her arm to stop her from clicking it. "Lucy wouldn't do this for free. See if you can find a spreadsheet with matching amounts."

It took only minutes of checking recently opened files to find the relevant spreadsheet. Down the left column were dating sites, each linked to a set of initials. The rows across were divided into twelve months, and each month's box held a dollar amount.

"Is that what she charged them?" Emy looked dubious. "That's a lot of money."

"Not really. Think of all the work. Clever jokes, little asides, comments on the day's news. Viral video clips. Instant messaging at all hours. Maybe Lucy's clients were professionals who were too busy to keep up with it all. Or..."

Emy eyed me thoughtfully. "Or what?"

"Or—she may have charged extra to keep the arrangements confidential."

"Blackmail?"

"Not exactly. Some of these people might be married. Or anxious to hide their online identities for other reasons. Maybe they paid Lucy extra for... discretion."

Emy's fingers fluttered on the hollow at her neck as she studied the spreadsheet. "Should we be prying into this? I don't want to uncover any scandals. I only want to clear my mom."

"Me, too. But if the people on this list have something to hide, wouldn't that make them suspects in Lucy's death?"

Emy sighed and pointed at the screen. "Those initials are probably aliases."

Guessing cryptic names and passwords was a hobby of mine, thanks to a smattering of Latin gleaned from my mother, a professor of ancient languages. But I doubted it would help in this case. "Let's print it out and guess their identities later. The ones we think are harmless—or none of our business—we'll destroy."

"Deal." Emy tapped on the mouse. With a whirr, the printer in the corner spit out two copies of the spreadsheet. I slid them into my bag.

"What about this romance writer's website?" Emy clicked to open it. "It's marked as a favorite."

"Try that button," I suggested, pointing to an *"Excerpt"* icon under the title, *Dishonorable Intentions*. The cover that appeared featured a young man with an impressive six-pack, wearing jeans that barely...

We leaned in to read.

"Oh, my," I said.

"Wow," Emy echoed. "That's really... something."

We leaned in closer.

"There's a whole stack of those books over here," Lorne said.

We jumped, not realizing he was standing behind us.

With a smirk, Lorne pointed to the table.

The Officer Who Wasn't a Gentleman was on top.

That title was familiar. I closed my eyes, picturing the list of names in Sue's bird blind. Then I reassessed the titles on the table.

Red-Hot Rogue

To Trap a Tycoon
Kiss of the Mermaid
So, not birds, then.

Picking up the first paperback, I riffled through a few pages, then stopped to read a passage. Emy came over and stood at my elbow. We read silently for a few minutes.

"Hmm," Emy said, picking up half a dozen books. "We should take these for research."

"You're right." I took a few more.

"Forget about that," Lorne said with an impatient shrug. "Check out these stories about the Black Widow trial. There are dozens of clippings here."

He handed me one illustrated with a photo taken at the Strathcona bus station. Protestors—held back by a police officer—watched an elderly woman with black hair climb into an SUV. The same picture had been on the flyers handed out by the Leafy Hollow Protection Society.

But this one wasn't printed on red paper so I picked up the clipping for another look at the driver. Still, the reflection in the windshield obscured the finer details. I studied the sunglasses, the fedora, and the mustache, then held it out to Emy. "Take another look. Are you certain you don't recognize this man?"

She squinted at the photo and shook her head. "Sorry."

Lorne pulled out another box to paw through. "Why would Lucy want all this stuff?" he asked, dumping its contents onto the table.

I drew up straight, pointing. "What is that?"

Emy swiveled to follow my gesture. Her eyes widened. A gray fedora peeked out from the mound of clippings.

Lorne picked up the hat and flipped it over. A fake mustache was tucked under the leather rim.

My mouth gaped. "Lucy Carmichael drove the Black Widow here? Why?"

I reached for the hat. Before I could grab it, a yell sounded from the sidewalk at the front of the house.

"Ver-i-ty!"

I froze.

"Who's that?" Emy whispered.

"*Ver-i-ty*. Are you in there, hon?"

No. It couldn't be. *Impossible*. I darted down the hall. At the front window overlooking the street, I craned my neck to peer through a gap in the curtains. The porch roof hid my view of the person standing below.

The visitor stepped onto the sidewalk, and I drew back with a gasp.

Patty Ferris stood with her head tilted back, gazing up at the second-story windows. She cupped her hands around her mouth and called again, ponytail bobbing.

"*Ver-i-ty*. It's me, hon."

Emy darted up the hall to stand beside me at the window. Her eyes were wide. "Who is that?"

"A friend from Vancouver. But she didn't say she was coming here."

"*Ver-i-ty*."

"You've got to get her to stop yelling or that cop will come back," Emy said.

My mind raced over Patty's earlier mention of a vacation. It never occurred to me that she meant Leafy Hollow. Her timing was a little off. I sighed. Patty's timing was frequently off. I chewed my lip, hoping she hadn't brought any baked goods with her.

Emy shook my arm. "Hurry. That cop will be back soon."

We darted down the hall and into the office.

The crash of breaking glass on the first floor caught us up short.

"That sounded like a window." Emy looked alarmed. "Your friend wouldn't break into the house, would she?"

"*Ver-i-ty!*"

I closed my eyes for a moment, vaguely recalling a GPS tracking app Patty had installed on my phone back in Vancouver.

Then I scooped up the fedora, the mustache, and as many clippings as I could grab with two hands, dumped them into a box and shoved it at Lorne. "Use the back stairs," I said before turning to jog down the carpeted steps at the front.

When I was a few steps down, the front door opened and swung back, crashing into the wall of the foyer with a bang.

"Verity, watch out," Emy called from above my head.

I slammed to a halt, teetering over a pile of glass shards scattered over the steps. It looked like the remains of a crystal vase. Someone had deliberately broken it—possibly to slow me down.

And that someone might be Lucy's killer.

My eyes widened as I realized Patty was standing outside the front door.

A high-pitched squeal came from the sidewalk.

"Owww! Why don't you watch where—"

With a desperate glance at the broken glass, I planted both hands on the wooden railing and leapt over the banister, landing with a thud on the hall below. The front door was wide open. I raced through it.

Patty lay crumpled on the sidewalk. She wasn't moving.

I ran up and bent on one knee beside her. "Patty?" I shook her shoulder. "Patty?"

No response.

"Are you okay? Talk to me."

Patty groaned and sat up, pressing a hand to her head. "Who was that?" she asked groggily.

After glancing at the deserted street, I helped her to her feet. "I didn't see him. Can you describe him?"

"I'm afraid not, hon. I was looking at my phone, checking our app to see if I was in the right place... and somebody barreled right over me. Bloody cheek, if you ask me."

She gave her head a rueful rub while bending over to search the grass. "Do you see my phone anywhere?"

Patty's bright pink cell phone cover was covered in sparkly fake gemstones that spelled P-A-T-T-Y in heart-shaped letters, so it was easy to spot. The glass on the front was cracked.

"Drats," she said, staring at the screen. "That's a shame."

I jiggled anxiously beside her. "We have to go." A quick check of the street showed no sign of the cop yet.

Patty wasn't listening. "I love this phone. Daaaaarn it." She gave the screen an experimental tap. "Oh, look, it's still working." She held it up. "See?"

Grasping her elbow, I propelled her down the walk toward the metal pergola, swinging the gate open with my other hand. "That's great. Why don't we take it home and look at it there?" I urged her onto the sidewalk.

Patty was still tapping. "I'll send Clark a text that we're on our way."

"Clark is here?"

"Of course he is, and he's dying to see you. He's at a funny little sports bar on Main Street. You weren't answering my texts, and the app gave this address as your last known location, so I left him at the bar and..."

This was too much information for me. I zoned out so I could concentrate on getting Patty out of there before the constable returned.

Too late.

A police car drew up alongside us and the officer got out.

"Ladies." He tipped his hat. "Out for a stroll?"

"Yes," I said. "Nice day for it, too."

He inclined his head toward Lucy's porch, where the front door stood wide open. "What happened there?"

Before I could deny anything, Patty put her size-six right in it.

"Verity, you forgot to close the door. We'd better go back," she said brightly, twisting around.

I gripped her elbow more tightly and swiveled her back. "No need. The constable will look after that door. Nothing to do with us," I said, nodding in his direction while I marched Patty by.

At the next corner, I made an abrupt right turn and frog-marched her a quarter of a block before stopping. "Patty, what are you doing here?"

She gave me a startled glance. "Visiting you, naturally. Hey, were you surprised? I told Clark you'd be really surprised. Were you surprised?"

"Definitely. How did you find me, exactly? And what app were you taking about?"

"Hail+HeartY." At my confused glance, she added, "You know—that one we have on our phones? I wouldn't have thought of it, except you weren't answering my texts."

I winced, recalling Patty telling me to use that app to "call for help." I slipped the phone from my purse and clicked it back on. It beeped to inform me of twelve waiting texts. All from Patty.

I made a mental note to scour my phone of any and all mystery apps.

Then I stepped back to assess her injuries. "Patty, your knees are skinned and your forehead's scraped. You've been assaulted. We should report this."

She brushed grass clippings off her yoga pants with one hand while waving the other dismissively. "It wasn't his fault. I stepped onto the walk just as he was running down the path. Couldn't be helped."

"So, it was a man?"

"Couldn't say. I told you, I didn't see him—or her. So there's not much sense in reporting it to the police."

I mulled this over. If we reported it, I'd have to explain why we were in Lucy's house. Still, we'd uncovered vital evidence—

My heart caught in my throat. I had asked Lorne to remove that vital evidence. Why had I done that? I scrunched up my eyes. Just once couldn't I reflect on the consequences of my plan before springing into action?

"Verity?" Patty placed a hand on my arm. "Are you sorry I'm here?"

Opening my eyes, I reached out and wrapped her in a bear hug that surprised even me. Tears pricked the back of my eyes. For a moment, I couldn't speak. Then I took a step back, and smiled.

"I'm delighted to see you Patty. And it was a *huge* surprise."

She grinned in return. "I knew it. I told Clark so. I said..."

"Where did you say Clark was?"

"Down the street. There was a big bird on the sign. It looked like a heron. Or maybe a parrot. Or—I know—it was a..."

I nodded. The Tipsy Jay's attraction for Clark was obvious—three big-screen TVs tuned to sports channels. "Let's go get him."

Patty hobbled gamely beside me as I walked away. Hopefully the rest of the team had managed a cleaner escape.

CHAPTER FIFTEEN

IT WASN'T easy to pry Clark away from the big screens at the Tipsy Jay. I had to mention to Katia, *sotto voce*, that if she ran out of Guinness, it might be easier for Patty to get her husband out of there.

Katia readily agreed. Clark had been rather loud in his insistence that she change the channel to a football match between Leeds United and Manchester, even though the other patrons wanted tennis. There may have been a bit of shouting before we arrived.

Once we regained the street—Clark was swaying, which Patty blamed on jet lag—I offered to drive them to Rose Cottage and get them settled in. After that... I had things to do. Well, only one thing, really—check in with Emy and Lorne to make sure they hadn't been arrested.

Patty insisted on going to a B&B, but since their suitcases were propped up by their feet, she was only trying to be polite.

"Don't be silly," I said. "You'll stay with me. There's plenty of room."

Patty opened her mouth to object, but before she could say anything, Clark threw his arms around me in a mushy hug.

"Exshelent. Good show." He stepped back and looked around, then raised his hand with a flourish. "Lead on."

I ushered them down the street toward my aunt's truck. As we passed Anonymous, I glanced through the window. Fritz was conferring with a man in a chef's hat. Probably ordering more sea urchins.

Then, because apparently there weren't enough mysteries to keep me busy, I pondered the name. In my younger days, I'd thought "urchins" were wily youngsters like Dickens' Artful Dodger. When I moved to Vancouver, I discovered they were spiky ball-shaped creatures with edible gonads. Some of the world's tastiest sea urchins were harvested off Canada's west coast. Still—yuck. No one could mistake me for a gourmet.

Since the spare room at Rose Cottage held only a cot, I moved Patty and Clark into Aunt Adeline's bedroom after removing some of my clothes. After explaining the kitchen layout to Patty, and making coffee for Clark, I bowed out.

"I'll see you later for dinner." After contemplating that for a moment, I added, "We'll go out."

When I glanced back from the doorway, Patty was bent over, peering into the cupboards next to the stove. I closed the door, fervently hoping she wasn't contemplating any baking.

By the time I slid gratefully into a chair at the 5X Bakery, Lorne and Emy were already seated. Lorne was working his way through a slice of chocolate cake, so he only nodded at me, mouth full.

Emy pulled the hat and mustache from a box on the floor beside her. "What are we going to do about these?" she asked, twirling the fedora on her outstretched finger and raising her eyebrows.

"We'll have to come clean."

"Give them to Jeff, you mean?"

I nodded ruefully. "Maybe we can do it... anonymously."

Emy rummaged in the box for the newspaper clipping, and placed it on the table. Next to it, she laid the mustache. It was the same shape as the one in the photo. The fedora was also identical.

The idea that Lucy had driven a known killer to Leafy Hollow days before her death made me queasy. But what if it *wasn't* Lucy in that picture?

I picked up the clipping for a closer look. The driver's features were impossible to make out through the windshield, so I concentrated on the hands resting on the wheel. Were those small hands, like Lucy's? Or large, like...

Replacing the clipping on the table, I pictured Sue's outdoor-roughened fingers as she adjusted the scope on her binocular. She had often been in Lucy's home office. Often enough to plant evidence. But evidence of what, exactly?

"Did Sue Unger inherit a lot of money?" I asked.

Emy looked surprised. "Sue? Not that I know of.

Although..." she said, her forehead wrinkling. "She lived in an apartment over the jewelry store until a few years ago. Sue worked as a plumber back then. Then she bought that land and spent a fortune renovating the house."

"And building her blind?"

Emy nodded. "Exactly. No one has any idea where the money came from to buy that property. Sue doesn't work as far as anyone knows."

"Has anybody asked her?"

She rolled her eyes. "What do you think?"

Emy was right. Sue normally rebuffed questions about her personal life. I'd assumed that her whispered conversation with Lucy at our book club meeting was literary chitchat. Until my discovery of the book cache in Lucy's office, it never occurred to me they might have something in common—something they wanted to discuss. But still—why keep it confidential?

I shoved the hat, the mustache, and the newspaper clipping back into the box, uncertain what to do next.

"Uh-oh," Emy intoned.

Lorne and I jerked our heads up at her warning.

Emy was staring at the front window. She drew a finger across her throat. "Busted."

I swiveled around as the bell tinkled over the front door.

Jeff walked through and let the door close behind him. He regarded us with a no-nonsense expression, his police cap firmly on his head.

Emy jumped to her feet. "Hi, Jeff. Are you looking for a lemon cupcake? I didn't make any today, sorry. But I do have—"

He held up a hand. "No cupcakes, thanks Emy. Just a few questions. I see the usual suspects are here."

"I don't know what you mean," she said.

"I mean—it saves me having to round you all up."

I lowered my head into my hands. *Great.* Just when we'd been getting along so well. I parted two fingers to take a look.

"Jeff," Emy said, in her best wheedling tone. "You're jumping to conclusions again."

Sighing, I rose to my feet. "Never mind, Emy." Turning to Jeff, I said, "Yes, we went to Lucy's. And yes, we went inside—which wasn't illegal, since Emy's mom has a key. Lucy and Thérèse were friends, you know."

Jeff opened his mouth, but I sliced a hand in the air to stop him. "The broken glass on the stairs had nothing to do with us. That was somebody else."

His eyes narrowed. "What glass?"

"Somebody broke in while we were there," Emy said. "They smashed a vase in the stairwell."

"I think they were there all along," I said.

Emy raised a hand to her mouth with a gasp. "Oh, *crackers.* You mean, while we were searching the office, somebody was..."

"Wait a minute," Jeff said. "You were searching? For what?"

With my gaze fixed on Emy, I ignored his question. "I think we interrupted them. Remember that cluttered table in the office? Lucy was a bookkeeper. She had a tidy mind. She wouldn't have left her office like that. I think someone rifled through those papers because they were looking—"

Jeff raised his voice. "For what?" He pointed at me. "Spit it out, Verity."

Emy, Lorne and I exchanged glances.

Then I retrieved the fedora and mustache and handed them over, along with the clipping.

Jeff glanced from one object to the other. "You'll have to explain this."

By the time I brought him up to date—and Emy had made coffee, placed a raisin-walnut scone on a plate, and pulled out a chair for him—Jeff was shaking his head. He sat down, scrutinizing the objects.

Emy casually pushed the butter dish closer to his plate.

"This makes no sense," Jeff said. "Are you telling me that Mrs. Rupert had something to do with Lucy Carmichael's death?"

We nodded in unison.

"Why? What possible motive could she have?"

"Um..."

Jeff rose to his feet, leaving his walnut scone untouched. "It's a shock losing a friend, and it's always difficult to accept suicide—but there's no evidence to support this theory of yours. I'm sorry."

"There is," I said. "Dozens of villagers paid Lucy to monitor their online dating apps and flirt on their behalf. We believe she was blackmailing them."

For once, Jeff was speechless.

"A ghostwriter for online dating?" he said finally. "I didn't know that was an option."

I gave him a sharp look, and he held up a hand.

"I'm not interested for myself. But it does open up a new line of inquiry."

"Lucy charged big fees, according to the records on her computer. But some payments were larger than others. We think those were people who had something to hide."

"We'll search her computer, but"—Jeff held out his hand, palm up—"I'm guessing you already have a list."

I retrieved my purse and handed over the spreadsheet we'd printed in Lucy's office.

He perused it. "These initials could be—"

"Aliases, yes. We haven't worked them out yet."

Jeff nodded, folded the paper with a decisive swipe of his hand, and slid it into his notebook. "If you have any thoughts on who these aliases represent, don't keep them to yourself."

I nodded miserably. Jeff was deep in his professional persona. Hopefully, it wouldn't interfere with our Friday night dinner. Probably not a good time to bring that up, though. I looked away, humming nervously under my breath.

He pressed his lips together before heading for the door. "Please," he said over his shoulder. "No more investigating."

Emy gave me a shove and tilted her head in the direction of the door.

I followed Jeff. We stepped outside.

"Are we still on for Friday?" I asked.

"I hope so." He smiled—one of those deep, soulful smiles.

The effect on my spine was such that I propped my arm on a lamppost to keep from melting into the pavement. I smiled back, a little more goofily than I'd intended.

Jeff's smile vanished, his expression turning serious. "Verity, you should curb your curiosity."

Huh? I released my hold on the lamppost.

Jeff fanned his fingers to forestall my protest. "Only when it comes to police work. Otherwise, it's—an admirable trait." He smiled again.

I relaxed again. Then his expression turned solemn once more, and I stiffened.

A woman could get whiplash this way.

Jeff stepped nearer. A whiff of Old Spice tickled my nostrils as he bent his face to my ear. "I don't want to have to worry about you all the time," he whispered, his breath warming my neck. Then he stepped away and gave me a searching look. "Why don't you let the authorities handle this one?"

I nodded wordlessly, then watched as he walked away.

Back in the bakery—I'm not quite sure how I got there—I sank into my chair and fingered the tablecloth. "Well, that's it. We're done investigating," I said dreamily.

I looked up to see Emy and Lorne staring at me incredulously.

"You're not giving up that easily, are you?" Emy demanded.

Dropping the tablecloth, I said, "I don't see what else we can do."

"We can visit Mrs. Rupert and ask if she knew Lucy."

I sat up straight. "You're kidding, right?"

"No, I'm not. She's been the target of a lot of criticism around here, and I bet she'd welcome a friendly visit from three Leafy Hollow residents who don't wish her ill."

The idea of interrogating a total stranger—never mind

one with a criminal record for murder—set the vein in my neck pulsing. "I'm not doing that," I stammered.

Emy ducked behind the glass-fronted counter to fill a plate with coconut-maple butter tarts. She walked back to the table and set it in front of me. "You haven't tried these yet. It's my latest recipe. I really need your opinion."

I eyed the plate. Maybe I should try Emy's new butter tarts, in case some inedible tea-time treat waited for me at home. That way, I could beg off as having already eaten.

I bit down, savoring the burst of syrup, followed by chewy coconut, with just a hint of...

"Is that cardamom?" I asked, once I'd swallowed.

Emy grinned. "Do you like it?"

"It's hard to tell after only one bite." I raised the butter tart for another nibble, then drew back. "Wait a minute. You're bribing me."

Emy grinned and leaned against the counter, arms crossed. "Is it working?"

"I guess it can't hurt to talk to her. But you'll have to do the actual talking." I crammed in another bite. Mowing lawns and edging perennial beds took a lot of energy.

After Emy swung her CLOSED sign to face the sidewalk and locked up, we walked across the street to the hardware store. Derek Talbot was perched on a bench, sandwiched between the blue-haired girl and Sue Unger. The women's protest signs lay propped up on the bench beside them, and they were sipping soft drinks with Derek. I looked about. There were no other marchers.

That was the trouble with protests—everybody's gung-ho for a day or two, but participation tends to drop off.

"How's your hand, Derek?" I asked.

He brandished a bandage-free palm. "Great, thanks."

Emy raised her eyebrows. "No chanting today?"

"We're taking a break," Sue said. "It's so hot. Derek lined up for half an hour at the corner store to buy us cold drinks." She took a sip of her diet Coke.

Derek looked sheepish, but pleased, at her praise. I wondered when detente had broken out and if it had anything to do with blue-haired girl. She was cute once you got past the piercings.

Emy, Lorne, and I ducked up the alley that led to the parking lot behind the hardware store. We halted at the metal fire escape that led to the second- and third-floor apartments.

"What's our approach here?" I asked. "Should we rehearse?"

Lorne chuckled. "Can't we just ask her if she's offed another one? And take a look around her apartment for dead husbands?"

Emy poked him hard with her elbow. "Stop that." She giggled, then passed a hand over her face. "That's not funny," she said solemnly. "We have to gain her confidence, make her like us. Then we can ask her about Lucy."

I snorted. *Gain her confidence.* Sure. That was easy for Emy. Everybody liked Emy. Even a convicted killer could fall under the spell of her mesmerizing smile.

Emy gave me a bemused glance, no doubt reading my mind.

She gave my arm a squeeze. "You can do it, Verity. You're very likable."

"Whatever. Follow me."

We trooped up the first flight of the fire escape stairs, walked the length of the building on the metal landing, and started up the second flight, halting outside the door to the third-floor apartment.

While Emy knocked, I scanned the rooftops and billowing trees around us. We'd been up here once before, but that was after dark. In broad daylight there were no raccoons to chide us, although squirrels chattered on nearby branches. Or maybe those were finches. I craned my neck to listen.

Emy knocked again, then bent to place her ear against the door. "I can't hear anything. She must have gone out."

"Wouldn't the protesters see her?"

"Maybe not, if she came out the back. Although..." Emy frowned. "She'd have to walk past them to get onto Main Street. Unless she's acquired a car."

We swiveled our heads to the tiny parking lot below us. Of the two spaces reserved for tenants, one held the same rusted Toyota sedan as always. The other spot was empty.

"Knock again," I urged.

As Emy raised her knuckles, Lorne leaned over her to prop a palm against the door with a sigh. "This is a waste of —" He drew his arm back with a sudden intake of breath. "It's open." He pointed to the gap where his arm had pushed the door ajar.

Emy gave us a pointed look. We nodded in unison, and she pushed it a few more inches. "Hello?" she called. "Anybody home?"

Silence, except for the chattering finches... er, squirrels.

A shiver rolled down my spine. "That's odd. I could understand if she forgot to lock it, but it wasn't even latched. This could be a burglary. For real, I mean."

Emy fished in her shoulder bag for her phone. "I'll call nine-one-one. They always say you shouldn't go inside if you suspect a break-in. The burglar could still be in there."

Lorne pushed the door wider. "There's three of us. We're not in any danger." He held out an arm to hold back Emy. "I'll go in first."

I followed him in, with Emy bringing up the rear. I missed our camouflage gear—especially Lorne's blue balaclava with its fluffy wool pompom and Maple Leafs hockey logo. Unfortunately, it was tucked away in an evidence locker at police HQ—along with Emy's deer-head mask with yellow button nose, and a red-lace D-cup bra, which certainly hadn't been mine.

That wasn't all that differed from our previous visit. Last time, the apartment had been covered in clothes and knick-knacks, with files and books strewn everywhere. The kitchen sink had been filled with dirty dishes and the counter laden with takeout containers.

But today it was pristine. Lace curtains covered the front windows. A threadbare sofa and faded rocking chair sat on the floor—which was bare, like the walls. Either Marjorie Rupert hadn't unpacked yet, or she had nothing to unpack. A table under the window bore two pens with a hardware store logo on them, a pad of lined yellow paper, and a handful of framed photos. Two loose pages had drifted onto the floor. I walked over and pulled them from behind the table.

Justice Denied: A Widow's Ordeal was printed in square letters at the top of the first. The *"D"* and the *"O"* had been colored in with red and blue ink. Both pages were covered with closely spaced handwriting, with the first letters of each paragraph meticulously filled in like the title. Doodles covered the margins, including crude pen-and-ink drawings of faces—a little boy, a man.

Two pages. That was all. Perhaps Marjorie Rupert suffered from writer's block.

I placed the pages on the table and reached for the nearest framed photo. A much younger Marjorie, wearing a pink knit dress, stood outside a restaurant. Next to her was a beaming man in a full-length apron. A teenager stood to one side, hands in his pockets. Written across the photo in silvery ink were the words, *Sydney's restaurant in Strathcona.*

The picture had been taken years earlier, judging from the age of the cars parked on the street. Electric street-car wires cast a shadow along the sidewalk. Strathcona, the nearest big city to Leafy Hollow, was a two-hour drive. But who was Sydney? I put the photo back, carefully aligning it between the others.

"There doesn't seem to be much here to entice a burglar."

Emy stepped up beside me, dropping her phone back into her purse. "I called the police." She tilted her head toward the bedroom and raised her eyebrows. "Might as well take a look, since we're here."

I followed as Emy walked across the bare floor and

pushed open the door. Then she jerked back, crashing into me. She whirled around with her hands clasped to her face.

Lorne swept past me to grasp her shoulders. "What is it? What's wrong?"

Emy pointed helplessly to the open door. I ducked past her and halted.

A woman lay on her back on the bed, her head lolling over the bottom edge and her vacant eyes staring straight at us. Her arms were flung out to either side.

Even from six feet away, there was no mistaking the red bruises that circled her throat.

Marjorie Rupert, the Black Widow Killer, was dead.

CHAPTER SIXTEEN

JEFF SENT us over to the bakery to wait for an officer who would take our statements. I think it was more to get us away from the murder scene—and out of his hair—than because we might have something useful to say.

My teeth chattered as I paced up and down alongside the bakery's glass-fronted counter. No matter how many homicide victims I saw—and since arriving in Leafy Hollow, I'd seen more than my share—I never got used to it. I rubbed my throat, picturing those bruises on Marjorie's neck.

Emy slumped in a chair at the table, mumbling under her breath. Lorne sat beside her, rubbing her back and murmuring to her.

My stomach felt nauseous. I averted my eyes from the pastry display. It was the first time I'd been in the 5X Bakery and not wanted to eat.

A half hour earlier, the police had whisked Sue Unger away in a cruiser. I had no idea why, since she'd been sitting outside the hardware store all morning. It was probably routine. I stopped pacing with a start, remembering something else I'd seen in Marjorie's apartment. In my horror over the marks on her throat, I'd forgotten. A referee whistle lay on the floor next to the bed.

Like the one Sue Unger brought to her protests.

"Who do you think killed her?" Emy asked.

Lorne gave a snort. "Lengthy list of suspects, I bet."

They both looked at me.

"It could have been anybody," I said uneasily. "She made enemies."

Had Sue's protection campaign extended to harassing Marjorie in her home? An argument could have led to violence, even murder. Marjorie wasn't quite... normal. What if she became enraged and attacked Sue, who had to defend herself? But if that was the case, why didn't Sue hang around and tell the police what happened?

The bell over the front door tinkled, and Jeff walked in.

"What did she say?" I asked.

"I don't know who you mean."

"I saw the whistle, Jeff."

He frowned. "Sue says she misplaced her whistle. Mrs. Rupert could have found it on the street. Maybe she was using it to call for help."

My hand shot to my throat as I recalled the scene. "She was strangled, wasn't she? That takes a lot of strength. Were there signs of a struggle?"

"Let's leave that to the professionals," he said.

"What about the bottle of pills and water glass on the nightstand? If she was groggy, she wouldn't be able to fight back. It wouldn't take much strength to kill her in that state."

"You didn't touch anything, did you?"

"Of course not," I protested. "You can see the nightstand from the bedroom door. Anyway, the Black Widow could have taken those pills before she was attacked. Any consensus on time of death?"

"Let's not call the victim the Black Widow, okay?"

"Sorry. Mrs. Rupert, I meant."

"Why were you in the apartment?"

Emy, Lorne, and I exchanged glances.

"You first, Verity," Jeff urged.

With a black look at my compatriots—who failed to meet my glare—I straightened up and adopted my most innocent expression. "We wanted to ask her about Lucy."

"Why?"

Emy stared at the tablecloth in front of her. Lorne stared at the floor. They were throwing me to the wolves—or the lone wolf, in this case.

"When we were in Lucy's office, we found multiple references to the Black Widow murder trial."

"Many people in Leafy Hollow were interested in that case," Jeff said. "That doesn't prove anything."

"But Jeff, there's a killer out there. You have to reopen the probe into Lucy's death." I started to pace again. "And another thing—"

"We have."

"—what about the broken fence? Don't you..." I trailed off, staring at him. "What did you say?"

"We have reopened the investigation into Lucy

Carmichael's death," he repeated. "But that has nothing to do with today's homicide."

Even though I wanted to ask what it did have to do with, I refrained. Because what if he said, *Lucy's will?* I kept my gaze averted from Emy.

"Could the killer be the person we surprised at Lucy's?" I asked. "What if they think we found evidence that links them to the crime?"

"And what if they come back for it?" Emy asked, rubbing a hand across her throat.

⁂

I tilted my head back, the binoculars pressed to my eyes, and fiddled with the focusing knob.

Emy tugged on my sleeve. "Can you see anything?"

"Not yet... wait." I slowly swept the binoculars past the main Pine Hill Peak lookout, three hundred feet above us, to scan the densely wooded section farther east. When I reached the spot I wanted, I readjusted the knob. "There it is."

"Are you sure that's where she went over?" Lorne asked, a hand shading his eyes as he looked up.

"No, I'm not." My gaze swept the edge. "But I recognize the opening between the trees, and I can see the broken fence. That's the closed trail. The one Sue showed me." Something caught my attention, and I readjusted the knob. "I see something."

"What?" Emy asked, tugging again. "Let me look."

I handed her the binoculars. "Look for the gap in the foliage. See it?"

She nodded.

"Directly under that, the ledge that runs along the escarpment about twenty feet down?"

Emy tilted her head back and peered through the lenses for a moment, slowly moving the binoculars. She halted, her mouth open. "You're right. I do see something there and it looks like..."

She lowered the binoculars, and we exchanged glances. Emy handed the binoculars to Lorne. We watched as he studied the same spot.

"Definitely pieces of wood. And they're straight and even, not like branches. I think you've found the smoking gun, Verity. Those are broken fence railings."

"But what good will it do us? We can't identify them from down here. And Jeff doesn't believe my theory that Lucy fell from somewhere other than the lookout. He's not likely to send a crew up there to retrieve those railings—if that's what they are." My shoulders slumped. "We're no further ahead."

Emy let out a disappointed groan. "I was sure this would clinch it. Mom's in such a state. I so wanted to help her." She dropped onto the bench beside us.

"Don't worry," Lorne said. "We can do this."

We swiveled our heads to gape at him.

"How?" I asked.

"By retrieving those railings ourselves."

It was a good thing the swelling over my hornet sting had subsided because the speed with which my eyebrows rose would have hurt otherwise. I pointed to the cliff. "Those fence railings are nearly three hundred feet up. How on earth would we get to them?"

It was meant to be a hypothetical question, but Lorne took me seriously.

"First," he said. "It's not three hundred feet. That spot where Lucy fell is closer to the ground. It's only about two hundred and ninety feet."

"Only?" He ignored me.

"Second, we don't go up to get those pieces. We go down. And from my reckoning, that ledge is only about twenty feet from the rim."

Emy let out a long sigh of recognition. "Ohh," she said, "I get it." She looked up at the ledge with a hand on her hip. "You're right." She twisted around to face me with an expression of triumph. "Lorne can get them."

"Have you both lost your minds?"

"I'll rappel down, grab the pieces, and be back up in no time," Lorne said. "Half an hour, start to finish. I'll just need a little help with the ropes."

"Won't it take longer than that to install the pitons?" Emy asked.

"I won't have to. They're already there."

"You're not talking about the ones you used in high school? Are they still safe?"

"They've installed new ones since then. Some of the guys used them just last week."

Emy gave him a suspicious look.

"That's what I heard, anyway."

This conversation would have alarmed me, except that in

high school, I took part in an Outward Bound canoe expedition in Algonquin Park. As part of the course, we'd been taught how to rappel down a cliff face. I remembered it as being enormous fun. We didn't go back up the cliff. And we didn't learn anything about pitons. But it was exhilarating to slide down those ropes and arrive breathless at the bottom.

So, I raised a thumb. "Great idea."

"We'll do it at night," Lorne said. "When nobody can see us."

I glanced from him to Emy and back again with a shiver of apprehension. "Is that... safe?"

"Sure. There's a full moon tonight, and no rain. It's perfect. We'll wear headlights on our helmets."

"Won't they be visible from the valley?"

"Not if we work fast."

CHAPTER SEVENTEEN

LORNE CARRIED the heaviest of the ropes slung over his shoulder as we climbed up the darkened trail that led to the peak. Emy and I trudged behind with the rest of the equipment. The lights on our helmets created ghostly shadows in the undergrowth. Several times I halted, convinced I heard muttering in the trees.

"It's the wind," Emy hissed, giving me a poke. "Go on."

When we reached the lookout, Lorne strapped into his harness and attached the rope to a piton just under the rim. We did a dry run of a few feet. Everything was going well until we realized that Emy and I weren't strong enough to pull Lorne back up the cliff. He hauled himself up, hand over hand, and stood at the top where we exchanged glances.

Lorne insisted he could grab the fence pieces one at a time and hold onto them while climbing back up with one hand.

"You're absolutely not doing that," Emy said. "What if you slip?"

"I'll be tied in. Nothing can happen."

"Yes, it can. You could slide and bang against the cliff and break your ankle. Or a wrist. Or your head. Then what would we do?" Emy shook her head decisively, which made the lamp on her helmet dance. "Absolutely not."

"Do we have a bag that Lorne could put the pieces in?" I asked. "We could haul it up separately." I pawed through our climbing harnesses and other gear. *Nothing.* "I'll go back to the truck. I'm sure there's a tarpaulin we could use."

Emy looked unconvinced.

"There's no time. We've been up here for fifteen minutes already, and someone in the valley may have reported us by now. Even if you run, it will take half an hour to get to the truck and back. We have to do this now, or not at all."

"Then I'll climb up," Lorne said.

"No!" Emy countered. "We have to scrub the mission."

While they bickered, I walked closer to the edge to gaze at the stars. Somehow, the Peak was less forbidding after dark. Maybe because I couldn't see as far.

I pivoted on my hiking boots and marched over to Emy and Lorne. "I'll do it. Suit me up."

"That's an even worse idea," Emy insisted.

"No, it's perfect. Lorne can pull me back up."

Lorne nodded. "Verity's right. And it's completely safe."

Emy bit her lip. I suspected she was weighing the chance to clear her mother's reputation against the fear something could go wrong.

"It's fine, Emy," I said. "I've rappelled before. It's easy.

The only hard part is coming back up, and Lorne will take care of that."

She hesitated.

"I'm not going far," I added.

Emy turned to Lorne. "You're certain you can pull her up?"

"Scout's honor."

He helped me with the harness, checked the connections, and tied me in. Lorne reviewed a few safety rules—most of which I recalled from my Outward Bound excursion.

I walked backward until my heels hung over the rim and the rope was taut.

"Okay," Lorne said. "Here we go."

I stepped off the edge.

At first it was exhilarating to slide down the cliff, my feet bouncing off the rock face. A breeze ruffled my hair, and crisp night air filled my lungs.

Within seconds, my feet connected with the solid heft of the ledge twenty feet down. "I'm here," I called.

Lorne tightened the line while I bent my head to light up my surroundings with the lamp. The light shone on pieces of fence railing—several with signs of a fresh break—nestled in a few shrubs growing on the ledge. I leaned over to reach for the nearest one, but the taut rope held me back.

"More slack please, Lorne," I yelled.

He complied. This time when I bent, I could tickle the end of the railing with my fingers. Grunting, I stretched as far as I could and closed my hand around it.

"Got it!" I hollered. With another grunt of effort, I drew the railing up against my chest and grabbed it with my other arm. The movement pulled my torso away from the rock face. Which made my feet slip. And then my entire body was twirling in midair, my feet flapping.

As I swung helplessly out from the cliff, still clasping the fence railing, I looked down. My lamp lit up the first fifty feet or so of the vertical rock that plunged beneath me. The rest was in blackness.

I hung for a second in mid-air, my chest heaving in ragged gusts. When I tried to speak, nothing came out.

Then I swung back, hitting the rock face with a thud. As my feet regained the ledge, I flattened my right arm against the cliff and tensed my grip against it, clinging to the rough rock as if my fingertips had suction cups on them.

I gulped in air until my breathing gradually slowed.

With my left hand, I inched the fence piece higher until it was nestled under my chin. Then I slapped my left arm, too, flat against the cliff, sighing deeply as my fingertips gripped the rock.

I closed my eyes.

"Are you all right, Verity?" Lorne called. "I'm going to haul you up now. Hang on."

My fingers wouldn't release their hold on the rock.

"No," I said feebly. "Not yet."

"What?" Lorne called. "We can't hear you."

"I said..." The words caught in my throat, and I raised my voice. "Not yet."

Emy's face, white in the moonlight, appeared over the edge. "Did you find something else?"

"No."

"Lorne's ready to pull you up."

"Please don't."

"I don't understand."

"Give me a minute," I hollered in what I hoped was a cheerful tone. I nudged the piece of railing a fraction of an inch down my chest. Tentatively, I lifted the fingertips of my left hand away from the rock. Carefully, I slid that hand toward my chest.

I swayed, and the rope creaked above me. I slapped my hand back flat against the cliff.

With my face smooshed against the rock face, I closed my eyes and tried to stave off the anxiety attack that threatened to close my throat. I tried to concentrate on breathing, but my reptilian brain was running in circles, hollering, *You're going to die! Forget the stupid breathing exercises!*

I resorted to gasping for air.

Much better.

"Verity? Are you ready now?" Emy called.

"I can't," I wailed. "I'm sorry."

"What do you mean, you can't? We have to get out of here."

"Go without me," I mumbled, wondering if dawn would illuminate my desiccated body, still clinging to the rock.

"What did you say?"

I opened my eyes, anchored my feet on the ledge, and angled my head to the side to look down.

Big mistake.

The floor of the valley rushed up, all rocks and branches and terror. A wave of vertigo swept over me. With a gasp, I slapped my cheek against the cliff and closed my eyes again.

"Verity?" Lorne called.

"I think she's stuck," Emy said, her voice rising. "Lorne, do something."

The voices overhead were muffled, but then Lorne called again. I assumed he was leaning over the edge, but there was no way I was going to look.

"You can't fall, Verity, you're tied to the rope. And it's tied to the pitons."

Sure, I thought. *Unless the rock cracks and those pitons slip out and...* I fought the urge to look down again.

Physically, I was rigid. Mentally, I was slapping myself silly. *Rappelling is fun, you said. I've done it before, you said. Are you a complete idiot?*

Lorne's voice interrupted my inner lecturer.

"The line is taut, Verity. I'm pulling you up."

"No!" I screamed. I swallowed hard and attempted to modulate that response. "Just give a minute or two," I yelled cheerily. "I'll be fine." Even to my ears, my optimism sounded forced.

More muffled conversation above me, followed by the rustle of equipment and the snaps of a climbing harness being adjusted.

Then Emy called, "I'm coming down, Verity. Hang on."

"Please don't," I mumbled. "Not a good idea."

A rope slapped against the cliff. Emy rappelled down and stopped beside me.

"Why did you do that?" I wailed with my cheek flattened against the rock and pebbles permanently embedded in my face. "Now we'll both die."

Emy gave my shoulder a reassuring pat. "We're not going

to die, Verity. Lorne is going to pull me up, and you'll see how easy it is."

A gust of wind dropped a clump of soggy leaves on my head.

"I'm sorry to be so much trouble," I said as a pebble followed the leaves to bounce off my forehead.

"Verity?"

"Yes?" I croaked.

"You're hyperventilating. Take a deep breath." Emy gave her rope a tug. "Ready, Lorne."

Emy's rope went taut. The toes of her running shoes started up the cliff face, one step at a time. "See?" she said, swiveling her head to face me. "It's easy." Her expression changed. "Wait, Lorne..." Emy tried to pull up her trailing foot. It was trapped in a shrub. "Oh, crackers." She yanked her leg. Her foot still didn't move.

The rope creaked above her, growing tauter.

"Stop, Lorne," she called. "My foot's stuck."

He must not have heard her over the wind, because the rope continued to drag her upward until her legs were far apart. One foot was stuck in the shrub, and the other had almost reached her head. As a teenager, Emy had been a gymnast—but there are limits.

"Stop!" I screamed, trying to swivel my gaze upward without prying my cheek from the cliff.

Emy joined in. "Lorne! Stop!"

Lorne stuck his head over the edge. When he saw Emy's contorted figure, he panicked. "I'll be right there," he yelled.

"No. Don't do that..."

Emy's voice was lost in the wind. Within seconds, Lorne

had flung another rope over the edge and rappelled down. Gently, he pulled Emy's captured foot free.

Emy rappelled back down to the ledge, followed by Lorne.

The three of us stood there, hundreds of feet above the valley. Pine trees creaked and moaned around us. An owl hooted. A cool breeze ruffled our hair.

"Good job, Lorne," Emy said.

I winced, recognizing that tone.

"No problem." He hadn't caught on yet.

"How are we going to get out of here now?" She thumped him with her elbow.

At Lorne's surprised "*Oof*," the owl burst from its perch, wings flapping, to soar over the valley.

With my one eye—the one that wasn't glued to the cliff—I watched the owl glide past the full moon and into the velvet blue beyond. "At least it's dry tonight," I said.

The words were barely out of my mouth when a whoosh rattled the branches above us and a cold wind sliced across our faces.

"Uh-oh," I said, wincing. "I think it's going to—"

Rain pelted down.

I shivered as water ran down my neck and under my collar.

"Well, Lorne?" Emy asked, wiping water from her face. "Now what?"

Before he could answer, a muffled "Hallo!" drifted from the rim above. "Anybody down there?"

Still gripping the rock face—now slippery from the rain—I swiveled my head far enough to make out two faces peering over the edge. They wore identical helmets with white mono-grammed patches on the fronts.

Firefighters.

Someone had seen our flashlights and reported us. No chance of a low-key escape now. I groaned and smooshed my face even tighter against the cliff.

Despite my terror, my mood lightened. Not only was I not going to die, but I was about to fulfill a lifelong dream of being rescued by firefighters. Wait till Patty heard about this.

"We'll have you out of there in a jiff," the first man called. He pointed to Lorne. "We'll bring you up first, son, and you can help us rescue the others."

Lorne looked grim as he was hauled up the rock face. When he disappeared over the top, I said to Emy—out of the side of my mouth—"Don't be too hard on him. He panicked because he thought you were in trouble."

She winced. "It's not that. Lately, he's been a bit... standoffish."

"What do you mean?" Given that one side of my face was flattened against a cliff, I thought this heart-to-heart could have waited, but—

"He goes off somewhere and he won't tell me where. He makes up excuses, and they're pretty feeble. A couple of times, he even said he was working with you when he wasn't."

"And you know this because..."

"I may have checked up on him. Once or twice. But don't tell him," she whispered. Emy's rope tightened. "You'd tell me, wouldn't you? I mean, if Lorne was..." The rest of her sentence was lost in the wind. Soon she was also at the top. More muffled conversation followed.

A firefighter rappelled down to the ledge, landed lightly, and turned to me with a smile. "Now then, Verity. My name is Bob. You and I will go up together, nice and slow. If you get nervous, you just let me know and I'll signal them to stop hauling on your rope. Okay?"

The wrinkles around his eyes and the gray in his hair assured me this was a veteran, well able to save my embarrassed butt. Still...

"You've done this before, right?" I asked.

"Many times," he assured me. "Are you ready?"

I scrunched my eyes closed. At least with the rain, my face was already wet so no one would notice if any tears of gratitude welled up.

"I'm good."

"One last thing," he said.

I opened my eyes. "Yes?"

He grinned. "Don't look down."

Our ascent was a blur, probably because I kept my eyes closed the entire time.

Once I was back on the rim and several yards from the edge, I turned to my rescuer. "I'm so, so sorry."

"Don't worry about it. We don't get called out that much. Haven't had a good blaze in weeks."

His firefighter buddy, reeling in the last of the ropes, looked up. "Well, there was that big brush fire near the racetrack."

"Oh, I forgot about that. But no house fires, thank goodness. And this is only our third rescue this summer. It's good practice. We don't usually get called out at night for these though."

"That's not true, Cap'n. Remember those teenagers last month?"

"Oh—right again. But they'd been drinking."

"True." They turned to look at me.

I shook my head vigorously. "We weren't drinking. Not a drop."

I whirled at a man's deep voice behind me. "Who wasn't drinking?"

Jeff arched his eyebrows at me. His shirt was untucked on one side, his cap was nowhere in evidence, and he was panting slightly, as if he'd been running. After scanning me with a head-to-toe sweep—checking to see if I'd lost any body parts, maybe—he turned to the firefighters. "What happened?"

They told him.

Jeff ran his hands through his hair and let out a long breath before replying. "Thanks, guys."

"No problem." They headed down the escarpment trail, carrying their equipment. "Take it easy, Verity," the captain called over his shoulder.

I turned to face Jeff.

Lorne and Emy tried to melt into the underbrush. When I glared at them, they stopped backing up, looking sheepish.

"Before you say anything..." I looked around for the broken fence railing I'd dropped at the top and found it near the edge. After I retrieved it, I handed it over.

"That's a fresh break," I said while Jeff examined the

railing under the light of my helmet lamp. "Lucy was pushed through that fence. It wasn't suicide."

"I know," he said, shading his eyes from the light. "You can turn that off now."

"Sorry." I switched off my lamp. "What do you mean?"

"When the coroner examined her body, he found bruises that he believes could have been inflicted before she fell."

A memory of swinging on a rope hundreds of feet above the valley flashed through my mind, along with a wave of fear. I sank onto the nearest boulder and rested my hands on my knees. "So..." I swallowed back my renewed panic attack, "We did this for nothing?"

"That's right." Jeff swiveled on Lorne and Emy, who straightened up. "You two can leave. I need a word alone with Verity."

They gathered the equipment, backed up until they hit the trail, and vanished down it without a word.

I snorted. *All for one, eh?*

Jeff said nothing for a while. Then he sat heavily on the rock beside me and heaved a sigh. "Verity... I can't do it."

My throat tightened. "What do you mean?"

"Dinner. Friday night."

I let out a sigh of relief. "Did something come up? That's okay. We can go another time."

He clasped his hands before him, not looking at me. Moonlight shone on his face, but not bright enough that I could make out his expression.

"No... we can't," he said.

I considered sliding closer, but something in his voice dissuaded me. "Why?" I asked.

He drew in a breath and let it out slowly. "You get into too much trouble, Verity. I can't deal with it."

For a moment, I thought he was kidding.

When he added, "I'm sorry," I knew he was serious.

Jeff rose and extended his hand to help me up. I clasped it, but he let go as soon as I'd regained my feet. He picked up the fence railing and started walking. I followed him down the trail. Neither of us spoke.

Hoots and bird calls erupted in the surrounding trees, but I didn't try to identify them. Any woodcocks or night herons or whip-poor-wills were on their own.

Emy and Lorne were waiting in the cab of the truck. I climbed in behind the wheel. Lorne handed me the keys, and I revved the engine. Emy put a hand on my arm, but I shrugged it off.

While I drove through the parking lot to the exit, I glanced in the rearview mirror. Jeff leaned against his cruiser, watching me. I gunned the accelerator and sped off down the road.

CHAPTER EIGHTEEN

THE NEXT DAY, sitting at the bakery table with Patty, I glumly contemplated the maple-bacon cupcake on my plate. This time, no amount of baked goods, not even Emy's signature concoction, could erase the sting of defeat. Miserably, I reviewed my lack of progress.

I had failed to clear Thérèse.

I had embarrassed myself in front of the entire village, judging by the comments of the residents Patty and I passed on our way to the bakery: "Verity! *Drop in* any time," and "Verity, you're looking a bit *Peaked*." Followed by gales of laughter. That's Leafy Hollow for you—comedy central.

I could no longer flatter myself that my panic attacks were under control—unless sheer terror was an improvement over ordinary anxiety. I'd have to check the *Ninja Guide* on that one.

But worst of all, I'd driven away the only man I'd been

interested in since Matthew died. That knowledge weighted the pit of my stomach like an entire bushel of sunchokes.

Maybe the cupcake would help. I raised it to my mouth and took a big bite of maple goodness. I chewed, mumbling under my breath. Nope. Not working.

"What's that, hon?" Patty asked. "I couldn't hear you." She was rummaging around in a tote bag at her feet, pulling out oblong Tupperware containers with bright red lids. She resurfaced and placed them on the table. "Did you say something?"

I paused mid-mumble to blink at the plastic boxes. "Patty?" I said, my voice rising a little. "What are those?"

"Ah." She patted the top lid fondly. "Last night, when you were out with your friends on your secret mission"—she flexed her eyebrows conspiratorially, looking delighted—"I whipped up a few things to help out. I knew Emy would be too tired this morning to bake much."

I dropped the cupcake on my plate, my gaze riveted by the red plastic.

Uh-oh.

I swiveled my head to check out Emy's glass-fronted counter, full to bursting with freshly baked butter tarts, scones, and cupcakes.

"Really?" I said weakly. "That was nice of you."

The faint tinkle of the doorbell in Emy's vegan shop next door announced the departure of her latest customer, no doubt bearing a barbecued sweet potato sandwich, or her ever-popular avocado and grilled faux-cheese. No mention was ever made over there of the bacon-maple specialties that lay only a few feet away.

Emy appeared in the doorway that linked her two shops. She rubbed the heels of her hands into her eyes before staring blearily at us.

"I'm exhausted," she said. "I got no sleep last night, and I was up at four as usual. More tea?" She turned to flick the burner on under the kettle and leaned on the counter as if it was the only thing holding her up.

"Actually..." Patty stood and picked up a plastic container in one hand, "I took the liberty—"

I slapped a hand on the lid, forcing the box down to the table. *Later*, I mouthed. Patty, looking confused, sat down.

Emy filled the teapot, brought it to the table, and slumped into the third chair. "Isn't this nice?" she said, forcing a tired smile. "I'm so glad you could visit, Patty. Verity misses you."

"Does she?" Patty perked up, her ponytail bobbing.

"You know I do, Patty," I interjected.

Emy nodded. "She talks about you all the time. And Clark, too." Emy's gaze fell on Patty's plastic containers. "What have you got there?"

I cleared my throat, eager to change the subject. "Talking about Clark—where is he?"

Patty sighed. "I can't get him out of that Tipsy Jay place." She consulted the black-cat clock on the wall. "He'll be watching rugby by now. They let him pick the channel in the morning and since the games are in the U.K., that's prime time for Leeds United." She leaned back in her chair with a sorrowful look. "I told him it was rude, Verity. Especially after you've been so kind to let us stay in Rose Cottage."

Emy poured three cups of caffeine-heavy Assam tea and handed them out. "You were neighbors in Vancouver, right?"

She raised her own cup, still black, to her lips. Having drunk Assam before, I reached for the milk.

"Yes... where I do a lot of baking." Patty glanced at the containers. "Verity loves my caramel-Worcestershire tarts, and I thought—"

Emy's brows narrowed over the brim of her cup.

"I've been meaning to ask you, Patty," I broke in. "Whatever happened to that marijuana grow-op down the hall? The lights that were so bright you could see them from the street?"

Patty looked confused for a moment. "Oh. That turned out to be a tropical fish tank. Nice couple. He's a biology professor or something." She added milk and sugar to her cup and took a sip.

"Um," Emy said, her brow furrowing. "Did you say caramel-Worcestershire? That sounds like an odd combination."

"Oh, it's delicious. I have some right here. I thought you could use them"—Patty pushed the containers across the table with a proud look—"to fill out your bakery counter today. Since you've been so busy." She flipped off the first lid and held the container out to Emy. "Try one."

Carefully, Emy replaced her cup on its saucer. "That wasn't necessary," she said, with an overtone of frost in her voice.

"But Verity told me how busy you were last night, so..."

Emy turned on me. "Did you expect me to leave my regular customers without their morning scones?" she asked huffily. "Not to mention the vegans—you know how they get."

Patty turned to me as well.

I looked from one to the other, wishing desperately that someone—anyone—would walk into the bakery and mock our hilarious rescue again. But there was no welcome tinkle of doorbell this time. I was on my own.

Clearing my throat, I said, "Patty was only trying to help, Emy. It was nice of her. Naturally, you don't need assistance, but..."

"Please, try one," Patty urged, holding out the container.

Emy forced a weary smile. "Verity's right. It was very thoughtful of you, Patty. And I do like to try out new recipes." She reached for a tart and raised it to her lips.

"I have to get going," I said, jumping to my feet and turning to the door. "Sooo much to do today. Lorne and I have to..."

A muffled choking noise made me wince.

Turning, I saw Emy with her eyes wide and a hand clapped over her mouth. With difficulty, she swallowed.

"That was... not good," she said, once she could speak. "How can you call that a caramel tart?" she added, flinching at the sight of the container full of them.

Patty's mouth dropped open. "How dare you? I suppose you'd rather sell your boring, pedestrian..." She gave a snort of derision. "Maple-bacon? How derivative."

Emy got to her feet, eyes blazing. "This is a successful bakery." She planted her hands on her hip and straightened up to her full five-foot-one, swaying slightly, fighting exhaustion. "How dare *you*?"

"Ladies," I warned. "Let's keep this civil."

Ignoring me, Patty opened her mouth to respond.

"No," I said, clapping my hands on the table. "This is pointless. Why don't we let a third party decide?"

They turned their chilly gazes on me.

"Not me," I blurted, trying to conjure up someone diplomatic enough to make this work. "How about Fritz Cameron? He adores your desserts, Emy, yet he's enough of a forward thinker to appreciate Patty's... unique take on things." I raised my eyebrows. "What do you say?"

They were still glaring.

"Listen." I attempted a forlorn look. "I don't want my two best friends to fight. I love you both."

They mulled this over, arms crossed.

Emy pressed her lips together and thrust out a hand to Patty. "I'm sorry. You were trying to help, and I was rude. Friends?"

Patty shook heartily, ponytail swerving from side to side. "I'm sorry, too. It was thoughtless of me to barge in here like that. Please accept my apology."

They stood awkwardly, looking at each other. I suspected they'd never be soulmates, but it was a start.

My phone beeped with a new text and I pulled it from my pocket. The message was illustrated by a full-screen image of a gray ventriloquist-dummy head.

Verity. We need to talk.

Oh, for pity's sake. *Now* Control wanted to chat?

B right there, I texted.

"I really do have to go," I said. "If I see Fritz, I'll ask him to drop by."

I headed for the door, then turned around to pick up my cupcake. *Later*, I mouthed as I jammed it in my mouth.

Outside, a glance at Marjorie's apartment triggered another bout of anxiety.

"Hey! *Stop.*"

Startled, I whirled around with my fists up, ready to strike.

Fritz easily parried my attempted hook punch. "Hi there," he said, unfazed by my belligerence.

"Sorry," I said, lowering my hands. "But you sneaked up on me."

"Did I?" He raised a finger to smooth his mustache with an amused look. "I thought you were coming this way. My mistake."

"I'm looking for Lorne. We have a lot of work this afternoon. But I'm glad I ran into you because—"

He wasn't listening. "Since you're not busy, can you do something for me?"

Puzzled, I followed him to Anonymous, where he halted on the sidewalk, pointing to the four-foot-wide window boxes on either side of the entrance. "Can you help with these?"

"You want me to plant flowers?"

"By tomorrow, please. They should have been done before the opening, but there was no time. I need them ship-shape before the weekend traffic. We have a lot of reservations."

"Fritz, I'm really busy..."

"This is what you do, isn't it? At that little landscaping business of yours? Because if it's beyond you..." He shrugged his shoulders. "I can get someone else. But Ryker recommended you. I'm sure you wouldn't want to let him down."

"Of course." Lips pursed, I pulled a tape measure from

my pocket and extended it over the window boxes to estimate the soil and plant material needed—while also estimating the time it would take away from my other projects. I stood back, rewinding the tape. "I suggest red geraniums and coleus to fill, purple and white pansies for contrast, and sweet potato vine to trail over the sides. Unless I find something at the nursery that's better." I committed the measurements to memory and slid the tape into my pocket.

"Can you do it now?"

"I'm sorry, Fritz, but I have to check in at Rose Cottage. Can it wait?"

Fritz sidled nearer. "You're going home? Now?"

"Yes, because..." I stopped talking, because I couldn't tell him the real reason.

"If you have that much time to laze about at home, you can't be very busy. And these window boxes are on the first floor. It's not like you have to climb anything." His cheek twitched.

I really wanted to wipe that smirk from his face. But I couldn't—not if it meant Ryker might stop sending clients my way. "Fine," I said evenly. "I'll pick up the material now, and plant these boxes first thing tomorrow."

"Great." Fritz gave me an annoying thumbs-up. After glancing up and down the street, he got into his BMW and drove off with a brief wave.

Too late, I remembered my promise to ask him about Emy and Patty's bake-off. It would have to wait until I returned with the flowers. I climbed into my aunt's truck and headed for the first of the nurseries on Coming Up Roses' purchasing list.

It would add an hour to my day to arrange the foliage for Fritz's window boxes. Back at Rose Cottage, Carson was waiting for me to approve the new paint color for the exterior window frames. And Control... I scrunched up my face, trying to remain calm.

My despair over our Peak misadventure had almost banished my concern over Aunt Adeline. Almost. The knowledge that she was out there somewhere and I was doing nothing to help was a continual worry, nibbling away at the edges of my consciousness. Control had said nothing would happen for weeks. So its latest message would likely lead to another pointless skirmish.

On the other hand, if I let my aunt's landscaping business fail, that would mean giving up Rose Cottage. Then she'd have nothing to come back to.

Control would have to wait.

CHAPTER NINETEEN

I WAS on my way home from the nursery with the flowers for Fritz's window boxes in the back of the truck when the first fire engine raced up behind me, siren wailing. After swerving onto the shoulder, I watched as the truck whooshed by. Before I could follow, another siren wailed—an ambulance this time. More sirens. Another fire truck swept past, followed by a police car with its blue and white light bar flashing.

Sirens always sent a shiver up my spine. Hopefully no one was hurt. It wasn't the season for house fires, according to the firefighters who'd rescued us, so this must be a traffic accident. Or maybe a heart attack.

I pulled out onto the road and headed for Rose Cottage, intending to drop off the rose bushes that I'd picked up at the nursery for the front garden. There was just enough time to tuck them into a shady part of the driveway, have a word with Carson and duck downstairs to find out what Control wanted. Although I hoped it would be an update on my aunt's whereabouts—or Gideon's, at least—I wasn't getting my hopes up. Control had disappointed me before.

Meanwhile, Lorne was waiting at the next house on our list—a half-acre lawn that took an hour to cut.

Turning onto the road that led to Rose Cottage, I caught a whiff of smoke. Not a heart attack, then. I lowered the side window of my aunt's truck. Sure enough, an acrid smell filled my nostrils. It might be someone burning brush. It wouldn't be the first time one of those fires had raged out of control.

The smoke got thicker as I approached home. None of my neighbors had been burning brush when I left that morning. With my heart in my throat, I tamped on the accelerator and roared over the hill.

What I saw took my breath away.

Two fire trucks were parked outside Rose Cottage, lights flashing. A firefighter on the front lawn had a hose trained on the newly shingled roof. Water surged out, bathing the roof and gushing along the eavestroughs. A police car—also with lights flashing—was angled across the road, barring my way.

I slammed on my brakes and jumped out of the truck, leaving the driver's door gaping open. A police constable on guard reached out an arm to stop me, but I raced by him, almost knocking him over.

"That's my house," I yelled over my shoulder.

Outside Rose Cottage, I stuttered to a halt.

The porch was burned through. The fieldstone walls behind it were black, as were the wooden window frames and the front of the roof. The smell of smoke was sickening.

With a hand clapped over my mouth, I whirled to the

firefighter behind me. "Was anyone inside?" Without waiting for an answer, I ran over to the crumpled and still-smoking porch stairs.

Two gloved hands grabbed me around the middle, holding me tight. I struggled against the firefighter's grip, my feet swinging off the ground. "Let me go," I hollered over the roar of the gushing fire hose.

"You can't go in. It's not safe," he yelled in my ear. "There's no one in there."

"*Ver-i-ty*," a woman's voice called.

The firefighter loosened his grip. I whirled to face Patty, who stood on the driveway a few yards away.

"Over here," she called, waving a hand. "We're all fine."

Clark stood beside her. Carson was there too, watching the firefighters with concern—no doubt dismayed to see his hard work going up in smoke.

I sprinted over. "What happened?"

"No idea," Patty said. "We just got here. I'm so sorry."

"I was in the trailer, having a lie-down," Carson said. "Didn't see anything. Sorry. But..." He flinched and pointed at the front lawn. My heart caught in my throat at the look on his face.

I whirled around.

One of the bulky-suited firefighters was bent over something on the lawn. He reached to one side for his equipment, revealing a gray-and-white bundle lying on the grass beside him.

"Oh, no," I whispered, fighting back tears.

I raced over and dropped to my knees as the firefighter fit a tiny plastic mask over General Chang's mouth and nose.

"He's not breathing, is he?" I asked. *"He's not breathing."*

"Give him a chance," the firefighter said. "A little oxygen can work wonders."

"Please save him," I said, sniffling. "He's such a good boy."

Part of me protested, *Since when?* But it was only my inner curmudgeon, preparing for disappointment.

The tiny oxygen balloon swelled and sighed under the firefighter's hand. The General's fur was wet and matted, and he smelled of smoke. I don't know how long I knelt there, but it felt as if time had stopped.

"We found him on the porch, lying on that rocker," the firefighter said, not lifting his eyes from the General. "He must have been asleep, and breathed in the smoke."

The General's feet were curled against his body, and his good eye was shut tight.

Carson walked up to crouch beside me on the wet lawn. "He's gonna pull through. That little guy's tough as nails. Tougher."

I patted Carson's hand without taking my eyes off the oxygen mask. The General *was* tough. He'd once stopped a killer in his tracks—and possibly saved my life. And now, I was helpless to save his. My vision blurred.

The firefighter glanced up. "He's coming around."

Holding my breath, I watched the furry face behind the mask.

The General coughed. And then again.

The firefighter took off the oxygen mask. "See?" he said.

I chucked the old tabby under the cheek with one finger. His eye stared blearily at me, his breathing raspy.

"He's got a little smoke damage, that's why that eye is so red. I don't know what happened to the other one, though," the firefighter said. "There are no burn marks."

"Oh." I laughed. "It's always been that way. Thank you."

"No problem. Let's leave the oxygen mask on him a while," he said, showing me how to operate it. "But check with your vet as soon as possible."

"I'll take him to Dr. Naz right away. Thank you so much, Officer... Sorry, I don't know your name."

"Yes, you do," he said, grinning, and took off his helmet to reveal gray-streaked hair. "Bob Valens, at your service."

It was the leader of the squad that rescued Emy, Lorne and I from our ill-fated climb.

"Yikes," I said, feeling a flush color my cheeks. "I don't know how to thank you."

He chuckled. "Maybe you should consider a house closer to the fire hall."

I forced a smile.

"Seriously, that's what we're here for," he said. "Happy to help." He winked, tucked his helmet under his arm, and walked over to direct the crew members who were retracting the hoses.

Within minutes, the second fire truck had packed up and driven away.

Captain Bob returned to bend over the General, whose tail swished at his approach. The General batted a paw at the oxygen mask, obviously annoyed.

"Let's take that off so you can hustle him along to the vet's. Before you go"—he winced—"I'm sorry to say we found evidence of arson. The fire marshal's been informed. The police are leaving a cruiser on the road for now. Do you have somewhere to stay for the night?"

I tried to take it in. "Arson?" My head whirled. *Who would want to burn down Rose Cottage?* Bewildered, I glanced over at Patty and Clark, who were talking to a fire-fighter. Patty was doing most of the talking, gesticulating wildly. Even from there, I could see a glazed look in the fire-fighter's eye that indicated Patty was only getting started.

"We'll be fine. Thank you for everything you've done, especially for the General here. I really, really appreciate it."

Captain Bob bent over to pat General Chang's head and pick up the oxygen mask. The tomcat narrowed his eye at him, arching his back a little.

"Is that specially made for cats?" I asked.

"All small pets. You're lucky we had one on the truck. We don't have them on every vehicle."

"Do you need more?"

He smiled. "Wouldn't turn 'em down." He stood up to go. "See you, Verity."

"Oh, I hope not," I said with a fervent sigh.

His lips twitched.

"I didn't mean it that way," I hastily added.

"I know." With another wink, he climbed into the truck and the second crew drove off, leaving only the police cruiser on the road, lights flashing.

Carson drove the Coming Up Roses truck to Dr. Farah Naz's surgery, so I could hold the General. Emy was on her way.

After taking Carson back to Rose Cottage, she intended to move Patty and Clark into her apartment over the bakery.

I called the vet's office from the truck while the General squirmed in my arms.

"Best if you bring him in right away," she said. "So long as he's breathing fine on his own, he'll likely be okay, but I should check him for signs of carbon monoxide poisoning."

"Can you keep him overnight?" I asked. "I'm not sure where I'll be."

"Yes, of course. I was going to suggest it, so we can watch for complications."

A few minutes later, I deposited the soggy tomcat on Dr. Naz's metal examining table. The General was not pleased. Possibly he recalled returning from a previous visit to Dr. Naz with some very undignified nip-and-tuck.

"Sorry, fella," I said. "Liver treats to come. Concentrate on that."

He huffed his disdain, for liver treats in general and me in particular, before hunching down to glare suspiciously at the vet.

"How's Rose Cottage?" Dr. Naz asked, bending her hijab-covered head over the General. "Still standing?"

"It didn't look like there was serious structural damage, although we'll have to start over on the roof and the eavestroughs. A lot of exterior wooden trim was damaged. And the porch is a write-off." I sighed. "I haven't been inside yet. The firefighters said the blaze started outside, against the wall, but there will be smoke and water damage indoors."

"Sounds grim. I'm so sorry. Adeline would be devastated."

"I know you and my aunt are good friends, Dr. Naz..."

"Please, call me Farah," she said, reaching for her stethoscope.

Like everyone else in the village, Farah believed my aunt was dead. I was tired of arguing—and the subsequent pitying glances.

"Adeline would be proud of the work you've done," she continued. "You've got home insurance, right?"

"I hope so. I assume my aunt had insurance on the cottage. I don't know how much it covers though." I made a mental note to call Aunt Adeline's insurance agent the minute I left Farah's office.

"Adeline was very conscientious. I'm sure you'll be fine," Farah said in a reassuring tone as she held the stethoscope to the General's chest and listened. After a few moments, she released him and lowered the earbuds. "As fine as you can be, given that you've been forced from your home. You're welcome to stay with me until Rose Cottage is repaired. I've got plenty of room."

"That's kind, but I have a friend in the village who's willing to put me up."

"If you change your mind, call me anytime. And call to check up on the General here. I think he's going to be fine. He didn't gag or foam at the mouth, did he?"

"Not that I saw. Is that likely to happen?"

"Not now. Those are signs of smoke inhalation in cats, so it's good he hasn't exhibited them. And his vital signs are stable."

"Will his eye stay red for long?"

"It should clear up on its own. We'll put in a few drops to help it along."

"Thank you. Can I pay on the way out?"

"Definitely not."

I halted on my way to the door. "Excuse me?"

"No charge. I'm happy to help Adeline's niece. I only wish I could have helped her." Farah's eyes misted. Then she picked up the General and walked briskly to the treatment room in the back, adding over her shoulder, "Call me tomorrow and I'll let you know how the General is doing."

By the time I emerged into the parking lot, I was near breaking. We'd come so close to disaster. What if Patty or Clark had been in the house? And what about—I halted, overcome by remorse. *What about Reuben?* I hadn't given my adopted rooster a thought. What kind of pet owner did that make me? I whipped out my phone to text Emy, then slid it into my pocket without dialing. I didn't want to disturb her while she was getting the Ferrises settled.

Anyway, Reuben was never indoors at Rose Cottage. He spent his nights in his makeshift coop—my aunt's ruined Ford Escort. The rest of the time, he wandered in and out of Carson's trailer. Plus, someone would have told me if Reuben had been injured. I needed to calm down.

And I did. Calm down, I meant.

Until Jeff pulled up into the vet's parking lot and jumped out, leaving his driver's door wide open. He jogged over, concern etched on his face. And to think I'd once thought his square jaw and sculpted cheekbones probably indicated shallowness. Today, they seemed downright nurturing.

He held out his arms. I collapsed into them, sobbing.

Neither of us spoke, but he held me so tight I could feel his heart beating, slow and steady and comforting, under his shirt.

After a few moments, I pulled away, wiping my face.

"Are you okay?" he asked.

"It was awful," I said, my voice breaking. "Patty and Clark could have been killed. I don't understand. Why would anybody do that? Who could hate me that much?"

Jeff pulled a handkerchief from his pocket and handed it to me. I wiped my eyes before loudly blowing my nose. A distant part of me wondered how many men still carried handkerchiefs. This one was clean, too, smelling a tiny bit of Old Spice. I blew my nose again, still pondering. Maybe it was a cop thing—they must deal with a lot of hysterical females. Handkerchiefs might be part of the standard-issue uniform.

"Thanks," I said with a sniffle.

"No problem." He inclined his head at the vet's surgery behind me. "How's the General?"

"He's going to be fine. How did you know?"

"Emy told me when I arrived at Rose Cottage. I just missed you. She said you were at the vet's and I figured she meant Farah's. I would have been here sooner, but I wanted to check in with the guys at the fire hall."

"They told me it was arson."

"I'm afraid so. The fire marshal will send us a full report. We'll find out who did this, Verity."

"I know you will."

Jeff looked worried. "You mentioned Patty and Clark..."

"Friends of mine, visiting from Vancouver."

"I know. My point is—it could have been you in Rose Cottage."

I closed my eyes as tears threatened to well up again.

"You're shaking. Come over here." He opened the back door of his cruiser and made me sit inside. "Lower your head between your knees," he said.

I complied.

"Breathe deeply and try to relax." Jeff rested a comforting hand on my shoulder. "I'm taking you to emergency for a quick look."

"No." Without looking up, I reached out to grab his wrist. Breathing slowly, I hung on. In. And out. I released his hand and stood. "I'm fine. I'm going to check in with Emy, then I'll get Carson to see what can be salvaged. And I have to call the insurance agent. Then I'll—"

"Not yet. That can wait. You're in shock and you need to recover. Give me the keys to your truck. I'll drive you to Emy's and drop the keys off with Lorne. He can check over Rose Cottage with Carson and see that it's secure."

"I feel a little dizzy, but I'm sure—"

"I'm so sorry, Verity."

I looked up sharply. "What for?"

"I never should have said what I did at the Peak. I don't know what I was thinking. And now... if I'd been around, I could have done something—"

I held up a hand to stop him, suddenly peeved. After the day I'd had, the last thing I wanted were second thoughts from a man who'd rejected me less than twenty-four hours earlier.

"You said I get into too much trouble. You were right.

Nothing's changed—in fact, this latest incident only proves your point." I straightened up, glaring at him. "You don't want to be my babysitter. And I don't want a babysitter."

"You don't understand—"

"Now I'm dumb, too?"

"That's not fair. I never said—"

Scowling, I held up both hands. "Spare me." I marched over to my aunt's truck and got into the driver's seat.

Jeff followed. "Please let me drive you to Emy's. You're hysterical."

I swiveled my head to face him, my eyes narrowed. "I'm what?"

He scrunched up his face. "Sorry! That's not what I meant."

"Excuse me," I said, reaching for the door. I was careful to keep my tone un-hysterical. After all, the man was a cop. He could stop me from driving if he wanted to. I pulled the door shut, rammed the gear into reverse, and backed up—leaving Jeff standing in the parking lot.

Hysterical? He had no idea how close he'd come to a head butt.

CHAPTER TWENTY

CARSON and I stood in the driveway on Friday, two days after the fire, contemplating a still-sodden Rose Cottage. Water dripped sporadically from its eaves under a gray, forbidding sky.

Reuben perched on the roof of the Ford Escort, looking dejected. The green caterpillars that had been dropping from the elm branches all week were gone. Whether from the heat of the blaze, the torrent of the fire hoses, or the lack of sunshine, those tasty larvae had decamped.

At least Reuben had sunflower seeds to look forward to—since his friend Carson always carried a bagful in the pocket of his sagging jeans. My concerns about the rooster had been unfounded. He'd watched the entire event from a front-row perch in a nearby shrub. And his nighttime roost in the back-seat of my aunt's Ford was undamaged.

The rest of the cottage's residents had to find other accommodations.

"I talked to the insurance agent. He said my aunt had fire coverage and he arranged a hotel room for me so I could move out of Emy's. I'm at the B&B down by the village hall."

"Hear it's a nice place," Carson said in a noncommittal tone.

"I can probably swing a room for you, too."

"Not my kinda thing."

"The agent also said I can hire a security guard to keep watch for a few days until the property's secure. The insurance company will pay."

Carson brightened. "I can do that."

"I was hoping you'd agree."

Carson would welcome the cash. Hiring a perpetually tipsy security guard might not be the best idea, but he'd been living in my driveway for months and I couldn't force him out now. Besides, I'd need his help repairing Rose Cottage's crispy bits. Carson knew more about mid-nineteenth-century architecture than anyone in the village. Even if the insurance company insisted on hiring an official construction company, Carson would make sure their repairs were authentic.

"The workmen arrive tomorrow," I said. "Will you be okay here again tonight?"

"Sure."

My forehead furrowed. "Carson, there's a killer out there. Maybe you shouldn't stay here alone."

He gave a snort of derision. "What would a killer want with me? Hey—how's the General doin'?"

"Great. Farah's spoiling him with liver treats and tummy rubs on demand. He might not want to come home from the vet's. Listen—Gideon's place next door is empty," I said, pulling my key ring from my pocket and extracting a key. "You can refuel there whenever you like."

"He won't mind?"

The thought of Gideon and his quest to find my aunt made me uneasy. I hadn't heard from him since his puzzling message —*Adeline found.* That wasn't surprising, since the note Gideon left when he originally disappeared ordered me to "stay out of it." Control, on the other hand, insisted he'd "gone rogue." I didn't believe that any more than I believed my aunt was dead.

At least Control had confided in me, for once. Although not willingly.

Rose Cottage's talking hologram had been indignant when I finally aired out the smoky basement enough that I could breathe down there.

"We tried to tell you," it said.

"I know. I'm sorry. But—"

"We could have been destroyed," it wailed.

"Oh, come on. You're not even human," I replied with a snort. "You're a... you're a..."

"Artificial intelligence unit?" Control thrust out its rows of gray chins, looking smug.

"Really? Then why don't you use some of that intelligence to find my aunt?"

"Plans are afoot, Verity."

"What are they?"

"We're not allowed to say."

Wrong answer. Seething inwardly, I leveled my gaze at the double rows of monitors. Everybody has a breaking point, and I had reached mine.

Calmly, I strolled over to my aunt's toolbox. My hand passed over the saws, the wrenches, the boxes of nails and screws, until I reached a claw-nosed hammer. I lifted it, assessing its weight, slapping it against my open palm. Placing it aside, I slid on a pair of protective glasses. Safety first.

Then I picked up the hammer and marched over to the monitors.

"Verity? What are you doing?"

I swung back the hammer and slammed it onto the first screen. It connected with a satisfying *crunch* that shook my arm. Bits of glass sprayed the console, sparks flew, and lights flickered.

I stepped back to survey the damage. Nice. I raised the hammer again.

"Verity. *Stop.*"

"Not until you tell me where my aunt is."

"We can't—"

The hammer swung through the air. There was just enough time for me to appreciate the appalled look on that gray face before the claw head connected.

More sprayed glass, sparks, and flickers.

"I can keep this up all day," I said, raising the hammer again.

"Stop."

"Not until you tell—"

"We don't know where she is."

The hammer slipped from my hand and dropped to the floor as I gaped at the monitors. "You lied to me?"

"Not exactly." At my raised eyebrows, Control added, "Gideon used to work for the Syndicate."

"The criminal organization that tried to buy up Pine Hill Valley? That can't be true."

"It is. Your aunt convinced him to change sides. Years ago."

I tilted the chair to let bits of safety glass fall off and then dropped into it. "Gideon said you were online marketers. The devious kind—black ops, even. He implied you make things... go away."

"Not exactly. We make things *appear* to go away. Unlike the Syndicate, we never use force." The gray faces frowned simultaneously. "It's a long story, Verity. We do have a plan, and it involves much more than just your aunt."

My flicker of anger over the words *just your aunt* did not go unnoticed.

"Don't worry," Control blurted. "Adeline's safety is a number one priority with us. Please don't smash anything else."

I withdrew the hand that had been reaching for the hammer. "Go on."

"Your aunt is gathering information to help us close down the Syndicate for good. But she's being watched."

"By who?"

"We don't know."

My fingers flexed, and Control hastily added, "But we have a good idea. Meanwhile, we need you to trust us for a little while longer."

"How long?"

"We told you. Ten days. Maybe two weeks. That's all."

Sighing, I got to my feet. "If I don't have news by then, I'm going to the press. Or the police. Or... somebody." I gestured helplessly at the broken glass. "And I'm not cleaning this up, either." Then I had stalked out of the basement and slammed the door.

It was a hollow threat to go public, as Control well knew. Who would believe such a crazy story? Especially since the hologram would simply fail to co-operate if I tried to produce it. Leaving only a dusty, unused console and rows of old monitors—some of them smashed—in my aunt's basement. The aunt whom everyone presumed was dead.

They'd probably lock *me* up. In one of those rooms with padded walls.

Standing in the driveway of sodden Rose Cottage, I uttered a sigh at the knowledge that Gideon's cottage would be empty a while longer. Then I pushed my shoulders back. I couldn't do anything about that for now.

Carson waved the key, bringing me back to the present. "Are you sure?"

"Gideon won't mind. Take it. You can air the place out for him."

Carson put the key into his pocket. "Thanks. I'll clean up a bit here—get some of this ruined wood squared away."

"The repair crew can do that."

"It'll be easier for them if the driveway's cleared. And it gives me sumthin to do."

"Go ahead, if you want. I'm heading for the fire hall, to thank those guys for everything they've done."

And also because, well, firefighters.

"Wait." I snapped my fingers. "I have something for you."

I trotted to the truck, where the passenger seat was piled high with white bakery boxes, and came back with one. "Emy sent these for you. Sausage rolls, veggie sandwiches, and butter tarts."

He brightened. "Well, now, that's nice of her. Thank Emy for me."

Reuben fluttered into the air to land on Carson's shoulder. The rooster cocked his head at the box. I should have tucked a few caterpillars in there.

"Take care," Carson said, sitting on his camp stool and cracking open the lid. "Everything will be fine, Verity. Houses can be fixed."

With a grim smile, I climbed into the truck and swung the door shut. *Yes, they can,* I completed his sentence as I backed out of the driveway, *but people can't.*

Carson meant to reassure me, but his comment only reminded me how close I'd come to disaster. Someone targeted Rose Cottage for destruction. It wasn't much of a leap to believe they meant to harm me—and my friends—as well.

My aunt loved this cottage, with its fieldstone walls, pine-planked floors, and cedar-shingled roof. I'd come to love it too. Not only did it represent some of the best times of my troubled childhood, but it was my last remaining link to my aunt as well as my mother—her sister. I'd worked hard to restore my aunt's magnificent gardens, and I put money aside every week to pay for Carson's meticulous work on the cottage itself.

Now all that hard work was ruined. Even the climbing roses along the front wall were singed black.

I felt deadened as well. What did I do to provoke this hateful act? Did the same person who killed Marjorie Rupert and Lucy Carmichael set fire to Rose Cottage? Did my insistence in probing those deaths anger someone?

A vision of the General lying limp and motionless on the lawn flashed across my mind. The scruffy tom would be fine. But worse things might happen if I didn't back off. Why did I have to meddle, anyway? How many murders did one person need to get involved in? My stomach clenched as I remembered Jeff's words. *You get into too much trouble, Verity.*

He was right. My actions had been foolhardy and provocative. If the arsonist's intention was to scare me off, they succeeded. The police could probe Lucy's death without my help. From now on, I would focus only on Coming Up Roses Landscaping, and finding my aunt.

But first, I had firefighters to thank.

A warm reception greeted me at the local fire hall—although I wasn't sure if the grins and whistles were for me, or the stack of baked goods I brought along. I staggered in with an armload of lemon meringue pies, sausage rolls, and double-chocolate brownies.

Smiling firefighters in short-sleeved black T-shirts that showed off bulging muscles surrounded me. I felt like I'd stumbled into the pages of one of those fundraiser calendar shoots. *Focus, Verity.*

"This is a little thank you for all you've done," I said. "I'm sorry I've been such a pest. And to prove it, I made a donation to the children's hospital. Also—" I fished a receipt out of my bag and handed it to Captain Bob. "I ordered three pet oxygen masks for the department."

He took the receipt with a grin. "Thanks. We'll put them to good use. How's your cat?"

"Doing great, thanks to you. You saved his life."

"All part of the job. Although..." he said with a grin. "If he wants to show his gratitude by cleaning up our vermin problem..."

That elicited guffaws from his crew. "The only vermin around here are the ones attracted by those stinky lunches of yours, Bob," a firefighter with *Tracy* embroidered on her T-shirt joked to general applause. The men on either side high-fived her while the captain rolled his eyes.

"I'd like to comply," I said with a chuckle, "but I'm afraid the General is useless at pest control. Maybe I can round up a pinch-hitter," I added, recalling the feral-cat colony down by the river. "I know a few crack mousers that might be willing to help out."

"*Mrrowww.*"

I jerked back, startled, as an enormous white cat leapt onto a shelf beside my head.

"Meet Oscar," the captain said. "Our own resident—and completely useless—mouser."

The tom stretched his neck, then languidly scratched his chin with his hind leg, unfazed by the insult.

"I thought fire halls had Dalmatians," I said.

Oscar turned curious blue eyes on me, no doubt expecting me to hand over a sausage roll.

One of the firefighters reached up to scratch under the

tom's chin. "No chance. Oscar would never allow a dog on the premises."

After more banter, and an invitation to the fire hall's community open house—which I promised to attend—I drove off, feeling good about one thing at least. The next kitty threatened by an arsonist had a better chance of survival now that the fire department was stocked up on tiny oxygen masks.

That left me free to concentrate on my other goal for the day—planting Fritz's window boxes. Then I intended to withdraw from any and all murder probes. I didn't care who dropped dead. As long as it wasn't me.

CHAPTER TWENTY-ONE

THE NEXT DAY, I stood on Rose Cottage's ruined lawn and brushed a lock of hair from my forehead, watching a hired crew of three men repair the damage to the roof. Carson stood below, shouting instructions. The foreman harrumphed once or twice, but overall, the workers were impressed by Carson's knowledge of cedar shingles and built-in eave-stroughs.

There was a nip in the air, a welcome development after the annoying heat of the previous week. The change in the weather did not lessen my discomfort, though. I couldn't shake the image of Marjorie Rupert's body flung across the bed in her walkup apartment. It was a sight I could have done without.

I'd vowed not to do any more sleuthing, but it wasn't that easy to put the two killings out of my mind. The previous night, tucked away in my tiny dormer room at The Stumble Inn, I revisited the murder scenes every time I closed my eyes. If only to give me something else to think about, I had pulled the second copy of Lucy's spreadsheet from my purse. A more intelligent person would have ripped it up and thrown it into the trash. Unfortunately, I've never been a candidate for Mensa membership. So, I waded right in.

Emy and I had guessed most of the aliases, and she had dismissed them as persons unlikely to inspire a blackmail attempt. But the last two had been impossible to crack. I puzzled over those two most of the night, whacking my head twice on the slanted roof above my bed when I thought I'd found a clue. I finally gave up and stuffed the list back into my purse in frustration. The remainder of my restless night was spent counting cabbage roses in the wallpaper by the waning moonlight that streamed through the open window.

This morning, I had risen with fresh resolve, determined to squelch my curiosity and stop getting into trouble. Besides, I had other things to worry about. Patty and Clark were wearing out their welcome at Emy's. Twice, I'd suggested we move them to the inn. But Emy insisted they stay on.

She was wavering, though. Patty's decision to try out her recipes in Emy's spotless bakery kitchen may have been the last straw. I winced at the memory.

Neither had heard my cheery "Hallo" when I innocently walked in on the latter part of that confrontation.

Emy was pointing a spatula at Patty. "Get out of my kitchen," she said in a tone that cut through the tinkle of the front-door bell like a knife through lavender icing. Then, apparently rethinking her tone, she added, "Please?"

Patty tossed her ponytail and marched out—bearing aloft

a platter of what turned out to be eucalyptus-scented panna cotta with mustard sauce.

I sighed as I remembered the ensuing scene as well as the chipotle-chocolate chip cookie I'd been forced to eat to keep the peace. The cookie was actually quite good. But while I was chewing on it, Clark had hollered plaintively down the stairs from Emy's second-floor apartment: "Are you sure you can't get SkySports?"

Tomorrow, I intended to pack up the Ferrises and cart them off, by force if necessary, to join me at The Stumble Inn, Leafy Hollow's premier B&B.

I started the truck's engine, shifted into reverse, checked the rearview mirror as I glided down the driveway—and slammed my foot on the brake.

Fritz was standing behind my aunt's truck with a smirk on his face.

Forcing a smile, I climbed out. "Fritz? What are you doing here?"

"Heard you wanted to see me." He sidled up beside me and stopped, way too close for comfort.

"No. I don't." I took a step back. "What made you think that?"

"Something about a bake-off? You needed a judge?"

Fudge. He'd been talking to Patty.

"Emy has a few items she wants you to sample. But I'm sure it can wait." I motioned to the truck. "Sorry, I have to go."

Instead of moving out of my way, he simply smoothed his mustache. It was like a nervous tic—or would have been, if Fritz had a single nerve in his body to tic.

"Why are you still here?" I asked.

"I heard you needed protection." He ambled onto the grass to watch the work crew.

"Protection?" My resentment bubbled over. If it hadn't been for Fritz's insistence that his precious window boxes needed immediate attention, I would have arrived home in time to spot the fire. "Protection?" I repeated, walking over to grab his arm and force him around to face me. "It's a little late for that, isn't it?"

"I don't know what you mean."

I took a deep breath, suppressing the urge to go all Krav Maga on him—on anybody, frankly. My therapist in Vancouver would have blamed my "unresolved anger." But if anything, the fact my accusation was unfounded only made me angrier. Funny how that works. I planted my hands on my hips.

"Where were you when someone tried to burn down my house?"

Fritz looked horrified. "You're not blaming me for that?"

We locked eyes. The brown pupils behind those rimless glasses looked genuinely confused. I released Fritz's arm and patted it. My fury was misplaced and we both knew it. "No, of course not," I stammered. "I'm sorry."

He brushed off his sleeve while keeping his eyes trained on me. "Apology accepted. You're not entirely wrong, though."

"Excuse me?"

"You were let down, Verity, but not by me. The entire village owes you an apology."

I eyed him suspiciously. "You mean for all the bad jokes?"

"I mean—the police should have found your friend's killer by now." He smirked at me again. You think he'd know better. "You've been sleuthing, haven't you?"

The Leafy Hollow gossip machine never ceased to amaze me. What else did Fritz know?

"Maybe."

"What have you found out?"

"Um... I'm not sure I should—"

"Why hasn't anyone been arrested?"

I gave him a good long look. "Did you have someone in mind?"

"Why ask me? You're the one investigating. You must suspect someone."

"I really don't."

"Okay. You don't have to tell me." He shrugged. "But I assure you, I'm here to help. In fact, Emy asked me to check up on you when we were discussing menu changes this morning."

I didn't know what to say to that. Emy hadn't mentioned any of this to me. But I'd been distracted of late. Maybe I'd forgotten.

"Look out!" came a shout from overhead.

I ducked just in time to avoid being beaned by a shovelful of blackened shingles.

Carson walked over. "Better move out of the way, Verity," he said ruefully. He shouted up at the roof, "Watch it, will ya?"

Fritz took my elbow and guided me onto the driveway. I yanked my arm away, massaging it to stress my dislike of being mauled.

"Did I hurt you?" he asked, eyebrows raised. "Sometimes I forget my own strength. It's all that weightlifting I do."

I really wanted to punch him. Instead, I said curtly, "I'm fine." He looked hurt by my tone, so I backtracked a bit. "Sorry. I'm a little edgy today."

Thérèse would have admired my use of euphemism.

Fritz narrowed his eyes. "Don't let your irritation with me confuse the issue."

"What issue?"

"You're not fine. There's a killer's on the loose. Who'll be next? You?"

I shuddered, remembering yet again the scene in Marjorie Rupert's bedroom.

Fritz eyed me intently. "Did you know Sue Unger is missing?"

"What?" I swallowed hard, hoping my sudden gust of fear didn't show on my face. "Who told you that?"

"It's all over the village. I'm surprised that an experienced sleuth like you would be the last to know. Well, don't worry," he added with a mocking tone. "I'm sure the police will get around to it eventually."

Would they, though? Suddenly, I wasn't so confident. I had no intention of sharing that concern with Fritz, however. Turning back to the truck, I said over my shoulder, "I'm sure they will. Now, if you don't mind—"

He placed a hand on my arm to stop me. I stared at it in a meaningful way.

Fritz stepped back with an apologetic expression—and both hands raised. "Sorry. But I'm serious, Verity. If you need help, you can count on me. I won't let you down." He lowered his hands with a snort of disgust. "Certainly that moronic Jeff Katsuro isn't accomplishing much."

"Excuse me," I said coldly. "I have to go."

After climbing into my aunt's truck, I roared down the driveway, narrowly missing Fritz, who jumped out of the way at the last second. When I looked back, he was coughing at the dust churned up by the truck on the road's unpaved shoulder.

I didn't do that on purpose, honestly.

My wholly inappropriate delight at Fritz's discomfort fizzled quickly. His lecture had reawakened my misgivings about the official investigation into Lucy's death—or lack thereof. And now Sue was missing. What if...

I forced that thought away with a shudder.

Was it so wrong of a concerned citizen to seek explanations? I answered my own question with a resounding, *Certainly not.* In fact, it was our civic duty to help the police.

So long as they didn't find out about it, of course.

Emy, Patty, and I sat around the table in 5X Bakery, brainstorming over a pot of tea and a platter of—I eyed the baked goods suspiciously, wondering if the yellow sugar cookies had been flavored with lemon or mustard.

"Fritz was only trying to help. And he has a point," Emy said, bringing my attention back to the topic at hand. "There have been two deaths so far and not a single suspect. What have the police been doing?"

"They're doing forensic tests on that whistle, aren't they?" I asked.

"Yes, but on the day Marjorie was murdered, Sue was in full view all morning outside the hardware store. The police released Sue right after taking her statement. And Lucy was a friend of hers. Sue couldn't have killed them."

"I'm not saying she did. But no one's seen her for two days, apparently. Where is she?"

"What if she's dead, too?" Emy's eyes widened. "What if a serial killer is picking us off one by one?"

"Oh, my gosh," Patty squealed. Her hand flew to her throat. "A chill just went down my spine. Someone is walking on my grave." She gave an exaggerated shudder. "Or maybe your grave, Verity. It's hard to tell."

I sagged my head in my hands. "Thanks, both of you. I feel so much better now."

"The point is, we need to do something," Emy said, refilling my tea cup. "Mom's not out of trouble yet. This investigation needs a jump-start."

"Like what?"

"On television, the killer always makes a mistake. That's how the detective catches them. They wait for that one error and then... pounce."

Patty chimed in, her voice low. "We can't wait around for another person to die. What if it's one of us?"

"Exactly." Emy nodded gravely. "We need to force the issue."

Slowly, I said, "I'm not liking the sound of this."

"It wouldn't take much. What if we circulate a rumor

that someone spotted a figure standing behind Lucy before she toppled off the Peak?"

"Why didn't this hypothetical witness come forward earlier?"

"Maybe they didn't understand the significance of what they'd seen until now. Maybe they've been out of the country. Maybe—"

I held up a hand. "Okay, we could make something up. But how would it help your mother?"

"It would flush out the killer, don't you see?" Emy placed a cookie on the table and tapped it with a finger. "Say this is the new witness. The murderer"—she tapped on another cookie—"will try to silence that witness." She walked the second cookie over until it was touching the first. "Then the police"—Emy gathered a scone into her fist—"can pounce."

She slammed the scone down on the killer cookie.

"That's brilliant," Patty said, studying the pile of crumbs.

I hastened to point out the obvious hole in this theory—besides the fact the witness cookie was not looking too good. "You'd need an actual informant. Otherwise, who would the killer be trying to silence?"

"That's true," Emy said, nodding thoughtfully at the pulverized baked goods. "And it needs to be someone believable—someone who drives around town a lot during the day. Perhaps someone who chanced upon the scene right after Lucy's fatal fall. Someone like..."

Emy and Patty swiveled their gazes to me.

"Oh," I said, chuckling. "You've got to be kidding." I crossed my arms, my laughter dying on my lips at the expressions on their faces. "No," I said incredulously. "Not happening."

They held their stares while the black cat tick-tocked on the wall. Then Emy sat back, shaking her head. "You're right. It's a ridiculous plan. Forget I mentioned it."

Patty leaned in, her eyes shining. "No, it's a great idea. I can do it. I'm a tourist. I could have been waltzing about town, getting into all kinds of trouble. It's totally believable. Let me do it."

Recognizing the expression that signaled Patty had found a new project—and knowing she wouldn't let go—I slapped my hands on the table.

"*Absolutely not*. It's too dangerous."

Patty wasn't even listening.

"I can wander up and down Main Street," she continued. "Pop into a few stores, talk about what I saw..."

"No way." I raised my hands in a *I-give-up* gesture. "I'll do it."

Emy screwed up her face. "I don't know, Verity. I'm not sure it's a good idea."

"*Now* you have misgivings? You came up with this."

"I know, but... here's the thing," Emy said, tapping her fingers nervously on the table. "If we go through with this, you must promise to never be alone. Always have somebody with you. Rose Cottage isn't ready yet, right?"

"Correct."

"So you'll be fine at night, because there are plenty of people at the inn. But during the day, Lorne, me, Patty, or Fritz must always be with you. You have to promise not to go anywhere by yourself." She pointed a finger at me. "Promise?"

I made a face. "Do we have to include Fritz?"

"He honestly wants to help, Verity. But we won't call on him unless it's necessary. Promise?"

I nodded and made a cross-my-heart motion.

Patty looked a bit dejected. Then she brightened. "Verity, can you teach me a few Krav Maga moves? In case I need to defend you when we're together? Like maybe that thing you do with your foot?" She sprang up and adopted her idea of a martial arts pose, with knees flexed and hands up, then attempted a hook kick with her foot. The only thing she managed to hook, however, was the nearest chair, which went down with a clatter.

Emy's eyebrows rose as she regarded the toppled furniture.

"That won't be necessary, Patty," I said, picking up her fallen victim. "This killer only strikes people when they're alone. We won't be in any danger."

I smiled at them both, hoping my expression conveyed more confidence than I felt.

CHAPTER TWENTY-TWO

WE'D BARELY PUT our plan into action when news broke the following day of a development in the Black Widow murder case. The 5X Bakery filled up rapidly with friends and customers anxious to hear the news.

While we waited for the facts, Emy worked the crowd.

"Coming through." She hoisted her platter of baked goods above her head so she could sidle between two book club members who were disputing the use of euphemism as a literary device. They paused just long enough to grab a sample each before resuming their debate, mouths full.

I hoped Thérèse hadn't noticed their breach of etiquette. Although, when I caught a glimpse of her through the crowd from my position against the wall, she looked as if table manners were the last thing on her mind. Thérèse sat in the back of the bakery, head bowed.

Emy made the rounds, dispensing samples of nut tart and lemon shortbread. "My latest—try them," she said.

The group was centered on a beaming Wilf Mullins. Our diminutive councilor was stretching out the reveal. As usual. Eventually, he reached the pertinent nugget.

Sue Unger had cut short a birding trip to Costa Rica and come home after returning to base camp to find she was a "person of interest" in two mysterious deaths. She wasn't happy about it, though.

"As her recently appointed lawyer, I accompanied Ms. Unger to the police station," Wilf said. "Of course, she had nothing to do with either of these tragic events. Ironclad alibis." He winked, which I found incongruous given the severity of the possible charges.

The crowd pressed in, calling out questions.

Wilf held up his hand. "One at a time, please."

"What was her alibi?"

"On the day of Mrs. Rupert's death, numerous people spoke to Ms. Unger outside the hardware store. Several can testify that she never left that spot. The police had already been apprised of this. And when Lucy Carmichael met her tragic end, Ms. Unger was on a group field trip, stalking a rare bird. Some sort of finch, I believe," he said, brow furrowing. "In any event, the entire group can vouch for her presence. She was quite... memorable."

I wondered if Sue had a fit of pique over the day's menu.

But this news did not reassure me about her innocence, because I knew something that cast doubt on her alibi. Something I hadn't shared with the police.

A voice in the back called out, "Then who's the current suspect?"

All eyes swiveled to Thérèse, toying with the morsel of

nut tart on her plate and pretending not to notice their pene-
trating stares.

Wilf gave an expansive wave of his hand and public
attention returned to him. "No idea, I'm afraid. You'll have to
ask the police." After dropping a stack of his personalized
fridge magnets on Emy's countertop, Wilf picked up a white
bakery box tied with string. "Folks, I have to get back
to work."

He waltzed out the door, followed—as he knew he
would be—by the crowd. They continued to pepper him
with questions, some walking backward in front of him, as
the group made their way up the street toward his law
office.

The bakery door closed quietly—Emy had dismantled
the bell an hour earlier with an exasperated sigh—leaving
only the four of us: Emy, Thérèse, Patty, and myself.

Then it opened again, and Lorne strode in.

Instead of his usual jeans and work boots, he was wearing
khakis and a sports jacket. I gave him a puzzled glance. "I
thought you were mowing the Hendersons' lawn. Did I miss
something?"

"Going there now. I had an errand this morning at the
police station."

Relief surged through me. "You told them Thérèse's
alibi?" I'd figured it out during my restless night at the
Stumble Inn, but hoped someone else would reveal it.

"I did," Lorne said, crossing his arms.

Emy dropped her empty platter onto the counter with a
clatter. "What?" She turned to Thérèse. "Mom?"

Before Thérèse could answer, the door opened again and

Jeff walked in. He must have dropped Lorne off before parking his cruiser.

Jeff removed his cap, tucked it under his arm, and nodded at us.

Thérèse pushed her plate to one side and leaned her elbows on the table with an audible sigh. For the first time in days, the wrinkles on her forehead disappeared. "I couldn't tell the police where I was the morning Lucy died, because it was someone else's secret."

"Whose?" Emy asked.

"Mine," Lorne said. "Your mom's been teaching me to read, Emy. We had a lesson that morning. It was ludicrous to think anyone would suspect Thérèse. I expected it to blow over and that the real killer would be caught. Obviously, I was wrong." He gave an apologetic shrug. "I gave a statement at the station this morning. I'm sorry. I should have told you."

Emy stood stock-still, staring at him. "I don't understand," she said finally. "You know how to read."

Lorne flushed. "I do now."

Thérèse rose to her feet. "Lorne has dyslexia, Emy. I've been teaching him techniques to counter it. It's not unusual, but it interfered with his learning to read. His teachers didn't notice because he was clever enough to keep it hidden."

Emy's eyes never left Lorne's. Her voice wavered. "He kept it hidden from me, too."

Lorne flinched. "I wanted to tell you, but—"

"You didn't trust me?" She blinked rapidly.

"It's not like that..." he broke off at the look on her face. "Oh, Emy, I'm so sorry. Don't cry, sweetheart."

Emy wiped the back of her hand across her nose while

she looked away. "Your uncle should have noticed," she whispered. "Years ago."

Lorne shrugged. "He was busy. Oh, please don't cry."

"I'm not crying. I'm not. But I don't understand why you didn't tell me."

"I was embarrassed. I didn't want you to think our children—"

"Our what?" Her eyes widened. "Aren't you getting a little ahead of yourself?"

Lorne flushed even redder. "I meant... my children. Mine. Not yours. Yours would be perfect in every way." His voice trailed away, and he trained his miserable gaze on the floor.

I looked around for a shovel—or at least a big spatula. Lorne would need one to dig himself out of this hole.

"My cousin had dyslexia," a cheery voice said behind us. "She reads fine now."

I'd forgotten about Patty.

Emy wiped a tear from her cheek, ignoring her. "One word from you, Lorne, would have cleared Mom. Why didn't you—"

"It's my fault," Thérèse said. "I told Lorne not to go to the police."

Emy's mouth dropped open as she whirled on her mother.

I pushed off from the wall. "I think I'll get going."

Jeff nodded. "Me, too." He held open the door for me, and we walked out together. He closed the door and smiled at me.

"So," I said. "Thérèse has an alibi."

"Yes. You could have told me."

"I didn't know for sure. I only figured it out after our... climb."

The look on his face caught me up short. It was almost wistful.

He lowered his voice. "I know you don't want to hear this..."

I braced myself for a lecture.

Jeff trained his gaze on the sidewalk at his feet. "When that call came over the police band that a fire crew was at the Peak, rescuing climbers, I knew it had to be you. Who else would be that—"

"Dumb?" I finished the sentence for him and waited for his reply.

He chuckled, then raised his head until his eyes were locked with mine. "I was going to say bold. Or, maybe —daring?"

Bold? Daring? Those were not the adjectives I'd expected.

"But while I was driving there—much too fast, by the way —I realized how dangerous your actions were. And that by getting... involved, I might be encouraging you to continue that risky behavior."

He took a deep breath. "I didn't want you to get hurt, Verity."

I glanced through the window into the bakery where Emy was shaking a finger at Lorne. "You explained this already."

"But that wasn't the whole truth. It wasn't only that I

didn't want you to get hurt. I didn't want to *worry* about it. And that... was selfish."

My mouth opened, but I couldn't find anything to say.

"When my wife died, I blamed myself," Jeff continued. "If only I'd driven her that night. If only I'd asked her to wait out the storm. If only..."

"It wasn't your fault."

He nodded. "The thing is, Verity, you do get into a lot of trouble."

I bristled. "That's not always—"

He grinned. "I kind of like it, to be honest—the way you spring into action to help your friends."

My pounding heart was the only thing holding me up.

"Although..."

Oh, great. At the exact moment my backbone turned to mush, he discovered another objection.

Jeff stepped closer, mesmerizing me with his slightly parted lips. He ran his fingers along my bare arm, sending an electric tingle up my back.

I released a breath I hadn't known I was holding.

"Maybe," he said, "I could be the one to charge in and save you now and then? I mean, if it's not too..."

"Clichéd?"

He chuckled. "Not what I was thinking, but... sure."

I tapped the badge on his shirt pocket. "You already have the armor. Where's your horse?"

He covered my hand with his own, pressing it against his chest, and directed a brief nod at his cruiser. "Right there." Jeff tightened his grip on my fingers and grinned. "Care for a ride?"

What was left of my spine decided to call it a day.

It would have been so easy to cave. But I remembered how my stomach churned during our talk on the Peak. What if he changed his mind again? Could I handle another reversal? Could I go back to Rose Cottage once more, fling myself on the sofa, and stare at the ceiling while the General nuzzled my wet face?

Once had been enough, I thought with a wince.

Jeff raised his eyebrows, smiling.

I drew a deep breath and slowly, let it out. "No."

He released my hand and stepped back, looking startled. "Why?"

"I don't... trust you."

He tilted his head with a puzzled expression. "Sometimes, you have to take a leap of faith, Verity."

I shook my head. "Sorry."

Jeff looked away. His jaw clenched a moment. Then he slid his cap from under his arm and aligned it precisely on his head. It seemed to take a long time before he got it just right.

"See you around," he said. "Take care, Verity."

And walked away.

It was all I could do not to run after him.

What had I done?

I trudged back into the bakery, letting the door close behind me, and sighed heavily. One thing I hadn't done was reduce that agitation in my stomach. It was like a carnival tilt-a-whirl in there. At the sound of voices, I looked up.

Emy was standing in front of Lorne, biting her lip. "I knew you were going somewhere on those days—all those lame excuses. But I thought..."

He looked down at the floor. "I couldn't tell you."

She took his hand and pressed it against her cheek. "You should know by now that you can tell me anything."

He raised his eyes. "I'm sorry."

"Please don't apologize. It's my fault. I must have given you a reason—"

"There was no reason. I just..."

"Well," I mused aloud, unable to ignore the look of anguish on Lorne's face any longer, "there was one reason."

Everyone turned in my direction.

I made a face. "Oh, come on. We've all seen the way Fritz looks at Emy. You can't blame Lorne for being jealous."

"Fritz?" Emy scrunched up her nose in disgust. "Don't be ridiculous. He's a buffoon."

Lorne's face brightened into a grin.

Patty picked that moment to weigh in with her usual impeccable timing. "He likes my eucalyptus panna cotta though. He might even put it on the menu."

Emy gaped at her. Then she marched behind the counter, noisily filled the kettle, and placed it on the burner, muttering under her breath. She stood before the kettle with her back to us.

Lorne walked around the counter until he stood next to Emy. By the time Thérèse, Patty, and I were seated at the table in the back, he had his arm around her, and she was leaning against him.

"They'll be fine," Thérèse whispered.

The kettle boiled. Emy made a pot of tea and brought it over to us. She slumped into a chair with her raised feet planted on the table's central leg, pouting. "You should all be ashamed of yourselves," she said.

Lorne leaned over and dropped a kiss on her head. "Noted."

Thérèse cleared her throat. "Now that's over with, I need to come clean about something else."

Emy groaned and swiveled her gaze to the ceiling, but said nothing.

Thérèse shook her head sadly. "Lucy deceived me—deceived all of us." Emy looked up with surprise, as did Lorne and Patty. I was the only one who knew what was coming.

"She embezzled money from the book club charity fund," Thérèse said.

"How much?" Emy asked.

"All of it."

Patty gasped. "Is that why she was killed?"

Thérèse considered the question gravely. "I don't think so. No one suspected but me, and I didn't tell anyone. I had a hunch, but... I should have realized what she was up to. Verity checked the books for me a few days ago and confirmed it."

"Did you tell the police?" Emy asked.

"How could we? Your mom was a suspect in Lucy's murder," I pointed out. "Knowledge of Lucy's fraud could have been considered a motive."

Thérèse tilted her head with a quizzical look. "I never thought of that, to be honest. I didn't tell the police because I couldn't bear for anyone to remember Lucy as a thief. She was a good woman, I know she was. If it hadn't been for her obsession with that ridiculous house..." She shook her head.

"Lucy poured hundreds of thousands into that restoration. I never stopped to think about where the money was coming from."

Thérèse's eyes filled with tears—something I never thought I'd see.

"If only I had paid more attention," she said. "Maybe I could have helped her. Maybe she'd be alive today."

I pulled a tissue from my purse and handed it over. Thérèse took it with a nod of thanks and blew her nose.

Emy looked chastened. "You couldn't have done anything, Mom. Verity and I also have a secret about Lucy. We believe she was blackmailing people."

Thérèse went still, one hand holding a tissue to her nose. "What?"

We explained Lucy's online ghostwriting gig.

"I've never heard of such a thing," Thérèse protested.

"Neither had we," I said. "But many of Lucy's clients were high-earning professionals who lacked the time to create online chatter, so they hired Lucy to do it for them. Some of her conversations were a little sordid, I'm afraid. Not illegal, but nothing you'd want your boss, or your neighbors—"

"Or your spouse," Emy broke in.

"—to hear about. Reputations were on the line."

"What happened when these correspondents asked to meet in person?"

"I guess Lucy arranged the meetings and hoped for the best. Maybe she provided them with cheat sheets. 'Ask about Fluffy' and so forth."

"Are you certain?" Thérèse asked.

"We have no direct evidence of blackmail. Lucy had a list

of aliases that correspond with online dating accounts and each name has dollar amounts tied to it. We worked out most of the aliases—they were initials, so it wasn't hard. We think she charged those people for her services."

"But three of the accounts showed huge payments," Emy said. "Way more than the others. And they continued, month after month."

"Who?" Thérèse lowered the tissue.

Emy shot me a worried glance.

"Tell me," Thérèse demanded.

"We haven't been able to work out the aliases for two of them," I said. "We have no idea who they are. But the other"—I flinched, reluctant to disappoint Thérèse by casting doubt on another Originals member—"was Sue Unger."

Thérèse looked puzzled. "Sue?" she asked. "Why would—"

I leaned in, hoping to soften the blow. "Here's the thing, Thérèse. Lucy stole way more money than she needed for the house. That's why she had such a huge investment account. I think she enjoyed her little stings. I think she took the book club money for fun."

"No," Thérèse whispered. "Not Lucy."

"Maybe she couldn't help herself. A lot of white-collar criminals have psychiatric issues," I added, dredging up something I read in *Morally Bankrupt: A Primer*.

Thérèse knitted her brows. "That's true. It often originates in childhood."

"You see? So, it's not surprising you didn't realize what Lucy was up to."

Emy chimed in. "And even if you had, you couldn't have stopped her."

Thérèse rallied, tucking the tissue into her purse and decisively snapping it shut. "Maybe not, but I can put things right. With the money Lucy left me, I can repay the book club charity fund and return the blackmail payments. Without anyone else knowing."

I nodded, but my expression gave me away.

"Verity?" Emy asked.

"We have to tell the police about Lucy's sideline. I'm sorry, Thérèse, but one of those unidentified accounts could be her killer."

Thérèse got to her feet. "I'm leaving that up to you two. Meanwhile, I'm going to ask Wilf about transferring Lucy's money as soon as the estate clears." She headed for the door, but paused with her hand on the handle. "I think I know why Sue was paying Lucy, and it wasn't blackmail." She pulled open the door and stepped through.

"What was it?"

"Ask her," Thérèse called over her shoulder as the door closed.

Emy and I exchanged puzzled glances.

My cell phone thrummed on the table and I picked it up to read the text. "Our rumor's making the rounds," I said. "The Originals are all over it." I placed the phone down.

Too late to call it off now.

"What rumor?" Lorne asked.

"Verity saw someone up on the Peak the morning Lucy died." Emy's lips twitched in a smirk. "And she's going to the police station tomorrow to report it." She turned to me. "You can identify them, right?"

"Oh, yeah," I said, hoping a bit of mock hilarity would ease my jitters about our new plan. "I had binoculars, remember?"

Lorne looked puzzled. "But you didn't—"

Patty leaned over my shoulder, cutting him off. "I'll tell you later, Lorne. Are we still meeting for the fireworks?"

Fireworks. My face lit up. I loved fireworks. How had I forgotten about Founder's Day? "Definitely. I'll be there at nine."

Emy gave me a sharp look. "Not alone, I hope."

"Lorne's taking the truck to our last job of the day, while I run one last errand. Then he's going to pick me up at Rose Cottage and we'll join you at the park."

Emy frowned. "Rose Cottage? I thought it was still being repaired."

"There are a few things to do, but the roof's watertight again and we've aired everything out. I'm desperate to move out of that inn," I said, rubbing my head ruefully. "I'll be fine, Emy. Carson's trailer is right outside my front door."

"But where will you be in the meantime? What errand?"

"Visiting Sue."

"Alone?"

"Oh, come on, Emy. Sue can protect me if necessary. She's a big girl. Between the two of us, we could fight off a pack of grizzlies."

Well, raccoons maybe. If they weren't hungry.

Emy opened her mouth to object, but Patty cut her off.

"Sounds great," she said, still leaning in. "See you at nine.

Meanwhile, I promised Carson I'd drop by the hardware store to pick up some of those fancy nails he likes. He's not happy with the ones the crew's been using on your roof. He's very particular, is Carson. He explained all about your built-in eavestroughs when Clark and I went up there yesterday. It was really fascinating." Patty headed for the door.

I watched her go, trying to remember when Carson had complained about the nails. He told me he was happy with the finished job. Maybe I should stop Patty from making a useless purchase.

But she loved to be helpful, and a visit to the hardware store would get her out of Emy's hair for a while. I decided against going after her, although I hoped the real reason for her visit wasn't to buy the aluminum cookie sheets she'd pointed out when we were there a day earlier.

"Those would make a nice gift for Emy," she had said.

Derek had been serving us and I could tell he anticipated a sale, so I hadn't wanted to discourage her. But Emy was particular about her baking equipment. "Probably best to buy her something else," I said.

Patty nodded, a hand on her chin, while she studied the stocked shelves. "Can I see one of those?" she asked, pointing to a locked cabinet full of kitchen cleavers and chef's knives.

Derek selected a key from the chain jangling at his waist and leaned over to open the cabinet. "There must be a lot of stuff in Lucy's old house," he said. "Thérèse should hold a yard sale."

Patty brightened. "That house is *packed*. I sold Verity's belongings in Vancouver. I'd be happy to help out at a yard sale."

"You were in Lucy's house?" he asked.

"Sure. I saw that burglar too, the one who broke in and ransacked the place."

"Well," I muttered, "that's not quite—"

Derek seemed fascinated by Patty's disclosure. "Do you realize you may have seen her killer?"

"Oooh," Patty said. "I guess I did." She turned to me with an air of triumph. "Think of that, Verity."

"Let's not," I said, gently guiding her out of the store. "Thanks, Derek."

"No problem," he said, jangling the TPB bobble head on his key chain. "Let me know if there's a yard sale. I could use another bookcase."

At the door, Patty turned to look back at the store and narrowed her eyes. "You know…"

I shoved her through the doorway. "No time. You can shop tomorrow."

When I had reached behind to shut the door, Derek was staring after Patty, his mouth oddly twisted. When he noticed my gaze, he had turned back to the cabinet with the key in his hand and locked the door.

CHAPTER TWENTY-THREE

THE DOORBELL on Sue's massive front door was the strangest I'd ever heard.

"*Caw. Caw. CAW,*" sounded inside the house when I pressed the buzzer. Fearing I'd developed a hearing problem, I held it down again.

"*Caw. Caw. CAW.*"

And I thought Reuben was annoying. On the other hand, Sue probably didn't get a lot of visitors. I peered through the sidelight, shading my eyes with one hand, watching a figure approach in the darkened hallway.

The door swung open.

Sue stood on the threshold, glaring, her left hand holding the door ajar. In her right hand, she held an enormous pipe wrench.

I took an involuntary step back.

"Oh. It's you. Come in, then," she muttered, brandishing the wrench at the hall behind her.

I exhaled, then stepped over the threshold.

Sue closed the door and set off down the hall. "I'm in the kitchen," she called over her shoulder without waiting to see if I was behind her.

I followed her to the rear of the house. Banks of windows overlooked a full-length deck with breathtaking views of Pine Hill Valley. The kitchen cabinets were white, the counters were white, the floor was white, and everything was... immaculate.

Except for the area around the double kitchen sink, where a tool box, an empty pail, and an assortment of wrenches were laid out on a quilted mover's blanket.

"Did you have a leak?" I asked.

"A leak?" Sue looked confused. I pointed to the toolbox.

"Oh, you meant the sink. No, I never have leaks."

"Then why are you..."

"I change all the fittings on a regular basis. To keep my hand in." She dropped to her knees outside the open cabinet doors and twisted around to duck her head under. "Didn't Emy tell you I was a plumber?" she asked, her voice muffled.

"It never really came up," I lied. "Although we did hear that you'd been to Costa Rica. Was it fun?"

Sue slid back out and dropped the wrench onto the blanket. "Woulda been—if it hadn't been for the blasted police insisting I return." She assessed the selection of wrenches and picked up a new one. Even bigger than the first. "Why the honor of a third visit, Verity? I didn't think we were this close."

I wondered what to say to that, until I realized she was

kidding. Sue's sense of humor often left me confused. Which explained my next question.

"When you mentioned Derek's girlfriends, you were kidding, right?"

She shrugged. "Lucy said something once that made me think he was involved with someone." She ducked under the cabinet again and tightened the second wrench on a pipe.

"So you and Lucy were friends."

"You know we were. Or perhaps acquaintances is a better word." She gave the wrench a last twist and slid out of the cabinet.

"Was Lucy always so... difficult? I mean, when she was younger?"

Sue looked surprised by the question. "No," she said thoughtfully. "She wasn't. She was more fun."

"So what happened?"

"Don't know. Some guy, I think." She snorted. "It's always a guy."

"Someone she was involved with years ago?"

Sue shrugged impatiently. "I'm not sure why you're asking me this. Are you here for a reason?" Her tone implied that she would not be extending a dinner invitation.

I reached for my purse and pulled out a folded sheet. "Because of this," I said, handing her the list of book titles.

Her face flushed as she scanned the list. "Where did you get this?"

"Emy and I found it in Lucy's office."

We locked glances, and I held my breath as Sue's brow tightened.

Nervously, I noticed that she hadn't put down the second wrench.

"Nothing to do with me," she said, tossing the paper on the floor between us.

"Oh, come on, Sue." I pointed to the paper. "This has something to do with Lucy and her blackmail scheme. What did the two of you discuss when you pulled her aside at those book club meetings?"

Her mouth gaped. "Blackmail? What are you talking about?" Her knuckles turned white as her fist tightened around the wrench.

"Did you help Lucy with it? Is that where you got all your money?"

"Are you insane? I have no idea what you're prattling on about. And my money is none of your business." Glowering at me, she barked, "Get out."

I swallowed hard, aware that the pulsating vein in my throat might be about to burst. Nevertheless, I persisted. Like I've always said—*not* a Mensa member. "Two people are dead. Whatever you're hiding, Sue, it will come out."

She took a step toward me, her expression black.

I tensed, hoping I wouldn't have to fight my way out of there. Sue was a big girl. I anchored both feet, planning my defense and remembering Emy's words. *Not alone, I hope.*

Why hadn't I listened?

Sue halted, still glaring.

Blood pounded in my ears.

We stood there a while, glaring at each other.

Then Sue tilted her head back in a burst of laughter.

I took a hasty step back, not certain if this was an improvement in her mood, or an indication she'd finally cracked.

"All right, I'll tell you," she said, wiping a hand over her face and dropping the second wrench onto the blanket. "We discussed plots."

"Book plots?" I asked, insight dawning.

"I knew about Lucy's ghostwriting sideline, but I stayed out of it. None of my business." She paused. "I swear, I didn't know she was blackmailing anybody. Thing is, Lucy told me stories about her clients. Anonymously, of course. They were perfect for my purposes." She picked the printed list off the floor where she'd dropped it and held it out to me. "I write romance novels. The really steamy kind."

At my raised eyebrows, she added, "It's quite lucrative."

"That's why you were paying Lucy?"

She nodded. "Plot consultations. When you've written as many novels as I have, you appreciate new insights."

I took the paper and refolded it. "But why are your books a secret?"

"Lucy worried Leafy Hollow residents might recognize my characters. She was probably right."

"Which would have been bad for her blackmail business."

"I guess. Although, like I said, I knew nothing about that. I just didn't want Thérèse and the book club to know about my writing."

"Why?"

"Can you imagine the snickering, once people read them?

Like I said—they're really steamy. And I'm not exactly... the type." She made a face.

I slid the list back into my purse. "Your secret's safe with me. Although, if I were you—I'd tell the club members that your books are meant to be ironic. And give them all free copies. I think they'd love them."

She shrugged. "I might. Anyway, this latest development would make a great plot. Maybe I'll branch out into thrillers."

Back at Rose Cottage, I was seated at my aunt's desk, puzzling over the last two mystery aliases on Lucy's spreadsheet, when my phone buzzed again. After ignoring its pings for the past hour, I thought I'd better pick up. The latest text was from Clark. Apparently he'd looked away from the soccer game on his phone long enough to realize his wife wasn't with him at the park.

U seen Patty?

Lorne had taken the truck to our last appointment of the day, but he'd promised to drop by and drive me to the fireworks display. I rose to stretch my legs, walking toward the front windows, as I messaged Clark.

No. Did U text her?

I peered out the window as a copper convertible cruised past with Fritz at the wheel. It was the third time today he'd checked up on me. His car disappeared up the road. Lilac Lane was a dead end, so he'd be back. My phone pinged.

No answer, Clark replied.

I returned to my aunt's desk and put the phone aside.

Patty would show up. She could be at the hardware store, buying Emy a hostess gift. I hoped it wouldn't be a chef's knife. I smiled at the memory of Derek jingling his bobble-head Trailer Park Boys key chain in front of the store's locked cabinet.

At least the protesters were gone, so Derek wasn't arguing with them anymore. Although he probably missed blue-haired girl. In my horror at finding Marjorie's body, I'd forgotten their cozy circle of three. What had Sue said?

Derek lined up for half an hour at the corner store to buy us cold drinks.

It hadn't struck me as odd at the time, but it did now. It took two minutes, tops, to grab Cokes from the convenience store's cooler and pay for them. Occasionally, you got stuck in line behind someone buying a dozen lottery tickets. But still —half an hour?

With a sudden chill, I realized half an hour was long enough for Derek to duck around the corner and up the fire escape to Marjorie's apartment—with plenty of time left to buy Cokes on the return trip.

That's ridiculous. Derek Talbot was no more a killer than I was.

I remembered the heart-to-heart I'd shared with him in Thérèse's bathroom the night of the book club meeting. I also recalled the scratches on his hands. Not the ones inflicted by smashing Thérèse's favorite vase, but the other, older ones. Those could have been caused by pebbles and sticks and bits of bark. Especially if Derek had been grap-pling with someone on the Peak. Flattening the bushes. Even...

I puffed out a breath. My imagination was carrying me away.

Unless... With a shiver of foreboding, I traced a finger down the spreadsheet to the first of the mystery aliases—TPB.

I stared at it.

TPB. Trailer Park Boys.

Why hadn't I made the connection before?

Sue had mentioned Derek's "girlfriends," but I assumed it was a jest. If he'd found a girlfriend online, why would he hide it? Online dating was common these days. If anything, the book club members would be impressed. It showed... initiative.

I fluttered my fingers against my mouth, studying the spreadsheet. It must be something about the girlfriend, then —something Derek didn't want anyone to know. Could "she" be a "he"? Or married? Or a Montréal Canadiens fan?

Drawing my finger back up the spreadsheet, I stopped beside its last remaining mystery, the alias BWS. Initially, I suspected the two accounts were connected because their payments were made on the same day every month. I had dismissed that as wishful thinking. Now I studied the initials again. BWS. *Why was that so familiar? What did it mean?*

Tilting back on the wheeled chair, I gazed idly at the ceiling. A tiny spider was building a web in one corner. I watched, marveling how quickly insect life returned after a disruption. Even a fire hadn't dissuaded this insistent creature from returning to track his prey. I chuckled. What made me think it was a male? This could just as easily be a female stalking *her* prey.

My next breath caught in my throat.

I slammed the chair down and swiveled it around until I faced my aunt's bookcase, scanning the spines.

Risk Mitigation and Threat Assessment.

The English Garden, a Social History.

The World's Deadliest Insects.

I leapt from my chair, sending it spinning, and yanked *Deadliest Insects* from the shelf. With my hand shaking, I flipped through its pages, searching for the turned-down corner that marked that scary childhood encounter in my aunt's garden. I set the book on the desk and stepped back.

A bigger-than-life arachnid, with a brilliant red hourglass on its bulging black torso, filled the left-hand page. The title above it read, "Black Widow Spider." My hand went limp, remembering Emy's words. *Black widow spiders kill their mates.*

BWS. Black Widow Spider.

Or—Black Widow Killer.

With a shudder, I closed the book and dropped back into the chair.

No wonder Derek didn't tell his friends about his girlfriend. He couldn't, because she'd spent the last eight years in prison. Lucy must have introduced them online. Which meant Derek had been corresponding with one of the village's most-hated ex-residents. He probably arranged for her to rent the apartment over the hardware store, too.

No wonder he paid Lucy to keep quiet.

And now, the only people who knew his secret—Lucy and the Black Widow herself—were both dead.

My phone pinged again, and I reached for it without

taking my eyes from the desk. The last time I'd seen Derek, he gave Patty a very odd look. But why?

My stomach turned cold as I remembered her telling him she could identify the person who broke into Lucy's house. What was it he said to her?

Do you realize you may have seen Lucy's killer?

Patty had merely been showing off at the hardware store. She couldn't identify the burglar—she'd already told me so. But Derek didn't know that.

I glanced at my phone. Clark again.

STILL NO ANSWER.

My stomach clenched as I tapped out a message to Patty. R U OK?

No reply. I tried to slow my breathing as I waited, then sent another text. Still nothing.

Shadows had crept across the floor while I was working. With a glance out the windows, I reached over to snap on a floor lamp. It was starting to get dark. The fireworks display was due to begin in half an hour. Lorne would be back soon to take me to the park, where Emy, Clark and Patty should be waiting.

So where was Patty?

I had no reason to think she was with Derek, but I decided to call the hardware store just to make certain.

A woman answered. "Reginald's Hardware."

"Hi there," I said. "I'm looking for a friend of mine who was dropping by to pick up a present. A woman about thirty, blonde ponytail, very friendly? Her name is Patty Ferris."

"Oh, *Patty*," the woman said brightly. "That nice woman from Vancouver?"

I breathed a sign of relief. "That's her."

"She was here. Not long ago, in fact. But she left with Derek when his shift ended."

My stomach tightened. "Did they say where they were going?"

"He mentioned something about the Peak. Patty had never seen it and he offered to take her up there. It's getting a bit dark now, though, so maybe they went somewhere else."

After shutting off the call, I scrolled through four screenfuls of apps before I found the one I wanted—Hail+HeartY. When I clicked on Patty's name, a red dot flashed on and off. I zeroed in. "Patty Ferris" was... on Pine Hill Peak.

I began a text to Clark, but realized he'd have no idea where to go. Instead, I pocketed my phone and ran outside, intending to climb into the truck and head for the trail that led to the Peak. As I slammed the front door shut, I remembered Emy's words.

Don't go anywhere by yourself.

Halting on the porch, I reconsidered. Then I texted her.

PATTY ON PEAK WITH DEREK. DANGER.

No reply. By now, Leafy Hollow's central park would be jammed with people anticipating the Founder's Day fireworks. There would be music blaring from the bandshell, and hand-held sparklers glittering everywhere, and good-natured shouts and laughter. No wonder Emy couldn't hear her phone. Even if she did pick up the message, it would take time to thread through the crowd to reach her car which was probably parked blocks from party central.

Fudge buckets. What should I do?

Fear overcame caution. I tapped out another text.

Heading there now.

I darted down the front steps and toward the truck.

I stuttered to a halt, staring at the empty driveway.

Lorne had the Coming Up Roses truck. And Carson was at the park with the rest of the village. Reuben regarded me forlornly from the window of the Ford Escort, where he was settling in for the night.

My frantic call to Lorne went straight to voice mail. Pacing up and down the driveway, I listened impatiently to his message before barking out my own.

"Where are you? Call me back."

Possibly Lorne was already on his way to Rose Cottage to pick me up. Or maybe the last job of the day had taken longer than he expected and he was still mowing, taking advantage of the last half-hour of daylight. Buckets of rain during the past two weeks had left us way behind on our work. No chance of Lorne hearing his phone over the roar of the industrial mower.

Should I wait for him?

Don't go anywhere by yourself.

No choice, I thought grimly, trotting down the driveway. If I jogged the entire distance, I could reach the entrance to the trail in less than ten minutes.

I halted at the sound of a car.

Fritz's convertible turned up my driveway and crunched to a halt on the gravel. He angled his head out the driver's side.

"Need a lift?"

I was in the front passenger seat in less than a second, pausing only to toss a leather backpack off the seat and onto the floor. "Pine Hill Peak," I barked, gripping the dashboard with both hands. "Now."

With a bemused glance, Fritz backed out of the driveway and onto Lilac Lane. "You might want to fasten your seatbelt," he said, as the warning bell sounded.

My feet had trampled the designer backpack underfoot. Leaning over, I pushed the open bag to one side. A sheaf of papers tumbled out. With a flash of alarm, I stuffed them back in before straightening up and snapping on my seatbelt. *Breathe, Verity.*

"Sorry, is that in your way?" Fritz asked, slowing the car and reaching for the backpack. "I can put it in the backseat."

"It's fine." I gave the backpack another shove with my foot. "Just go."

"What's this about?" he asked.

"Probably nothing," I muttered. "Can you drive any faster?"

He picked up his pace. "Is it worth breaking the speed limit for? Because I'm happy to—"

"My friend Patty is on the Peak with Derek Talbot."

"Who?"

"Derek Talbot. He works at the hardware store."

"The one with the key chain?"

I glanced over at him. Fritz was more observant than I thought. "That's him."

"I don't see the problem."

"I could be wrong, but I think Derek pushed Lucy Carmichael off Pine Hill Peak."

"Whoa. That is a problem."

I leaned forward to pull my cellphone out of my pocket.

"Are you calling nine-one-one?"

"Maybe." I stared at the phone. What, exactly, could I say? *My friend's on the Peak with a suspected killer? Please save her?* What if they asked, *Who suspects him? Well, that would be... me.*

This was an overreaction. Probably.

The car veered around a corner and I slapped a hand against the door to steady myself. *Don't go anywhere by yourself.* It wasn't an overreaction. There was a killer on the loose.

I made the call.

"How long will it take them to get there?" Fritz asked once I'd clicked off.

"Fifteen or twenty minutes, they said. Most of the cruisers are at the park for crowd control." A police presence was required at such a large event, although they were unlikely to face anything more challenging than overly refreshed party goers.

"So they're not taking it seriously."

I pressed my lips together. "Hard to say. I'm sure they take all calls seriously." I turned to look at him, but his eyes were on the road. "Why were you driving past Rose Cottage, anyway?"

Fritz chuckled. "Good thing I was." He swerved around another corner—I swear the car almost went up on two wheels. "Emy asked me to keep an eye on you."

I shot him a surprised look. "Emy? Why?"

"She said there's a murderer out there and none of you should be alone."

Well, she had said—*if necessary.* I guessed this qualified. Still, I was surprised to hear Emy had taken her concerns to

Fritz after referring to him as a "buffoon." With a smile, I recalled that might have been for Lorne's benefit.

Before putting my phone away, I tapped out another text. WHERE R U?

Still no reply from Patty.

We made record time up the road to the trail entrance. Because it was midweek—and most everybody was down below, at the party—the parking lot was deserted. It was almost dark, with only a suggestion of purple clouds lingering on the horizon. We pulled into the lot and came to a halt.

Fritz got out, leaving the driver's door open. "Hang on a sec," he said. "Right back."

Then I heard the trunk open behind me.

When I turned my head, he shut the trunk with one hand, holding up a rifle with his other. I swung my feet out of the car and onto the ground.

"What are you going to do with that?" I spluttered.

"This guy could be dangerous." He shrugged. "This is just in case."

"In case of what? He's not armed."

"How do you know?"

The vicious-looking knives in the hardware store cabinet popped into my head. I pressed my lips together, trying to suppress my distrust of weapons like the one Fritz was carrying.

He walked up to me. "Hand me that backpack," he said, motioning to the leather bag.

I yanked it out of the footwell and stood up, handing it over. "Do you have a permit for that gun?"

Fritz draped the backpack over his shoulder and turned

to the gap in the parking lot fence that led to the trail. "Let's go. If anybody asks, this"—he held up the rifle—"is for rabbits."

Rabbits? It looked as if it might take down moose. Too bad rutting season was over. I would have liked to see that contest.

I slammed the door shut and followed him.

CHAPTER TWENTY-FOUR

THE CLIMB up the hill and along the trail was difficult at the best of times, but in the waning light it was impossible to avoid overhanging branches. Not only that, but twice I stumbled on gnarled tree roots and nearly fell.

When we reached the flat shale that marked the main lookout of Pine Hill Peak, streetlights were winking on in the village below. Bright yellow spotlights outlined the park in its center. Music and laughter drifted up from the Founder's Day celebration.

Derek and Patty stood near the edge of the lookout, facing away from us, their backs lit up by the waning moon. Derek pointed to something in the distance, and Patty nodded.

I stepped forward, motioning to Fritz to stay back.

"Patty," I called as I walked over. "Come away from there, please."

She turned her head, grinning. "Look, Verity. You

can see Lake Ontario from here. Hey, did you get my text? Is that why you're here? Derek said you might not get it. He said the cell tower is sometimes blocked up here."

I walked toward them with a faked casual air. "What text was that?"

"To tell you I was here, of course. Sorry, but Derek said it was an ideal spot to take photos of the fireworks. And it is— it's spectacular, in fact." She brandished her sad, broken phone.

"You're too close to the edge, Patty. It's not safe."

"Don't be silly. We're fine."

"Please, Patty. Clark is waiting for you in the park."

"Okay." With a shrug, she took a step toward me.

Derek grabbed her arm. "Stay."

Patty shot him a look of surprise.

"Derek, move away from the edge," I said. "A few steps, that's all I ask. Then we can talk."

Patty's face went white. "What's going on?"

"He won't hurt you, Patty. Will you, Derek?"

"Hurt me? Why would he..." Her voice trailed off, her gaze caught by something behind me.

Without looking, I knew Fritz had emerged from the shadows and into the moonlight.

Derek rubbed his thumb nervously in the palm of his injured hand. "Why is he here?"

"Ignore Fritz. He doesn't mean any harm. Let's all go to the party. It will be fun."

"How did you know?"

"I'm sorry?"

"About Lucy—how did you know?" Derek nodded at Fritz. "That's why you brought him, isn't it?"

An icy wave swept over me. So I was right.

"I don't know what you're talking about, Derek."

"It wasn't my fault. I didn't mean to kill her."

Fritz stepped up beside me and raised his rifle.

"I understand," I said, raising a hand to hold Fritz back. "Tell us what happened."

"I brought her here—well, not here, exactly. Farther down the trail."

Derek pointed to a path off to one side, which I knew from my previous visit led to the labyrinth of closed trails—and, eventually, the broken fence.

"I don't think she realized how close we were to the rim."

"Why did you take her there?"

"Because no one uses that trail anymore, so no one would see us. I wanted to talk to her, to make her see reason. I couldn't keep paying her."

"She threatened to reveal your affair with Marjorie Rupert, didn't she?"

He gave me a miserable look. "How did you know?"

Patty was frozen in place beside him, her mouth open.

"It doesn't matter," I said. "Tell us the rest."

"Lucy and I argued and I... I hit her."

He looked away, clasping his arms tightly across his chest.

I motioned frantically to Patty. She shuffled off a few paces, still staring at his face.

"Lucy hit me back," Derek said. "Before I knew it, we were rolling around on the ground. She whacked me in the face and poked me and..." He unclasped his arms and rubbed his hands together, over and over. "I picked up a rock and... bashed it against her head."

My breath caught in my throat as I pictured the scene, but I swallowed my disgust. "It was self-defense," I said. "The police will understand."

"I didn't kill her," he insisted. "She was on the ground when I got up to leave, but she wasn't dead."

"Why didn't you go for help?"

"Because..." His voice broke. "She stood up and staggered around a bit. There was blood on her face and I guess she couldn't see. She went in the wrong direction. I tried to warn her, to stop her, but it was too late. She was at the edge before I could reach her." He shuddered. "Lucy fell backward and crashed through the fence. There was nothing I could do."

Patty sank to her knees on the rocky ground, mumbling. Which was good because at least she was breathing again.

"Derek, come with us. We'll tell the police what happened. It was an accident."

"They'll put me away for life."

"No. At worst, it was manslaughter, not murder."

"That's not all he did," Fritz said behind us. He raised the rifle, pointed it at Derek, and sighted along the barrel.

Derek stepped back to the edge. "Don't come any closer, or I'll jump," he whimpered. "I'll jump."

"Go ahead," Fritz said. His voice was cold.

"Please don't, Derek," I said, trying for a reassuring tone. Which wasn't easy. My heart pounded so hard it threatened to come through my ribcage.

I swiveled to look at Fritz. "Please, put the rifle down.

Derek will come to the police station with us and we'll sort this out."

With a snort of irritation, Fritz lowered the weapon. "He deserves to die. You realize there are two people dead. This loser must have killed them both."

"I didn't," Derek wailed. "I never would have hurt Marjorie. I worked for years to get her parole approved. I wrote letters and petitions and articles."

"Under your real name?" I asked.

"No. I made up names."

"With Lucy's help?"

He nodded. "She was good at that." Derek stared into the distance, over my head, and his voice lowered to almost a whisper. I strained to hear him.

"When Marjorie finally came home and moved into that apartment over the store, she told me..." His voice broke again. "She told me to leave her alone. I'd served my purpose. Her parole was approved. What did she need me for? I went to her apartment that day to convince her to reconsider, but when I saw her body... I left."

"Then picked up the soft drinks and returned to the hardware store?"

"That's right." He looked away, sliding his hands down his cheeks, pushing in the sides of his face. "It was awful, seeing her like that."

"So you were present at two deaths, but not responsible for either?" I asked.

"I know how it sounds. But it's the truth."

Fritz elbowed me aside with an expression of barely

contained fury. "You killed them both." He raised the rifle again.

"I didn't. I'm telling you. I don't know who did that to Marjorie, but it wasn't me. I never would have hurt her."

"You're lying."

Derek shook his head miserably. "I loved her." At my incredulous look, he added, "You don't understand, Verity. We corresponded for years... Marjorie wasn't guilty. She didn't kill her husband. That was somebody else."

"Who?"

"I don't know, but she wrote about it in her memoir."

"Did you read it?"

"I never had the chance. But she told me—"

"That's enough," Fritz barked. He raised the rifle again, and leveled it at Derek's face. "Don't let him say another word. It's all lies." His face twisted with rage.

I froze, wondering what could have triggered so much anger over the death of a convicted killer. *Unless...*

The photo of Marjorie, her first husband, and a teenaged boy standing in front of a restaurant flashed through my mind. *Sydney's restaurant in Strathcona.* With a shock, I recalled that the boy's hair had been red.

"Marjorie Rupert was your mother, wasn't she? And your father was Sydney..."

"Wallach. Sydney Wallach." Fritz gave me a cold look, but did not lower the rifle. "Marjorie was my stepmother. My real mother died when I was born."

"But she raised you?"

"No. My father did that. Until she came along." His lip twisted in a snarl. "Suddenly it was *Marjie* this, and *Marjie* that. Prancing around in tight dresses, fawning over him. He owned a chain of restaurants, so we had plenty of money. Sydney promised me a sports car when I graduated from high school. Marjorie stopped that—said he was spoiling me. When really, she wanted all his money for herself."

"That must have been hard. But—"

He kept speaking as if he hadn't heard me. "I left home after that. Changed my name and never spoke to the old man again. Then one day, I got a visit from a private investigator. He said my father hired him to track me down because he wanted to tell me something."

"What was it?" I asked, intrigued despite my fear—and also to keep him talking.

"I don't know. I sent the guy away. I didn't care what the old man had to say. A few years later, I reconsidered. By the time I decided to find out, he'd been dead for two years. Heart attack."

"I'm sorry. It's too bad you couldn't say goodbye."

"Too bad?" He laughed. "Too bad? Like it was some kind of accident? No." He shook his head. "I think Sydney was rewriting his will and Marjorie killed him before he could finish it. I think he was on to her."

"On to her? What do you mean?"

"She was cheating on him, with Ian Rupert. She married Rupert two months after my father's death. Husband number two." He shrugged. "Assuming that's all there were." His face contorted into a terrifying grin. "The Black Widow Killer. That's what they called her." Then he laughed.

Cold fear gripped my gut as I realized why he was laughing.

"You killed Ian Rupert, didn't you? And let Marjorie take the rap."

Fritz chuckled coldly. "You should be a detective."

"But how did you—"

"Convince her to go along with it? That was easy. I told her a private investigator had been to see me and he knew my father intended to change his will to cut her out."

"The investigator didn't tell you that."

"No, but Marjorie believed me because it was the truth. I told her the police would re-consider my father's death once they heard the new evidence about his will. She'd be charged with two murders—and never leave prison."

"Why would they think she killed Ian?"

"Because Marjorie and Ian sold my father's restaurant chain and pocketed the cash. They burned through it pretty fast, with trips to the Orient and cruises and fancy cars and jewelry." Another snarl curled his lip. "The money was nearly gone. It wasn't much of a jump to suggest Marjorie wanted Ian out of the way so she could start over. And then there was the insurance money."

As long as he was talking, he wasn't shooting. So I kept him talking.

"How much insurance?" I asked.

"Half a million. If you were on the jury, who would you believe? And remember—not one murder, but two."

"It was very clever of you," I said, hoping to put him at his ease.

"Enough talk. Let's move this along."

"Fritz, the police are on their way. You can't possibly get away with this."

He raised the rifle again, pointing it at Derek. "Come to think of it, Verity, you might come in useful. Maybe I'll leave you alive for now."

My brain was buzzing with fear. The vein in my neck had given up throbbing in favor of pounding.

I played for time. "You picked Marjorie up at the bus station to gain her confidence. Then planted that ridiculous fake mustache in Lucy's office to throw everyone off the scent."

Fritz merely snorted, which made his own, real mustache jerk. "She was too dead to deny it, wasn't she? That was a lucky break."

I took a step closer, stifling my overwhelming urge to run. "So that was you in Lucy's house. We must have surprised you. You broke that vase and tackled Patty on the sidewalk."

He snorted again, then jerked the rifle in her direction. "Your friend got in the way."

Patty clasped both hands to her throat, eyes wide, unable to speak. For once.

"Meanwhile, Marjorie actually thought I had forgiven her." Fritz scowled. "She always was a fool."

I was surprisingly calm. There was an air of inevitability about this encounter. As if time itself had stopped, caught up in the breeze that swirled my hair and swept over the Peak. "Derek didn't kill Marjorie Rupert," I said.

Fritz chuckled. "Oh, I did that. And she deserved it. You can see that."

"But why did you set fire to Rose Cottage?"

"Because you did too much sleuthing." He shook his head

with a wry grin. "You really should mind your own business, Verity."

It was a good thing that Fritz had a rifle in his hand, because otherwise I would have delivered a vertical front kick that would have landed right in his... well, let's just say an area well above his knees. Narrowing my eyes, I said, "The police will arrest you for Marjorie's murder."

He chuckled again. "Why would they do that when this moron here is the guilty party?" Fritz motioned at Derek. "He pushed you and your friend off the cliff to prevent his secret from getting out. I'll tell the police a sad story about arriving seconds too late to save you. And how I had to shoot him when the crazed fool rushed me." Fritz slid his finger over the trigger. "Of course, the order of events may not be exactly as advertised."

"Derek," I warned. "Get away from the edge."

"Yes, do," Fritz echoed. "Because I won't be able to shoot you if you fall."

He raised the rifle to his shoulder and sighted along it. The explosion that echoed off the rock was so loud I gasped.

"What was that?" Patty screamed, clapping her hands against her ears.

Pinpoints of light shrieked across the night sky behind us. Then they burst, scattering showers of multicolored sparks.

The Founder's Day fireworks had begun.

Patty sunk to her knees with both hands clasped to her chest, looking as if she was going to be sick.

Fritz smirked. "Fireworks—what an excellent idea. No one will hear a thing."

Derek staggered back, eyes wide. "No, please..."

Fritz eased off a shot that missed him.

Derek dropped to his knees, whimpering.

Fritz laughed and lowered the rifle. "That was close, wasn't it?"

Two more fusillades soared into the sky, spitting and squealing. They exploded into cascading waves of golden light. Normally I loved fireworks. Today I just wanted them to stop.

Fritz raised the rifle again. "Time to beg."

Derek scrabbled backward, closer to the edge.

A series of explosions sounded, like the rat-a-tat-tat of a machine gun.

Derek jerked his hands up in terror, leaning back.

"No," I yelled, darting toward him. I dove for the rim, but I was too late to stop him from sliding backward and over the edge. By the time I reached him, he was hanging from the rim, holding on with both hands. I dropped to the ground, stretched to my full length, and reached for him.

Fritz squeezed off another shot. This one whizzed past my ears.

"For God's sake, Fritz—stop!"

His only reply was more laughter.

I grabbed Derek's wrist, holding on with both hands. His fingers curled around my arm, gripping it tightly, and his other hand gripped the edge. "Hang on," I said.

I knew I couldn't cling to him for long.

"Help me, Fritz," I yelled. "I can't hold him."

The next shot hit Derek's free hand, the one still grasping the rock face. With a scream of pain, he let go. The added strain on my shoulders almost pulled my arms from their sockets.

"Get out of the way, Verity, or I'll shoot you, too," Fritz called.

Patty snapped out of her stupor. "No," she shrieked, darting over.

"Or your friend," Fritz said, swerving the rifle toward her. "I don't care which."

"Patty—don't," I yelled, motioning her away with a shake of my head. "Stay back."

My shoulders burned with the strain of hanging on to Derek's wrist. I couldn't pull him up without help. And I couldn't hold him much longer. His hand started to slip.

A series of detonations transformed the night sky into bursts of cascading color. The fireworks illuminated Derek's upturned face. I saw fear in his eyes.

A single bang exploded behind me. A shot whizzed past, making my ears ring.

Fritz laughed. "Getting closer. Won't be long now."

I closed my eyes, took a deep breath, and then opened them. "He's going to shoot us all, Derek. I'm so sorry. You have to let go. Trust me. It's better this way."

He closed his eyes, nodding slightly. Then his hand slipped from mine, and he fell.

I scrabbled to the edge on my stomach and leaned over, listening, holding my breath. More fireworks exploded, drowning out any other noise.

Which was probably a good thing.

As the echoes died away, I twisted my neck to scream at Fritz.

"Why did you do that? You son of a—"

I gulped back my next words. The rifle was a foot away, pointed at my head.

"You're coming with me," Fritz said. "You know the way out of here."

I rose shakily to my feet. "I don't know what you're talking about."

"The closed trails. You're going to show me where they are."

"I don't know where they are. Anyway, the police will be here in minutes. I can't help you. I'll only slow you down."

"Nice try." Fritz poked the rifle into my chest, making me jump. "I'm not a fool, Verity. If the police were coming, they'd be here by now. Get going." He poked me again, harder this time. I hoped his rifle wasn't one of those hair-trigger things you're always hearing about.

"Verity?" Patty's voice was tremulous. "Where are you going?"

Fritz swung the rifle toward her.

"Please don't shoot her, Fritz. She won't stop you."

He paused, considering.

"Look, Fritz—Marjorie got her just desserts. After all, she and Ian killed your father. Your actions were," I racked my brain for a plausible excuse, "justifiable homicide." I wasn't sure that defense would fly in a Canadian court, but it was worth a try. "But if you shoot Patty, you'll have no defense. None. You'll be facing life in prison."

"Only if they catch me."

"Why take the chance?"

After a moment, Fritz lowered the rifle and barked an order at Patty. "Show me your phone."

She pulled the pink, crystal-covered cellphone from her purse with a trembling hand and held it up.

"Turn around. Throw it off the edge."

She did as he asked. I watched Patty's beloved device soar into the night and drop, moonlight glinting off its cracked screen as it disappeared.

"You. Verity," Fritz snapped. "Get moving. Hands on your head."

We crossed the shale lookout and plunged through the trees and onto the trail.

With my hands clapped on my head, I was helpless to stop branches from slapping into my face. I scrunched up my eyes, trying to avoid being blinded while still keeping an eye on the nearly black trail.

"Faster," Fritz said. "Turn to the right."

I swerved off the main trail and headed along the secondary path that led in the opposite direction from the parking lot. Before long, we reached the pile of tree trunks that marked the first of the old trails.

Fritz pulled a small flashlight from his pocket and turned it on to read the sign. *Trail closed. Caution advised.*

"Move," he said.

"I'll have to use my hands."

He merely grunted, which I took as permission to lower my arms before clambering over the pile of wood. I calculated the odds of overpowering him. Then I remembered his response to my attempted hook punch on Main Street. I hadn't thought about it at the time, but Fritz obviously had martial arts training. *Just my luck.* I'd been taken hostage by the only restaurateur in Leafy Hollow with a black belt to hold up his apron.

"Move!"

I scrambled faster.

Before long we were on the other side and plunging through the undergrowth. Thorns and twigs scratched my bare arms and I squinted, trying to see the path while ducking branches. Was that starlight ahead?

Timing was critical. If I moved aside too soon, Fritz would figure it out. Too late, and I'd plunge off the escarpment myself.

I picked up the pace. Behind me, I could hear him breathing heavily but keeping up. The rifle barrel was trained on the back of my head.

A beautiful star winked into view. Then another.

I ducked to my right and dove headlong into the bushes.

Behind me, Fritz kept going, straight toward the edge of the escarpment. For a heartbeat, I thought it was going to work.

Then he skidded to a halt and pivoted to face me.

Cowering in the foliage, I grunted in pain as Fritz rapped the butt of the rifle on my head. I saw stars again, but these ones weren't nearly as pretty.

"Get up," he barked. "And no more tricks."

Groaning, I rubbed my battered forehead and rose to my feet.

The valley loomed in the distance, only a few feet away. Fritz had stopped only inches from the edge.

"Turn around and find the right path," he said. "Another

stunt like that and I'll shoot you and leave you here to bleed out. Don't think I won't."

"It's hard to see in the dark. We need to slow down." I strained to listen for anyone coming along the path. An owl hooted softly—or maybe it was a chipmunk—and leaves rustled in the breeze. Nothing else.

Fritz slid the backpack from his shoulder with one hand and stepped to the edge. He kept the rifle trained on me while he swung the pack in a wide arc with his other arm. Then he let go and watched it drop. Unlike Lucy's body, the backpack was well away from the cliff before it dropped. It might have gone into the river. From there, it was a short distance to the lake.

"Move." He used his rifle to motion at the trail.

I stumbled back along the path and over the barrier, then pointed. "There it is. The trail to the back entrance. If you go straight down you'll come out on a one-lane road that skirts the escarpment. From there you can easily walk to the main road. I don't see what good it will do you—your car's back at the parking lot."

"Never mind about that. And I'm not going down there alone. Get moving."

"Look, Fritz, you can travel faster without me. Let me stay here. I promise I won't get in your way. The police are on their way. They'll find you."

"That's why you're coming with me." He poked me again with the rifle. "Hands on your head."

The trail started down at this point. It was slippery. I deliberately tripped on several tree roots to slow us down, mentally calculating how long it would take for the police to arrive in the parking lot and make the climb to the Peak.

Assuming they were coming. The dispatcher hadn't been impressed with my explanation. I'd heard a faint sigh when she promised to send someone. I couldn't blame her. Founder's Day was known for its hijinks. Like the time the villagers awoke the next day to find the statue's bronze sword had been replaced with a cell phone—and the founder was taking a selfie with it. That one trended on Instagram for days.

"Stop," Fritz hissed. I halted, trying to hear over the blood pounding in my ears. Was that someone running up the path behind us? Or merely a deer, using the man-made trail to speed its journey through the woods?

A lone light splashed off the branches ahead. I gasped. Could that be—

"*Halt. Police.*"

"Move!" Fritz yelled, prodding me with the rifle barrel.

I ran. His boots thudded down the trail inches behind me.

At precisely the right moment, I hit the deck, tucking and rolling into the bushes in my best approximation of a parkour action star.

Fritz roared an obscenity, but he couldn't see clearly enough to get off a shot. And he couldn't afford to stop and yank me to my feet. Instead, he ran right past.

A moment later, his footsteps thundered over pine planks.

I grinned through the leaf mold, pebbles, and mud that plastered my face. *Wouldn't be long now.*

Fritz reached the far side of the bridge.

Then the screaming started.

I didn't even try to suppress my giggles.

I extricated myself from the shrubbery in time to greet the police officers whose flashlights lit up the path.

"What the heck is that?" one asked, helping me to my feet. Judging by the freakish noise in the distance, someone was flailing in the dark, crashing into trees, and screaming like a little girl.

A nighthawk burst out of the pine trees to circle over our heads—no doubt sensing blood.

"That?" I asked. "That'll be the European hornets. If you wait a minute or two, I think you'll find Fritz Cameron will be back."

As the thrashing and screaming grew louder, I turned to the officer with the walkie-talkie.

"And call the firefighters. They have to rescue Derek Talbot. He's stuck on a ledge twenty feet down from the Peak."

CHAPTER TWENTY-FIVE

PANIC KEPT me on my feet until Fritz was in handcuffs, the firefighters had rappelled down the cliff to rescue Derek, and Patty was safely on her way to the bakery where a worried Clark was waiting.

When the cruiser drove away with Patty in the back seat, my knees suddenly buckled. I would have fallen had it not been for Jeff, who slid a steadying arm under mine.

"Whoa," he said. "Let's get you off your feet." He urged me toward a cruiser, where a back door stood open, and helped me to sit. "Head between your knees, please," he said, motioning to the cruiser's driver to join us.

I complied, my chest painfully tight.

"Breathe. And don't get up."

"Jeff—about Marjorie's memoir—"

"I know. It's gone. We'll never know what was in it now."

I made an impatient gesture. "No, it's—"

"That must be why Fritz threw his backpack off the Peak. With all this wind, those pages will be spread for miles—"

"No, they're—"

"And the forecast calls for rain. Even if we find them—"

"Stop," I said, raising my voice.

Jeff closed his mouth and gave me a quizzical look.

"I have to tell you something." I pointed to the tow truck driver who was loading Fritz's convertible onto his flatbed. "Don't let him take that away yet."

Jeff twisted his head to the car and raised his eyebrows. "Why?"

"Check the front passenger side, under the floor mat."

Jeff waved to the tow truck driver to stop. Then he walked around to open the door of Fritz's car and duck his head in. He emerged holding a sheaf of papers. "Is this..."

I nodded.

Jeff riffled through the pages. "How did you know?"

"When I got in Fritz's car for the drive here, I tossed his backpack off the seat. A few pages fell out. I didn't have time to read them, but I noticed that the capital O's and A's had been colored in—like on the two pages in Marjorie's apartment. I figured it had to be her missing memoir. And if Fritz had it, that meant he was her killer."

I drew in a long breath to steady myself before continuing.

"So when he opened the trunk to get his rifle, I took the pages from his backpack and slid them under the floor mat. I hoped someone would find them, even if—" I shuddered, remembering our moments of terror on the Peak. It could have gone so horribly wrong.

"If you knew Fritz Cameron was Rupert's murderer, why didn't you try to escape?"

"I couldn't, Jeff—not with Patty in danger."

He gave me a long look, then his face creased into a soft smile. "No. Of course not."

"Jeff," a paramedic called from the other side of the parking lot. Fritz had finally stopped screaming, now that he was pumped full of anti-histamine. His handcuffed hands were still flicking at his face, though, and he was mumbling to himself. Jeff walked over to supervise his transfer into a police cruiser headed for the station.

Captain Bob and his crew of firefighters emerged at the head of the trail, carrying Derek on a rescue stretcher. Two paramedics walked beside them. An inflated splint cradled Derek's broken ankle, and a bandage swaddled the gunshot wound on his hand. His face was pale under the parking lot lights.

The Captain winked at me as they passed.

The paramedics transferred Derek to the second waiting ambulance, settled him in, and closed the doors before driving away.

Jeff returned to exchange muffled words with the officer watching over me, then bent down to give me a worried look. "Are you okay?"

"I'm fine," I squeaked.

Jeff squatted beside me, one hand gently rubbing my back. "The paramedic's coming over to see you. You should go to the hospital, just to be safe."

"No need. I'm fine."

"You're not fine—you're covered with scratches, for one thing."

He stood as a paramedic with orange-streaked hair, wearing a blue uniform and stethoscope, walked over and squatted beside me. She attached a blood pressure cuff and inflated it.

"Hi, Verity. I'm Meredith. How do you feel?"

"A little woozy."

"Perfectly understandable." She checked the readout. "Your pressure's a little high. But you've had a lot of excitement, so that's not surprising. Let's take a look at those scratches."

Once she'd determined that nothing was broken, my shoulders hadn't been dislocated—I found that hard to believe—and none of my cuts were serious, she cleaned the minor wounds on my hands and face with antiseptic.

"You're going to have bruising. Are you sure you don't want to come in for a full checkup? You've had quite a shock."

A shock? That's how medics classify utter terror? Good to know. Sighing heavily, I ran a hand through my matted hair, picking out bits of leaves and insects and flicking them onto the gravel. "I'll be fine once I get home." The worst of my panic attack was over for now, but I desperately wanted to go back to Rose Cottage, lock the doors, ease into a hot bath— and never leave.

"Verity!" someone called from the road.

I turned to scan my surroundings. Vehicles jammed the parking lot. The first ambulance was gone, but the flashing lights on the fire truck, the fire captain's SUV, and four police cruisers provided ample competition for the village's fireworks display. Add in the rubberneckers—parked cars lined both sides of the narrow road—and Founder's Day had never been so exciting.

Fortunately, the police had blocked the parking lot entrance, so nobody could ask me any questions. Unfortunately, it also meant that Emy and Lorne were unable to run across the gravel lot to my side.

They waved frantically from behind the tape. "Verity!"

I leaned out to grab the officer's sleeve. "Can you let my friends in?" I pointed in their direction.

"Not yet, sorry. I have orders not to let anyone cross that line. But I can drive you home."

"Can you tell them to meet me there?"

"Sure."

He trotted off to speak to Lorne and Emy. I watched them confer over the yellow police tape. Emy was grabbing Lorne's arm and jumping up and down so she could see me over the crowd.

I waved. Lorne waved back.

My phone beeped with a text. I pulled it from my pocket to view Emy's message.

See U at home.

Great, I texted.

Then I turned my attention to the activity around me.

Jeff was directing the search of the Peak for evidence. One of the police officers retrieved Fritz's rifle and locked it away in the trunk of his cruiser. Jeff leaned over Derek's stretcher, now raised on collapsible wheels, to talk to him.

Derek lifted his uninjured hand to point at something. Possibly me.

I ducked my head back into the cruiser. Derek's frantic denial during our confrontation on the Peak played over and over in my head.

I never would have hurt Marjorie. I loved her.

Derek had never been violent. Not in public, anyway. His outburst at Sue during our book club meeting was the only time I saw him angry. And he told a convincing tale about how Lucy met her death.

Well, he would, wouldn't he?

My inner critic was insistent. I heaved a sigh. Not my problem. Someone else would decide Derek Talbot's fate. At least he wasn't dead.

My sympathy did not extend to Fritz Cameron. Considering how much one hornet sting hurt, I had a good idea of his suffering. It sparked no pity from me. Even as I winced at his swollen face and hands, my reaction had been coupled with satisfaction. The look of terror on Patty's face would stay with me forever—as well as Derek's.

Poor Derek. Whatever his faults, he had suffered for love. Marjorie played him, pure and simple. Or was that Lucy? There was more than enough deception to go around in their story.

I turned over another tale in my mind—that of Marjorie and Ian Rupert. Marjorie had embarked on a forbidden and doomed romance. You could almost call it a tragic love story. She gave up everything to be with the man she loved.

My inner critic gave me another slap. Marjorie Rupert was a gold digger, and the man she loved probably helped murder her first husband—which detracted a bit from the romance angle.

Still, if a pair of psychotic killers could make love work, what did that say about me? I wasn't even willing to risk a dinner date.

I straightened up and pulled out my phone. After typing in a long text, my hand hovered over the SEND button. My heart pounded, my stomach churned, and that vein in my neck... I put my phone on the seat beside me, and bent over for a little deep breathing.

"Verity?" the officer asked. "Are you—"

"I'm fine," I said, sitting up so suddenly I triggered a dizzy spell. What was the matter with me? After a few more deep breaths, I picked up my phone and punched SEND. I was tired of letting anxiety control my life.

As I slid the phone into my pocket, the officer gave me a curious glance. I wiped the smile from my face, determined to retain at least one secret.

Briskly, I fastened my seatbelt. "Can you drive me home?"

ONE WEEK LATER...

Emy, Patty, and I stood on Rose Cottage's driveway, with the Ferrises' suitcases at our feet. I sniffled back a few tears. "I'll miss you, Patty," I said as we hugged.

Clark stood off to one side with his earplugs in, listening to the latest Leeds United match. "You too, Clark," I called.

He waved distractedly. "Sure thing, Verity." Then, "Yes!" he howled, jumping up and down on the gravel, punching his fists in the air.

Patty gave an exasperated sigh. Then she patted her purse—where she'd tucked my signed sublet agreement for delivery to my former landlord. "We'll miss you, too."

Emy held out a Tupperware container. "I brought along a few things for your flight, Patty," she said cheerily. "Sausage rolls and strawberry scones. I'm sorry they're so pedestrian."

Patty gave her a look of horror. I held my breath.

Emy winked. "I'm kidding. But you know what—I decided to punch up a few of my flavorings. You've been a real inspiration."

"Thank you," Patty said, accepting the plastic container with a grin. "But the only person who learned anything about baking on this trip was me. You're an incredible pastry chef, Emy. Thank you so much for showing me how to make your maple-bacon tarts." She leaned in conspiratorially. "They even made Clark look up from the television."

Patty handed me the Tupperware box so she could wrap Emy in a hug.

When she stepped back, both women were teary. I looked away, not wanting to embarrass the two prior combatants. They weren't soul mates—not yet—but they'd grown a lot closer. And Emy had promised to visit Patty in Vancouver.

Which left me free to resume my search for Aunt Adeline.

Two weeks, Control had said. The clock was ticking. I only hoped I was up for whatever it had in mind.

The sound of a car crunching over gravel recalled me to the present. The limo had arrived to take Patty and Clark to the airport. The driver put their suitcases into the trunk.

Emy and I watched the car drive down Lilac Lane and turn in the direction of the highway.

"Are you okay by yourself?" she asked.

"I'll be fine. Are you and Lorne..."

"We're great." Emy did not move toward her car. We stood silently, enjoying the day.

A pair of red squirrels scampered across the roof of Rose Cottage. I smiled at them, wondering if they were the same rodents who'd greeted me on my arrival over two months ago. When I turned back, Emy's expression had become serious.

"Verity, I don't trust that thing in your basement. No," she held up a hand. "Let me finish. That doesn't matter. When you need us, Lorne and I want to help in any way we can. Do not"—she poked a finger at me—"shut us out."

I swallowed hard. "I won't. And thanks."

"See you later, then." Emy climbed into her Fiat and drove off, waving as she turned out of the driveway. I watched her go, thinking about the changes of the past two months. When I boarded that red eye in Vancouver, I never expected to gain some of the best friends I'd ever had.

Once Emy's Fiat was out of sight, I turned to admire—for the umpteenth time—my beautiful rebuilt porch and its brand-new wicker rockers. Rose Cottage had never looked so good. The insurance company had even replanted the rose bushes.

"Carson," I called. "I'm going in. Do you need anything?"

Carson looked up from his latest long-term project—repointing the cottage's fieldstone walls. Reuben strutted by his side, admiring the work.

"Nope," Carson said. "Calling it quits for the day. See ya tomorrow." He glanced up at the darkening sky. "Looks like rain."

As the first drops fell, he and Reuben crossed the driveway and headed for their respective roosts—Reuben to the Ford, and Carson into his tent.

I lowered the ramp on the back of my aunt's truck to unload the day's landscaping equipment. Within minutes, a hard rain was falling, drenching my hoodie and jeans. When I was done, I dashed across the lawn and into the house.

General Chang was stretched out on the back of my new, and as yet unscratched, sofa. He opened his eye, saw it was only me, and closed it again.

"Some pets greet their owners at the door," I said, peeling off my hoodie.

The General huffily shifted his position to face the wall.

I walked over to ruffle his fur. "You'd be off there in a shot if I opened a bag of liver treats." He yawned, then nudged his head against my hand. I smiled as he broke into a rasping purr.

By the time I'd taken a hot shower, changed my clothes, and run a brush through my hair, the sky was black and rain was pelting against the windows. I turned on a few lamps and considered lighting a fire.

A soft knock sounded on the door. I walked over to open it.

Jeff stood in the doorway. Rain dripped off his chin, but his eyes were twinkling. "Are your houseguests finally gone?"

I nodded. "You're wet."

"What are you going to do about it?"

I stood on tiptoe to wrap my hands around his neck. "Hmm. Let me think."

He lowered his face to mine.

A crack of lightning lit up the yard, followed by a tremendous boom. The General flew off the sofa and into the basement. Every light in the cottage went out, leaving us in darkness.

"Power outage," I whispered in Jeff's ear.

"Perfect," he replied as he pulled me closer.

When not hunched over her computer talking to people who exist only in her head, Rickie spends her time taming an unruly half-acre garden and an irrepressible Jack Chi. She also shares her southern Ontario home with three rescue cats and an overactive Netflix account.

CPSIA information can be obtained
www.ICGtesting.com
ted in the USA
W10s2022250118
005LV00001B/168/P

9 781988 881010